The Lost Weapon

Sophie Jay

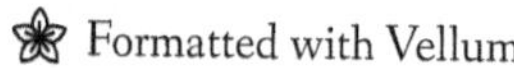 Formatted with Vellum

For the women who build walls so strong you forget they are
there. And for the people willing to make a door.

Author's Note

This novel contains mature themes such as torture, violence, death, consensual sexual activity, and *light* kidnapping (he forgives her rather quickly).

Ice Dominion
The portal
Bruma

TIRLUN

Chapter One

Sage

I reach into my boot and pull out my hunting knife.

Why did he have to be a runner? And thirty feet from the portal too.

I fling my knife with expert precision and it imbeds in a tree less than a foot from Aiden's head. He freezes. Good. Maybe now he'll take me seriously.

I casually stroll toward him, maintaining eye contact with his piercing blue eyes once he turns around.

"What did I say?" I ask with a tilt of my head.

He grumbles his response.

"Sorry, what was that?"

"That I'd regret trying to escape," he says, slightly louder. I'm not sure if it was stupidity or straight misogyny that led him to not take my warning seriously.

He seemed respectful of women when I was spying on him in the bar.

Less respectful when I tied his ass up and dragged him

through the woods. But that's to be expected when you're kidnapping a grown man.

"Can we please keep moving now? I'm antsy to get my magic back."

He eyes me warily; I know he thinks I'm crazy. Humans from Earth don't believe in magic anymore — it's been relegated to children's fairy tales. And those novels that the women seem to be obsessed with.

But I have nothing to prove. Once we cross the portal, Tirlun's magic will be undeniable.

I try to ignore the small lurch in my stomach. The one that makes me disappointed that he hates me. It's because he's hot — his caramel-brown skin contrasts with those stunning blue eyes. At least, that's what I keep telling myself.

Besides, it doesn't matter if he hates me. All that matters is that we find this Mother-forsaken weapon. And we need him to do it.

"After you, Pretty Boy," I sneer and gesture for him to walk in front of me. A cutting glare is his only response as he trudges once again through the woods.

Five feet now. I can practically feel my magic bursting under my skin.

Shit. I forgot to warn him. "Wait."

"What is it now?" he rolls his eyes as he turns to look back at me. This close to him, I have to crane my neck to look him in the eyes — he must be close to two heads taller than me, but I still manage to find a way to be the one looking down at him.

"Thought I'd warn you. Once we cross through the portal, it may tingle. You've been without your magic your entire life, so we don't know how long your body will take to adjust to having it run through your veins again. Just want you to be prepared."

I can tell he's about to respond with something snarky, but he pauses. "Hold up — who's *we?*"

I'm surprised he didn't ask about the portal or the magic, but maybe in his confusion he didn't even process that. He's probably still feeling some of the effects of the drugs I gave him. I do feel a little guilty about that, but there will be no lasting damage. It was better than the plan Del had suggested.

A grin stretches across my face. "Keep walking and you'll find out."

Aiden turns back around and cautiously moves towards the fog that begins to fill the forest. To any other living creature, this fog would be enough to disorient and scare them from crossing into the portal. And if they accidentally stumbled into Tirlun, the vicious animals in the forest on our side would handle them swiftly.

But in our entire world's history, someone from Earth has never been to Tirlun.

Until now.

Chapter Two

Aiden

Sage wasn't wrong about that fog tingling. If that's even her name. Who knows what she's lied about to get me this far? And I fell for it like a fucking fool. I thought we were just going back to her place.

She approached me at the bar, which in retrospect should've tipped me off. But at that moment, I couldn't help thinking how hot it was. How hot *she* was. She was so much shorter than me, but her body was filled with curves that sadly still make my dick hard even after she's kidnapped me.

And those eyes. Sage green, the only reason why I don't think she lied about her name. Those eyes saw right through me and I felt something I haven't felt in a very long time.

And then we left the bar. And then she drugged me, tied me up, and dragged me through the woods.

I must have regained consciousness earlier than she expected me to because she was pissed when I managed to run away, even though it was only a couple feet before a knife came flying at my head.

Who knew a woman that small and curvy was hiding a shit ton of muscle and aggressiveness?

But that tingle from the fog must be more drugs, because when it clears, all the colors around me are impossibly clearer. The air smells almost sweet, and as I turn to Sage to gauge her reaction, she has a bright smile on her face.

She's gorgeous. Her smile lights up her entire face and I'm reminded of that glimpse of hope and something more I managed to feel after just a few hours together at the bar.

Fuck. No. She kidnapped me. It's just a physical reaction. My body's thinking with my dick instead of my head.

I continue to involuntarily stare at her and what looks like a stream of water swirls out of her right hand and a small fire emerges from her left. She definitely drugged me, but I might as well enjoy this high. Whatever it is, it's strong. And I am no stranger to hallucinogens.

Weirdly, my body itself doesn't feel much different, only the world around me.

The two warring elements twirl around one another like a choreographed dance, twisting around Sage as she slowly moves in a circle. The water and fire act like snakes and nuzzle up against her arms and legs as they weave between her limbs. The sounds of a crackling fire and a soft stream combine around us, creating a symphony of sounds. The heat of the fire melds with the soothing cool of the water to create a warm summer breeze on my face.

Her eyes meet mine. "See? Magic."

Yeah, magic. The magic of drugs. Before I can respond,

her eyes widen as she looks down at my body. She slaps a hand over her mouth to poorly cover a laugh.

I look down — I'm naked. Completely butt naked.

I quickly move my hands to cover my cock and grimace as I feel a blush begin to creep over my cheeks. It's always annoyed me that when I blush it's visible, even on my dark skin.

But right now, I'm more angry than anything else.

"Care to explain why I'm naked?" I ask with as much confidence as I can muster at this current moment.

Sage removes her hand from her mouth, but a soft chuckle still manages to escape. "Sorry, I completely forgot that would happen."

I narrow my eyes at her. "*What* would happen?"

"That your clothes would disappear." She gestures towards my body. Clearly my clothes didn't disappear, that would be impossible. Maybe I'm hallucinating because of the drugs? But then, Sage wouldn't be laughing. Could she have stripped me without me feeling it? I doubt it.

"And why did my clothes disappear?" At this point, I just need an explanation, even though it's going to undoubtedly make my usually extremely patient self angry.

Sage takes off her large fur coat and hands it to me. Before answering, she pulls off her pack and pulls a pair of pants out of her bag.

She glances up at me as she takes my hands by the rope that's still tied around them. "I'm going to untie you now," she says softly, like I'm a spooked animal. "Please do not try to run away again. It will only embarrass you and annoy me." I give her a small grunt in confirmation.

Her knife cuts through the ropes and the tension against my wrists suddenly gives way. I rub them for a few minutes before beginning to put on the coat as Sage answers my question.

"So, if you hadn't been too busy trying to run away," she cuts me a glare, "I could've explained this *before* we crossed the portal." Is that what she's claiming that fog was? Either she's crazy or is trying way too hard to convince me she didn't drug me again.

"Do you know anything about magic?"

"You mean, like from children's books?" She rolls her eyes at my question — like I'm the one being ridiculous.

"I suppose that's all you would know the word from," she responds as she lightly bites her lower lip. "Anyway, as our two worlds evolved side by side, ours developed magic while yours developed technology that destroys your planet. Humans here," she adds, gesturing to herself, "and I guess you too, have been born with magic and enhanced physical capabilities."

What the fuck is she talking about? Magic? Enhanced physical capabilities?

Maybe those drugs from the fog are messing with her too. Although I vaguely remember her saying the word magic before we crossed through it. I was too busy being worried about me meeting more kidnappers than processing those words.

So she's not high. Just crazy. I can work with that.

Maybe if she believes I'm playing along with her delusions, she'll relax and give me a chance to escape. I need to pretend that I accept this nonsense. It shouldn't be too hard considering I pride myself on being a polite man. I've gotten pretty good at making others feel understood and heard, even when I completely disagree.

I take a deep breath before continuing down this rabbit hole. "What do you mean 'you guess I do too?'"

She smiles. "Well, Pretty Boy, that's the whole reason why I kidnapped you." That Pretty Boy nickname has got to go — it's so condescending. But I can only handle so much at once. Sage is obviously oblivious to my racing thoughts as she continues. "Your ancestors have most likely stopped sharing this, but three hundred years ago, your family lived in Tirlun."

I must make some sort of face at that last sentence because she adds, "Tirlun is where we are — our world. Like your Earth?" She phrases that last part like a question. Like she doesn't know the planet she lives on. Maybe in her fairy-tale world she really does live in this supposed Tirlun.

I just nod as if she's being completely reasonable. She nods in agreement and continues. "Long story short, there was a great war that ended only when your family created and wielded a powerful weapon. They fled to Earth to prevent themselves from ever being manipulated into using the weapon again." Right, right, right. Super casual and normal. A massive war no one's ever heard of.

My family made a crazy powerful weapon. Sure. And then they fled to "Earth." And *that's* why I've never heard of any of this or know what she's talking about. Makes perfect sense.

Now that we've begun this conversation and Sage can see I'm not trying to run away again (I don't want the knife to actually hit me this time), she gestures to me to begin walking forward again.

Massive spruce trees tower over us, scattered with the occasional aspen or pine. And although the colors are crisper, I inhale deeply and try to center myself in the familiar. The crunch of the snow beneath my borrowed boots and the squawk of a bird are occasionally interrupted by the sound of Sage's supposed magic in the air.

She lets us walk in silence for a while, almost as if she's giving me time to process everything she's said. As if *any* amount of time will be enough to make me comprehend what's going on.

Sage starts to hum a soft tune under her breath and it's beautiful, but my mind's running through everything she's already told me, and as I adjust the too tight pants I've borrowed that fit me like shorts, I realize she never answered my original question.

"Wait, wait, wait, you still never explained why my clothes disappeared after we walked through the fog." I can't wait to hear what wild explanation she'll give me for this. Although, I can't even think of one that would make sense.

She makes three fireballs and starts juggling them in her hands as she answers. These are some strong drugs. "While our two worlds evolved side by side, some things exist in one that can't exist in the other. Any material or product that was created from something toxic would never have been made in our world — we value Tirlun too much to create anything that could damage it. Your clothes were clearly made of synthetic materials, so they disintegrated as soon as we went through the portal."

I guess within the confines of her delusion that would make sense. And why she was able to keep all her things. I study the fur coat and pants I'm wearing and the fabrics all feel very natural.

I look over to Sage — she's in leather pants that hug her ass so fucking perfectly. Nope, not going there. Her being so attractive is what got me into this situation in the first place. I'm just going to have to find things that are unattractive about her; not her legs as I've discovered, not her face with those gorgeous eyes. I look at her torso; she's in a tight long-sleeve with a brown leather corset.

Both pieces of clothing unfortunately shape her upper body in a mouth-watering way. But strapped to her vest are several knives, including the one she threw at my head. Okay, that's unattractive, right? Wanting to kill me? My dick does not agree.

I try to distract myself from thinking about Sage and turn back towards the forest. Out of the corner of my eye I see Sage shrug at my lack of response and follow my lead.

A caw of a bird screeches overhead. I look up, expecting to see a hawk or robin, but instead I'm greeted by a rabbit with wings. I've never had drugs like this.

"What the fuck is that?"

Sage follows my eyes into the trees. "An avis — they're like your birds."

"That's not a fucking bird."

Sage makes a trilling sound and the rabbit-bird flies down closer to us. I cover my head with my arms, waiting to get clawed to death by this monster thing.

She laughs as the creature gracefully lands on her shoulder. Petting under its chin, she says, "This is our bird. Somehow, they started breeding with the rabbits and this is how they evolved. They're sweethearts — to us, anyway — but are wicked hunters."

This time, it's the "bird" who trills, like it's agreeing with Sage.

"Mhm, okay, sure. Are there any other weird animal combinations I should be aware of?" I don't want to believe what my eyes are telling me, but I should at least be prepared to see more of these wild mirages.

"Um, weird?" Sage shrugs and the creature takes off back into the trees. "Weird for you, probably." Her voice gets serious. "Whether or not you'd call them weird, there are dangerous creatures, to be sure. These woods guard our realm from yours and the animals take their jobs very seriously. We're considered the apex predators, so they mostly leave us alone. But that doesn't mean you should relax. The weakest creatures can be the most ruthless when desperate."

Yeah she has no idea. I'm drugged, disoriented, and clearly out-weaponed, so I think that makes me weak. And I'm pretty fucking desperate to find a way out of this situation.

"I don't think there's any way I could possibly relax right now," I say.

Sage's eyes shift to mine. "Don't challenge me, Pretty Boy," she purrs.

There goes my dick again. I clear my throat in an attempt to clear my thoughts. "Right, well how much longer until we get to..." I trail off. Where are we going? There's nothing in these woods except for forests and mountains. She kidnapped me from a ski resort that's fairly secluded within Colorado. I've been so distracted from the kidnapping and this magic nonsense that I didn't even realize that we were walking *away* from civilization.

"Bruma," she responds. "That's the capital of the Ice Dominion." Ah, yes, the *Ice Dominion*. More nonsense words.

"How long until we get to this Bruma?"

"We'll camp in the woods tonight and get there around late afternoon tomorrow. My family is waiting for us with food, tents, and a fire," she says.

My stomach grumbles in response. In all of this chaos, it's been almost an entire day with no food. Sage kidnapped me in the early hours of the morning and we've been walking all day.

The sun begins to set and I would rather not be stuck in a dark forest with my potential murderer.

Sage must've heard my stomach. "I'm starving too. Don't worry, we're almost there."

It's as if her words summoned them as voices pop up and I can see smoke rising from a fire.

Now there's even more people I'm going to have to escape. But maybe these people can be reasoned with and they'll convince Sage to let me go. I just need to stay positive.

Chapter Three

Sage

The first thing I see is Aneira's wide grin. Her blue eyes sparkle in the light of the fire, looking even brighter against her obsidian skin.

"Sagey," she squeals, getting up from her log to give me a hug. As she embraces me, I make eye contact with Idris across the fire and give her a small nod.

Before I can even straighten completely from Aneira's hug, I'm wrapped in a massive embrace by my cousin and his bear hug lifts me off the ground.

"Alright, alright, Del, it's been two nights, relax," I say, lightly patting his back.

"Two nights that we should've been with you," he grumbles as he lightly sets me down.

They all wanted to come with me through the portal, but it was faster and safer for me to go alone. It took a lot of convincing and by the end, we compromised that they would wait for me just over the border in case things went wrong.

Considering that the Queen of the Ice Dominion is Del's mom and my aunt, we're able to more or less decide our own missions and their approaches.

To anyone else, Queen Neve has a heart of ice. But when it comes to her children — and I suppose to a certain extent, me — her heart melts. Since the Fire Dominion attack fifteen years ago, her heart has been harder to thaw, but we can always find ways to get it to melt enough to cause some mischief.

Hence the glimmer in Del's storm-blue eyes. I don't know what the three of them planned while I was gone, but Del's punchable grin currently pasted on his face does not bode well for me.

Del looks behind me to where Aiden stands awkwardly with his hands clenched at his sides. "This must be Aiden Columben," he says with that idiotic grin still on his face.

Aiden glances at me before making eye contact with Del. "How do you all know who I am?"

I roll my eyes in response as I find an empty log and plop down. "Our records were right," I begin, taking a skewer of meat from Idris. "He knows nothing."

Idris smirks in response. She's the embodiment of a sunset — golden skin, eyes, and hair, all wrapped up in a lethal model's body. I'd be jealous if I wasn't so attractive myself.

Del claps an arm around Aiden, all but dragging him towards the fire. Somehow, Aiden looks small next to my cousin, a hard feat considering they're both well over six feet tall. But Del is a literal bear; tall, muscular, and wide. If he didn't constantly have a smile plastered on his pale face he'd be intimidating.

I groan in pleasure as the juicy, tender meat fills my mouth. I missed the amazing food of my home. Just two days without it and I began craving our flavorful meats, fruits, veggies, and desserts.

"There's no way you cooked this," I say to Idris.

"Of course not," she says. "But I did create the flame. The perfect temperature for roasting meat." Considering she's the only one out of them with fire magic, I don't know who else would've done it. But I'll let her take the win.

Aiden sits hesitantly next to Del. Aneira walks over to them and hands him a meat skewer. "Hi, I'm Aneira," she says with a warm smile.

Aiden takes the meat. "Aiden." I can tell he wants to keep his stoic demeanor but no one can resist Aneira's warmth. That's why she's in charge of training my soldiers when we're not on our smaller team missions; they can never get mad at her for working them so hard.

A small smile creeps across Aiden's face. Maybe we're finally getting somewhere. "You guys are pretty friendly for kidnappers," he adds before taking a bite of his food. "Holy shit, this is delicious."

Del bellows a laugh. "If we went with the plan I wanted to use, Sagey wouldn't have needed to kidnap you at all." Yeah, Del's plan was to have me take my seduction even further; sleep with Aiden, then convince him, somehow, to travel with me through the woods. There were way too many unknowns so my plan won in the end.

Before Aiden can question Del further, I butt in. "Our food is better than anything you have in your world for the same reason your clothes disappeared."

Aneira giggles next to me. "I was wondering about that."

A smirk crosses my face. "Yeah, I forgot about that. He had to borrow some of my clothes. Del, maybe you can lend him some of your stuff— you'll be a much better fit."

"Oh right of course. Magic." Aiden shakes his head in disbelief.

"He doesn't believe you?" Idris asks.

I shrug, throwing a stream of water and making it wind through everyone around the fire. "I did show him. He's convinced I drugged him and it's all a hallucination."

"Because you did drug me!" Aiden exclaims.

"Only in your world. It wore off once you woke up and I haven't given you anything since."

He scoffs. "What was in that fog then?"

"I told you." Now I'm getting annoyed. Does this man not listen? I explained all of this to him already. "It's the portal. There's nothing in it."

"Sure," he says before taking another bite of his meat. "And I'm sure there's not another dose in this food. I'm too hungry to care."

I gesture in his direction as I look at my friends. "See what I've had to deal with for the last day?"

Aneira gives me a sympathetic smile before turning to Aiden. Good. Maybe he'll listen to her. "Aiden," she says gently. "Even though Sage drugged you to get you here, why would she need to drug you again? Not only could she overpower you quite easily by herself, but now there's four of us against you. There's no way to escape and there's no reason for her to lie."

I watch Aiden's face as he processes what she's said. He opens his mouth as if to respond, before shutting it again. We sit in silence waiting for him to gather his thoughts, the crackle of logs in the fire the only sound. I finish my food and snatch Aneira's leftovers. Mother, how I missed this food.

Aiden heaves a sigh. "How else do you explain everything I've seen since the fog?"

His constant questioning is causing me stress. The more stressed out I get the more my joints hurt; they're already screaming at me for not taking good enough care of them over the past two days. It's so unfair that anyone else who trains as much as me can last three weeks on the road without needing to rest, but after two days my body rebels.

Slowly rolling each joint, I stretch my body. My hands are definitely swollen. I'm going to need to wear my compression gloves tomorrow.

I hide a wince as pain shoots through my knees and look at Idris. "I'm going into a tent. Id, care to join?" Idris hears what I don't say and nods as she follows me away from the fire.

Pulling my various salves and tinctures out of my bag, I take off my pants and lie down. Id grabs a salve, adds some heat with her magic and massages it into my legs.

I can't help the small groan that escapes at the immediate relief. Id gives me a small smile. "It's been a bad two days?" she asks me.

"I forget how much more my joints hurt when I can't constantly ice or heat them," I say through a wince as she hits a particularly tender spot. "That, plus the fact that I had to drag a man a mile through the woods did not do my body any favors."

She chuckles. "At least he was pretty to look at as you were dragging him."

"He might be pretty, but he's not very cooperative. He doesn't believe anything I say, but I can't get a read on him."

That more than anything, stresses me out. I'm an excellent judge of character and can usually assess other's moods really well. But his are all over the place; one minute he looks at me like he wants to kill me and the next like he wants to fuck me.

And then there's the way he speaks to me; it's like he's trying to be polite but can't help but snark. The constant back and forth of both his words and actions is giving me a headache and making it impossible for me to tell which version of him is real.

I don't even think he realizes he's doing it — it's like he has this mask that he can't maintain. But it's a mask he doesn't even realize he wears.

"How that must aggravate you." Sarcasm bleeds through Idris' tone.

"You know I hate not being able to predict the outcomes of our missions. And he is a huge variable."

Idris finishes her massage and hands me back my tins. "I know. Once we're in Bruma tomorrow, there will be no way for him to deny the truth. An entire city filled with magic? He can't blame *that* on drugs."

I sigh. "I hope you're right."

"I'm never wrong," Id replies. She's almost as cocky as I am — just much more silent about it.

"How's the rest of our plan coming along?" I ask.

"Everything's in place. I have a couple more things to take care of once we're back in Bruma, but we should be good to go."

Relief runs through my body. This mission and my plan have the power to change the very fate of Tirlun.

"This has to go perfectly," I reiterate to Idris. "If anyone even catches whiff of what we're doing —"

"I know, Sagey. I got it." She knows the importance of this mission as much as I do, but I can't help but remind her.

I nod in agreement. "Are you sleeping in here tonight?"

Idris shakes her head no and makes her way out of the tent. Which leaves Aneira... or Aiden.

Chapter Four

Aiden

When Sage and that other woman leave to go into a tent, I turn back to the other two. They at least seem friendlier than Sage. "So, back to my question. How do you explain everything that's happened since the fog?"

They glance at one another, most likely trying to figure out how to lie in unison. "First of all, my name's Delwyn," the man reaches out and shakes my hand. "I know Aneira already introduced herself." The woman smiles at me. "The golden-haired beauty is Idris. And well, you've met Sage." He gives me an impish grin.

"I will answer your question," he continues, "but from what Sage has already said, you're just going to think we're all crazy."

I nod in agreement. There's no use in lying — I probably will. Regardless, the more information I have, the better. If I can figure out their logic, I can figure out how to convince them to let me go home.

The thought of home sends a pang through my heart. Home hardly feels that way since my parents died.

"Most likely," I shrug. "But I still want to understand why you've felt the need to kidnap, drug, and lie to me."

Aneira ignores my comment and says excitedly, "I guess it's time to tell you a little more about Tirlun. There are two dominions: the Ice Dominion and the Fire Dominion. We're all part of the Ice Dominion."

Ice and fire? So obvious and vague.

"Delwyn here is the prince, but he's second in line — that's why he's allowed to come on these missions with us."

Missions? Is that what they call kidnapping?

"Besides, he wouldn't make a very good king anyway," she says, sticking her tongue out at him.

Why are they treating this like some big joke? My life is not a joke.

Delwyn sticks his out in response. She's right; not very kingly. Any definition I have of royalty does not match up with any of Delwyn's behavior.

"If you're born in the Ice Dominion, you have water and ice powers. If you're born in the Fire Dominion, you have fire and heat powers."

But Sage...

I look at her again. "How does Sage have both?"

"Before the lovely tension that the dominions find themselves in today —"

"So I'm entering a world of tension? Doesn't sound very nice," I interrupt. Seriously? If they expect me to believe there's magic and princes, why would there be tension?

Aneira continues like I didn't even speak. "Anyway, nobles from each dominion often formed political marriages to increase diplomacy between the two. Most children of these unions have a little bit of both magics, although there's usually a dominant side."

Nobles? "Why would you need nobles?" I ask.

"It's the way it's always been." Delwyn says.

Right. Because something's always been a certain way means it should stay like that. Getting back to their magic and powers, I look back at Aneira. "Which of Sage's magic is stronger?"

Aneira looks back at Delwyn before responding. "Honestly, hard to say. She's insanely strong." She's been the most level-headed so far, but now she's trying to act like Sage is some all-powerful witch? I look at Delwyn for some reassurance of Aneira's exaggeration.

Delwyn says, "She's not wrong. She's one of the strongest magic wielders in both dominions. Her ice powers are probably only second to my family's."

"Your family?" I ask him. This is the first time any of them have mentioned anyone else in their world. Maybe I can use this.

"Yeah, my sister and my mom."

"What about your dad?"

The first glimpse of something other than happiness crosses Delwyn's face before he says, "He passed away."

Fuck. Wrong thing to ask. I can't start to sympathize with them even though I know how much it hurts to lose a parent.

This is a lot of information to take in, especially as I'm tripping balls. Surprisingly, it all makes sense within the confines of whatever crazy cult they belong to. This lie that they are living in is definitely thorough.

Before I ask for somewhere to sleep so I can process it all, there's one thing Aneira said that I need to clarify.

"I have one more question. Idris mentioned that she started this fire. Does that mean she's also a noble from both dominions?"

Idris walks out of the tent as I finish my question. "My parents were both from the Fire Dominion. I-I don't have any ice powers." I definitely asked something wrong.

"How are you a part of the Ice Dominion then?" The tension in the air shifts. I should've kept my mouth shut. This is not going to make it easier for me to escape.

Delwyn stands up from his log and before Idris can answer, he says, "I think that's enough questions for tonight. Why don't you head on into that tent and get some sleep. You're probably exhausted."

He directs me to the tent Sage is in. Because of course.

If I'm going to be kidnapped, couldn't they have at least put me in the tent with the other guy?

I pull the flap back on the thick canvas and walk into a surprisingly cozy space. Two bed rolls are lying on the ground about a foot apart and between them is a gas lantern and Sage's bag.

She looks up at me as I enter, her green eyes shining in the fire light. "This explains Del's mischievous grin."

I sit down on the empty bed roll and stretch out my legs. "Why are you not sharing a tent with him?" They definitely seemed extremely happy to see each other.

"Delwyn is my cousin."

That's why he was so glad to see her. I was worried there was something more between them when he gave her that massive hug.

No, not worried. Why would I be worried? Just curious.

"If Delwyn's your cousin, why am I not sharing a tent with him?" That would be much more appropriate than being in such a small space with a woman I barely know.

I'm not a prude, but still, for all they know I could use this night to get back at Sage for kidnapping me. Well, at any of them, truth be told.

It's as if Sage reads my thoughts when she answers, waving a hand in the direction of the other tents. "Two main reasons: one, my cousin likes to fuck with me and thought forcing me to spend more time with you would be a fun way to do it and two, Del is the prince of our home, a fact which he only likes to use when it can benefit him." She shakes her head in annoyance. "For example, when he doesn't have to share a tent."

She glances at me out of the corner of her eye before continuing. "As for you wanting to use this night to escape and/or hurt me, I wouldn't try it."

Sage talks like everything she says is law and expects everyone else to fall in line. As if *she's* the royal one, not her cousin. Not that I believe *that*.

Which is why I decide when I answer her, I start by attempting to give her a nickname as condescending as the "Pretty Boy," she called me.

"Princess," I begin, her immediate sneer proving I hit my mark. "I would be an idiot not to try to escape. And as for hurting you, I'm not a fan of violence, but I'll do whatever I have to to get out of here."

Even when I played lacrosse in college, I hated the more physical components. Not because I was scared, but because skills and speed were much better at accomplishing my goals on the field. Hitting my opponents was just lazy.

Her eyes flash in challenge, and before I know it, I'm pinned on my back with her hips securely on either side of my body. It would be hot if she didn't steal me from my home and drug me.

It might still be hot. My friends were right; one day my love of strong women was going to bite me in the ass.

She slowly lowers herself, until her mouth is just inches from mine. Her breath brushes my face and I inhale her intoxicating scent of cinnamon and something sweet.

"Pretty Boy," she breathes and I'm entranced. Her sage-green eyes are framed by thick, dark lashes, and her wavy auburn hair lightly tickles my face from where it fell out of her ponytail.

At this moment, I don't care that she kidnapped and drugged me. All I want to do is close the small gap between our lips and find out what noises she makes when she's not taunting me.

Her eyes drift down to my lips and she slowly licks hers. I feel my pants tighten in response, but I'm too mesmerized to care.

"Yes, Princess?" I respond. The nickname may sound slightly less condescending now, but I'm too turned on to care.

With my words, Sage seems to shake off whatever came over her and she clears her throat and leans back up.

She quirks her head down towards my pants and a flush spreads on my cheeks. Now that the moment's past, I'm embarrassed and she can clearly tell why.

Instead of commenting on my erection, Sage thankfully decides to answer my earlier question. "Here's why you're not going to escape or hurt me." A flame appears in her hand and even though it's probably some trick of my mind, I can still feel the heat.

"You would be an even bigger idiot to try to escape. You're in the middle of a forest that you don't know, it's dark, it's dangerous, and most importantly, you have no idea which direction to go in. And as much as you may be a little stupid," she says as a corner of her mouth lifts. "You're not dumb."

She extinguishes the flame in her hand and whispers something under her breath that I can't hear. In the next moment, it feels like we're trapped in a translucent ball. I lift my hand to the left and hit an invisible wall before I can even touch the tent. I try to push on it, but it's immovable.

Whatever drugs she gave me, there's no way it would suddenly make me feel like this. With a few more whispered words, it feels like the bubble popped and I slowly reach my arm back towards the tent.

And I can touch it again. The lifted corner of Sage's mouth turns into a full smirk. "*That* is why you're not going to try to hurt me. Whether or not you actually believe my magic is real, the fact of the matter is I can do a lot more damage to you before you can do any real harm to me."

She reaches between her breasts and pulls out a slim dagger. I have no clue how she managed to hide that in there without slicing her skin. "I also have more daggers and knives hidden in this tent than you have fingers. And you'll never find a single one of them." Sage slowly moves off of my body and back towards her own bedroll. "Besides your body, you have no weapons. Even though you're much larger than me, don't for one second think you would ever beat me hand-to-hand."

Unfortunately, she's right. I've already seen her skills with her daggers, so I can only imagine what she can do without them. And she's already proven how ruthless she can be so I don't doubt she would harm me the second I threaten her.

I heave a sigh. I need to be smart about this. Clearly, trying to escape tonight is stupid. Maybe the people in charge wherever we're going can be convinced to let me go. There's probably more than one Aiden Columben in the world and they have the wrong guy. I just need to prove that somehow.

Sage blows out the lamp and we're plunged into darkness. It's like she's talking to herself when out of nowhere, she says, "I can't wait for a bubble bath and a massage."

"Oh, the poor Princess can't handle a little dirt?"

I can practically hear her glare. "You have no idea what I can handle."

"Not a lot if you're complaining about one day in the woods."

"Yeah, you're really thriving out here in the wilderness."

"I have a reason. I was kidnapped and drugged. All things considered, I think I'm handling this pretty well." Is she serious right now?

"Whatever. I'm done speaking to you. Good night." I hear her turn over so her back is to me.

"Oh no, you don't get to decide this conversation is over because you're mad I'm right." I hear her roll back over, and feel her stare straight through me with her piercing eyes. She can't possibly see in this darkness, right? But I still feel as if her eyes pierce through every part of me, so I quickly settle onto my bedroll.

"I don't know you're right. In fact, I *know* how wrong you are, so it's not even worth my energy arguing. Listen, I get you're pissed at us for kidnapping you. Me especially, for my, um, more active role in it all."

Could that be guilt in her voice?

"But, like it or not, you're stuck with us for the foreseeable future. You've already tried to escape and failed miserably. So, you might as well get on board. Face it, Pretty Boy. There's no going back. You have to learn to take the punches, or you'll get knocked out."

This woman can't have any idea what it's like to have your whole life ripped out from underneath you. I highly doubt she's ever been kidnapped by crazy people who think they have magical powers.

I can't even think of how to respond with everything that's happened in the last day. "Thanks for the advice, Princess, but I don't think I'll be taking any help from a crazy person."

"First of all, I am *not* a princess. Second of all, I am the furthest thing from crazy. You just infuriate me like no one I've ever met."

"Good, I'm glad. Because as long as you're holding me hostage, I am going to make your life fucking miserable." I'm seething by the end of this conversation. Any earlier attraction has quickly vanished. How can she be so nonchalant about literally upending my whole life?

"One breath, one step," she whispers.

"I'm sorry, what was that?"

"Nothing. Do your worst. Now, can I please go to sleep?"

"Fine. But don't even think about straddling me again." There, take that. Maybe now she'll be embarrassed by our intimate moment too.

Her response is quiet. "I wouldn't dream of it, Pretty Boy."

Chapter Five

Sage

I dreamt of it. That asshole put it in my head.

I wake up to birds chirping and fire running through my veins as my body recalls all the things Aiden did to me in my dream. Then I remember what a dick he was last night, and the fire is quickly doused. I turn over to find his bed roll empty. At least I didn't wake up to the sound of another escape attempt. I assume things are running smoothly this morning as no one has come bursting into my tent.

As if I conjured her, Aneira opens my flap and says, "I thought I should warn you. Del and Aiden are working out together."

"Fantastic. And why did Del think it would be a good idea to train our captive?" Let's just have the man trying to escape from us learn our weaknesses and skill level. My cousin may be a beast when it comes to political plays but with literally anything else he acts like he has no common sense.

Aneira shrugs. "No clue, but does this mean you're going to yell at him?"

My friends love when I put our prince in his place; mostly because we still manage to bicker like children into our late twenties. I have no siblings of my own, so Del and his sister have become more like siblings than cousins.

Especially after my parents died and my aunt agreed to be my legal guardian.

I snort. "Most likely. I'll be out in a few minutes. I need to stretch." Aneira nods and leaves.

My joints are in even worse pain today after sleeping on the dirt. I go through my morning stretches, doing my best to release the stiffness.

I add a thin layer of ice to the inside of my compression gloves before putting them on. Hopefully the ice will reduce the swelling in my hands by the time we get to the capital city.

Tonight, I'm going to take a long bath and have Sana work out all the tension in my joints. I shouldn't have let that slip last night to Aiden. He probably thinks I'm some prissy, spoiled brat — not a cursed woman with a chronic illness. Nevermind the fact that he thinks we drugged him. I finish stretching and head outside.

Aneira forgot to mention the most important thing about Aiden and Del exercising. Del is teaching him how to fight!

"Del, don't you think it might not be the best idea to teach someone who's trying to get away from us to fight?" They both look over at me, panting. I can't help but admire the sweat glistening on Aiden's dark and very chiseled chest. They must have been out here awhile if they're sweating in the Ice Dominion.

I notice Idris has her hands splayed out by her sides. That little vixen — she's heating up the air around them.

"Don't worry, Sagey," Delwyn says. "It'll take him a very long time to get good enough to have any chance of beating one of us."

"Hey! You told me I was doing well," Aiden says.

"Yeah. You are. If you were a ten-year-old in Tirlun, I would say you're a whole year above your age level." Delwyn says this with such a straight face that I can't help but laugh.

"Okay everyone," I cut them off. "Let's pack up and head out. I want to reach Bruma by the afternoon at the latest."

Our group makes its way through the forest that separates the portal from Bruma. It should take us the rest of the day to make it to the capital, but it's a beautiful journey. The crunching of the soft snow underneath our boots is the only sound as we walk.

I can tell Aiden's trying to observe as much as he can about our journey. But everything about these woods is made to trick the mind; each towering aspen and juniper are almost identical, with no defining markers. Any animals that we hear are intelligent enough to avoid the apex predators in the woods — us.

The Mother blessed us with this particular forest as an extra ring of protection should any humans get past our sentries on Earth.

As we approach the city, I try to prepare Aiden. "Bruma is the capital of the Ice Dominion. It's where our palace is and where most of our population resides. It's going to be different than anything you've ever seen before. Magic is imbued into every aspect of our society — the structure of the buildings, the public transportation, even the food. If you genuinely still believe we drugged you — which we didn't — then this is about to be the biggest trip of your life."

He looks down at me as I speak and lightly flares his nostrils. If he wants to hate me for the rest of this journey, he can be my fucking guest. I can't understand why I'm the only one receiving all his anger.

"I'm surprised you guys haven't refreshed my dosage," Aiden says. "We ate and drank all the same things, so unless you're drugging yourselves too, I don't know when you would have."

"Because I didn't." There's nothing else I can do to prove to him this is real.

He clenches his jaw like he wishes he could bite my head off and storms ahead to walk next to Delwyn. They're already becoming fast friends. To be fair, anyone can be friends with Del — he's charming where I'm harsh, sweet where I'm rude. I guess it makes sense Aiden would be drawn to my polar opposite if he hates me as much as he claims.

The sun is just starting to set as we walk up a hill to exit the forest and the entire city comes into view. This has always been one of my favorite spots, where the trees finally clear and you're left with a winter wonderland. Snow and ice glisten over everything: the buildings, the grass, the port bordering the city, and even the sky, as soft flurries slowly drift down.

With Bruma straight ahead, its snowflake shape is clearly visible. Farms surround the city, dotting the landscape, but otherwise the land is open as far as the eye can see. This spot is the perfect middle between the populated city and the secluded wilderness. I come out here a lot when I need time alone to think, as I often feel myself pulled in two directions.

I take a deep breath and head towards the city gates.

Chapter Six

Aiden

As we walk toward the gates, Sage lightly grabs my arm to get my attention. "You should know, now that you're in Tirlun, there's a very good chance you'll be able to access your magic."

I scoff. "Yes, *my* magic." Before I let my sarcasm bleed through my voice any further, I need to gather myself and play this smart. This is my chance to learn more about these people and how I can escape them.

"What kind of magic?"

The most sensible plan I can think of right now is to learn as much information as possible and somehow convince them they have the wrong guy. I have to imagine even cult members have common sense.

"Well, since you're a descendant of strong Ice Dominion nobles, I would imagine some ice and water powers. Your family also had great strength in spells and blood magic, so that may emerge as well."

"Blood magic?" Even though magic isn't real, if they believe in blood magic, that can't mean good things for the blood currently pumping through my body.

"It's not what you're thinking. People on Earth like to distort our magic into something evil and cruel," she sneers. "There are some individuals who use their magic for more nefarious purposes, but overall, blood magic has been used to heal and cast protective spells."

"Ah," I say, even more confused than before.

Sage is clearly done explaining any more of their beliefs for the moment, so I turn back towards the city; I must look like a kid in a candy store. A fifty-foot wall surrounds the entire city, and a steady stream of people head through the open gates into the center of the city.

To the right of the gates, a port opens up to an ocean? That's not right, it must be a lake. It certainly looks like an ocean with the massive ships and waves rocking the shore, but we're in Colorado.

Shaking off that discomforting thought, I look back at the guards supervising entry into the city. They have shields and swords that look to be made of ice but have warm smiles on their faces. Everyone appears good natured and friendly, people chatting and laughing with one another as they enter the city.

I do a double take when I realize what I thought was a massive white horse is actually a fucking polar bear. "I'm sorry, is that a polar bear? I've never had drugs like this before."

Aneira looks at me with her sapphire eyes that sparkle no matter where the sun hits them. "If that's what you call them on Earth. Here, the animals are called ursas. Because they're so big, they're often used to help with farming or other manual labor, but we can also ride them and they're fierce fighters on the battlefield."

"Battlefield?" First, they claimed there was tension between the two dominions. Now I have to worry about an actual battle?

"There hasn't been an all-out war in about three hundred years, but there have been plenty of skirmishes along the border. Things are getting worse between the two dominions though, so we've been training with ursas for the last fifteen years in case the time comes that we need them for a true fight. Why do you think we were desperate enough to kidnap you just to access a weapon?"

I never thought of it like that. I was so wrapped up in the craziness of the kidnapping itself, I assumed that the reason they needed me was just as crazy. Even if I'm hallucinating some of what I'm seeing, it can't all be fake. And if anything that Aneira said is true, wherever we are is preparing for something big. More soldiers are along the border of the wall patrolling the area and street peddlers are selling personal defense devices.

As we approach the several guards at the actual city entrance, everyone notices our group at once.

Conversations quiet down and one of the soldiers at the gate addresses us. "Prince Delwyn, Captain Sage, Idris, Aneira." Captain? Sage never said she was a captain.

The soldier bows to Delwyn and gives the rest of them respectful nods. His eyes move over me. "And who is this?"

"*This* can speak for himself. I do have a name," I say. My

friends used to say my politeness had no limits but apparently I found it — getting kidnapped.

"Can't wait to hear it," he replies. This guy reminds me more of Sage than her supposed cousin.

Delwyn interrupts us before things can escalate further. I may not have the battle training as the rest of this kingdom, but I played D1 lacrosse in college and have kept myself in fairly good shape since then. I'd like to think I could hold my own should the need arise.

"Thank you for the warm welcome back, everyone," Delwyn says.

He must be well loved, wherever we are, as I look at all the people swarming us. They stare at Delwyn with either great deference, love, or something like lust — both the women and men. Truth be told, they stare at all of them like that.

When they look at Sage, it's more like fear than love. But definitely lust. That doesn't surprise me one bit. I can already tell she's ruthless. If that's the impression I got from a couple days with her, I can't imagine what it's been like growing up around her. And the lust, well, I get that too. I can hate her and still want to devour her.

When their eyes reach me, they look puzzled and wary. Maybe this entire weird town wasn't aware of this group's little kidnapping scheme. I try to give a reassuring smile. It's not their fault that this group of people took me against my will, and everyone here seems nice enough. Besides that asshole guard.

Sage decides that we're done being sidetracked. "As Prince Delwyn said, we appreciate all the warm well wishes back. The festivities tonight will double as a celebration of our successful mission. Until then, we're all pretty tired and need to rest up. We suggest you all do the same." Every single person who had been swarming our group quickly goes back to their days as soon as Sage finishes speaking.

Two polar bears — ursas, I guess — spot our group and slowly pick up speed. The people crowding our group scatter as the two animals barrel into Delwyn and Sage. Shit. These animals must not be as well trained as Aneira said. Delwyn and Sage's bodies are completely covered by the beasts, so I have no idea what's going on, but no one around me is worried.

I hear laughter so I turn back to Aneira, but her mouth is closed with a soft smile as she stares at the two bears. It's then that I realize that the laughter is coming from underneath one of the ursas. The ursas move and Delwyn and Sage both stand up, covered in slobber.

The laughter is Sage's, and it sounds like heaven — light and sweet one moment, and deep and a little gravelly the next. Her laugh is just like her — full of contradictions. This is the first time I've ever heard her laugh that genuinely and it's because she was tackled by a seven-hundred-pound creature.

"I missed you too, Blizzard," Sage says to the ursa as it continues to try to lick her face. She scratches behind its ears, and it shakes its leg like a dog.

"How you doing, Bluebell?" Delwyn says to the ursa that won't leave his side. Then, like this isn't already the most bizarre thing I've ever seen, they both climb onto the backs of the animals.

"Come on, *shifrah*," Sage says. "You're riding with me."

What the fuck does *shifrah* mean?

Either way… "I don't fucking think so."

"Oh, don't tell me you're scared of this teddy bear?" Blizzard decides to take this moment to turn his head and look at me. More like a grizzly than a teddy.

"Not scared. I'd just rather not break all the bones in my body before I have a chance to return home."

"There's no returning home now and Blizzard is the smoothest ride in town. Besides, you don't really want to have to walk *all* the way to the palace, do you?" I look up in the direction of the palace. Once the roads begin to turn, it's impossible to tell how long the journey would be on foot. As far as I can estimate, we're still at least a mile out and the road towards it looks almost excessively windy. Unfortunately, she's right. I'm already exhausted from this endless journey and need to have energy for what's sure to be another weird night.

"Alright fine, but if this thing so much as licks me, I'm pushing you off it."

"I think there's a better likelihood of me licking you before Blizzard."

"Princess, do you not remember? You already did." She didn't, but I almost wish she did when she sends a heated look my way.

I smirk at her as I climb onto the massive beast. His fur is surprisingly soft, like a fuzzy blanket. I wrap my arms around Sage's waist and my hands involuntarily squeeze her curves.

"Slow down there, Pretty Boy. Let's at least get inside first," she says, turning over her shoulder to look at me with a sexy-as-fuck smile. I quickly remove my hands from her waist, realize there's nothing else to hold onto, and gently put them back.

"You really should get some seat belts or something," I grumble into her ear.

"I'll keep that in mind for the next time."

Before I even have time to retort, we take off in a sprint down the smooth road. I turn back to Delwyn, Aneira, and Idris close on our tails on Bluebell and a focused look takes over Delwyn's face. He whispers something into his ursa's ear, and she picks up speed.

They get closer and closer, weaving around people, other ursa's, actual horses, and carts. I can't understand how these gigantic things aren't hitting anyone at the speed we're going, but they avoid everything. Delwyn gets close enough that we're now running side by side. Sage glances over at them, flashes a wild grin, and shoots something into the air above us.

We gain a lead, and I look behind me to see what she shot and it's fucking fire. She shot fire into the air. It could've hit any number of people, homes, or animals, but she clearly doesn't care. Almost as quickly as the fire was thrown, Delwyn throws his own ice into the air to put it out with a feral grin.

"How did you know he was going to do that?" I shout over the wind as we race through the streets.

"Because I would've done the same thing and he's a much better person than me." I now understand that this is a game, a race, and by Sage throwing fire in the air and forcing Delwyn to put it out, she slowed them down significantly.

I can't help but smile to myself. She may be ruthless, but she's also smart. As we race through the streets of Bruma, I look around as much as I can at our incredibly fast speed.

Some of the streets we run through are barely wide enough for Blizzard, while others are four car lengths wide. Most are smooth paved cobblestone, inlaid with ice.

I guess these people don't need to worry about slipping on something that's so common to them. So common that it's literally everywhere I look; not only on the roads, but the ice is part of the walls of shops, apartments, and restaurants, and even form their own structures like balconies and terraces higher above.

Everything is colored in cool tones — blues, purples, silvers, grays, and blacks. The roads are cleaner than any city streets I've ever been on, and although some people are startled at our quick approach, most just smile and wave. I study their clothes and notice a wide range of attire; from suits, dresses, comfy wear, and everything in between. Luckily, most of the outerwear looks warm and lined with fur, although I have to imagine they're all used to the cold.

On the main roads, there's some sort of trolley system that runs along tracks. I don't have enough time to study the technology because we move too quickly. I also see some form of a car, but it is so different-looking I can barely call it that. It's more like a sled/carriage/boat that's made of metal and ice and some other material I have no hope of guessing. They range in size, from those large enough for two people to those that can fit twenty. The interiors look very comfortable, with cushioned seats. Some of the tops are open to the elements, but most are covered with a clear ice top, allowing the passengers to have an unimpeded view of the city around them.

After a few more minutes of running, Sage says something that I can't hear.

"Did you say something?" I ask.

"No, sorry, I was talking to Blizzard."

"Blizzard, as in your ursa?"

"Yes."

"You're talking to an animal." Is she for real? Maybe she is crazy.

"Yes, Pretty Boy. You need to get out of your Earth mind. While we can't literally communicate through words, because humans and animals are both connected to Mother Nature, we're able to convey larger emotions or feelings to one another. The more time you spend with an animal, the more you understand one another and the more nuanced your messages can be."

"Mhm." Okay, yeah, crazy.

"Blizzard and I have been together since we've both been pups. For example, I can tell that right now he thinks you're an idiot."

"Hey!" Seriously? Maybe she's the one who thinks I'm an idiot. Why does that make me disappointed?

Blizzard makes a noise that can't be described as anything but a chuckle.

Great. Now the animals are anthropomorphizing.

We approach the inner gates that lead into the palace. We don't slow down as Blizzard sprints through the gates and stops at the bottom of the palace steps so suddenly that sparks fly from his claws. Sage hops off him mid stop, puts out the flames like it's not even a conscious thought, and I barely manage to hold onto Blizzard and make my way off his back as the rest of the group enters behind us on Bluebell.

Idris jumps off their ursa first, her golden-hair looking disheveled for the first time since I've met her. "Delwyn never wins. Next time I'm squeezing on Blizzard with you two," she mumbles as she heads into the palace.

Sage chuckles and moves to walk into the castle with Aneira and Delwyn. She walks around like she expects everyone around her to follow. So presumptuous.

We jog up the steps and enter two massive doors made of ice with intricate patterns swirling within. I try to slow down to study them more closely, but Sage grabs my arm and pulls me inside. I'm obviously nervous, but another part of me is amazed; everything I've seen so far points to a highly functioning society. I don't understand how they've remained hidden.

As we walk down the hallways, I can't help but admire the palace. It reminds me of one of those ancient castles in Europe but also modern at the same time. Intricate, bone white molding lines where the walls meet the ceiling and floor, and large arches cross over one another.

The architecture in this city brings me back to trips to Europe I used to go on with my parents. A pang of sadness runs through me — too much reminds me of them, even now. But if they were here, they would want me to take advantage of this opportunity and learn something while I try to figure out how to escape.

The art on the walls is detailed and painstakingly done, depicting battles, woodland creatures, and royal family portraits. The floor is tiled with white and blue stones that are so bright it's hard to stare at for too long. There's enough light to suggest modern lighting — although within old-fashioned looking fixtures — and there's definitely some sort of central air as the temperature inside is perfect.

We pass a few people as we weave our way through the

castle, and every single person has striking blue eyes. Their skin tones range from Sage's porcelain to Aneira's onyx as well as their hair color, but those could easily be dyed. But their eyes — they range from almost white to a stormy gray, but they're all clearly shades of blue. Every single person here has had blue eyes except for Sage and Idris.

Living in New York City, I was used to seeing a wide-range of people. Considering I've never even heard of this place, I don't understand how this diversity managed to end up here. All the blue eyes are a little creepy, but for once, I don't stand out. Being mixed-race with light-colored eyes always led to stares back home, albeit appreciative ones. Now, I'm one of many. I'd think that would make me sad, but strangely, I feel... home?

Everyone we pass bows quickly, then continues on their way. Their uniforms vary, probably based on their roles in the palace. Some have simple and plain light blue dresses or loose shirts and pants. Others wear more intricate dresses and suits, covered in jewelry, which I would assume signify more importance.

The soldiers stationed at the corner of each hallway wear armor that looks like metal but moves as flexibly as regular clothing. The soldiers don't bow as we pass, but salute as they keep their stiff form.

After we pass each group in the hallway, a few linger to stare at us, with me getting the longest looks. None of my companions register anyone we walk past, Sage most of all. It's not surprising, considering she thinks she's better than everyone else. Aneira is the only one who gives warm smiles and small waves at everyone.

We walk through another set of massive doors, this time

with ice that's inlaid with silver and gold, and enter a massive chamber. Pillars two people wide border the empty space and floor to ceiling stained-glass windows run down the walls to the left and right of us. Straight ahead is a raised stage with three thrones. Sitting in the largest one in the middle is an older, female version of Delwyn. Looks like I'm meeting the queen.

Chapter Seven

Sage

We approach the dais where Queen Neve waits for us, looking like the epitome of royalty. Dahlia isn't on her throne to the left, so she must be busy in a meeting or training session because she almost never misses greeting us when we return from a mission.

"Welcome back, Son, Sage, Idris, and Aneira," she says, working her way down our line, passing over Aiden. Her turquoise eyes track back to him. "And you must be Aiden."

"The one and only." I can tell he's nervous even though he's trying to put on a brave face. I have to admit, I've been astounded by how calmly he's handled all of this. Besides a few escape attempts and snarky comments, he's never seemed all that scared.

That is why I gave him his little nickname, *shifrah*. It's what my parents used to call me growing up. There are many meanings; beautiful, clever, calm, and fair. And he is beautiful, but more than that, he has this inner peace that has allowed him to adapt like no one I've ever seen before.

And of course, the name's usually reserved for females, but I need to knock him down a peg, even if he doesn't know it.

Part of the reason he's so calm has to be because his soul is home. But right now, his voice slightly shakes as he tries to act calm and collected. He stands a little too straight and his chin's just a little too high.

"You must not be all that thrilled to be taken from your home and thrown into what is undoubtedly a strange environment, but my dominion appreciates your sacrifice more than I can convey." Queen Neve has read his emotions even quicker than me. Then again, she's always been great at reading people. It's part of what's made her such a ruthless and efficient leader. As she speaks, Aiden drops his shoulders a little, as if he finally has someone sane to speak to.

"You're nice enough for a queen, and I'm not sure how this city has managed to remain this isolated, but I'm not who you think I am. I don't belong here. Whatever weird cult, religion, community this is, I want no part of it."

The queen gives a conciliatory smile. "I'm afraid that is not an option. I've been receiving messages from Sage as you journeyed here, and I assure you, you are who we've been looking for. I know you think we are crazy and that we drugged you to make you believe us, but I promise after tonight, you will no longer think that."

I snort at that. He's almost as stubborn as me. If he doesn't want to believe us, the festival tonight is certainly not going to convince him.

"Something you'd like to add, Sage?" The queen puts her piercing eyes on mine.

"Oh, no. I was thinking about tonight's festivities. I think it will prove very *enlightening* for Aiden." He glares at me through his peripheral vision, not wanting to turn his head away from the queen.

Aneira and Idris both try to stop their chuckles, but some noises squeak out. Delwyn can't help himself and bellows in laughter at us trying to contain ourselves. At his ridiculous cackle, we all hysterically laugh, the noise echoing through the empty throne room. Aiden tilts his head as he looks at us and Queen Neve shakes hers.

"Sounds like you guys are having all of the fun without me!" I look in the direction of the voice to Dahlia walking in from the doors to the right of the dais. She truly encapsulates an Ice Dominion princess. She could be made from snow itself — her hair is as white as her brother's and mother's, and her skin is just as pale. Even her eyelashes are white, which frame her turquoise eyes that match her mother's. Her dress accentuates her angelic frame and coloring. Diamonds and sapphires frame a plunging neckline with the dress tapering in at the waist and billowing out into a beautiful train. A small cape is attached to her shoulders as well. Her whole outfit sparkles like fresh snow, and if you look closely, you can tell that the sparkles make a million snowflakes all over her dress. It's stunning. I'm jealous.

She approaches all of us but gives me a hug first. As we embrace, she whispers in my ear, "You're right, he is gorgeous." I had sent her a wind message once we entered Tirlun.

"I forgot to add — he's a massive pain in my ass and an egotistical prick." He's really not, but Mother I wish he was.

"Those have always been your favorite." She gives me a knowing look.

We pull away and she hugs the rest of our crew. She stops in front of Aiden. "Aiden, this is Dahlia, my cousin and the heir to the Ice Dominion throne."

Aiden startles as he realizes I'm speaking to him. He hasn't taken his eyes off her since she entered the room, not that I've been looking. He gives her a respectful nod.

"Normally I would demand you bow, but Sage has made it clear that you think we are a bunch of lunatics, so I'll let it slide," she says.

Her voice sounds like the most peaceful snowfall; light, gentle, and soothing. I've always been jealous of her because of that. My voice is deeper than most females' and a little gravelly. Then again, I would never want to be heir to the throne — way too much responsibility — but the clothes and jewels are definitely a nice bonus.

Aiden blushes. I haven't seen him blush since the first night we met, and I was flirting with him. Now he blushes for Dahlia, and it feels like a stone has settled in my stomach.

Aiden crosses his arms over his chest. "I apologize, but I'm not familiar with crazy-people royal etiquette."

Dahlia smiles widely and her teeth sparkle almost as much as her dress. "Oh, I like him." Alright, we need to leave this room before I hurt someone.

"Okay, well we should rest and get ready for the party tonight," I say towards Dahlia, but make sure to look at the rest of my crew. Everyone gets the hint, and we bow again to

Queen Neve — even Aiden, to my surprise — and follow Dahlia out of the back doors she came in through.

We make our way through the palace and eventually come to our bedroom hallway. "Come on Pretty Boy. Your room is attached to mine."

"Again?" Aiden asks. "Will I ever be rid of you?"

"I would say in your dreams, but we all know I'm in those too." I give him a devilish grin and open my bedroom doors. Delwyn and Dahlia laugh behind us as we enter my room.

"Wow, this is massive."

My room is my safe space. I come here when I need time alone to breathe or think, or scream or cry. I've spent basically my entire twenty-five years creating a space that is perfectly mine. And now I have to share it with him. I'm the only one with a second bedroom in their suite, but that doesn't mean I can't be annoyed about it.

"I'll give you a little tour," I say begrudgingly to him.

The main doors lead to my sitting room, where a massive white fluffy couch sits in front of a giant fireplace. On either side of the couch are two deliciously buttery brown leather chairs. Massive windows look out into the city, with two small balconies leading out of two of the floor to ceiling windows. One balcony has a table with three chairs where I like to take my coffee and read in the mornings. To the left of the couch space is a small handcrafted wooden dining table. I had one of the local artisans make it to fit the dimensions of the space perfectly, as well as the six matching chairs that surround it. I try to keep my room clean, but a couple books are strewn about, as well as some melted candles.

"So, as you can see, this is my main living space. To the left is my bedchamber with my bathroom attached."

I walk towards the right as he says, "Do I not get to see your room?"

"Considering as you'll never be in it, I don't see why you should."

"Am I not in your dreams too?" I glare at him. He gets on my nerves. My glares aren't even as effective as they should be since he towers over me, and I have to crane my head up to make eye contact. Asshole.

"Fine. Follow me." We enter the door on the left into my room.

"What's that?" Aiden shouts. My eyes track where he's staring.

"That's Fluffy."

"Fluffy?"

"She's my fox." Fluffy's wagging tail gives her away, otherwise she would've blended in with my throw pillows "Oh, Fluffy, we need to work on your stealth mode," I say as I sit on the bed to give her the belly rub she's clearly begging for.

"I would never have guessed you would name a pet Fluffy."

"I didn't name her, my mom did," I say as a pang of sadness runs through me.

"So she's your mom's?"

"She was. She's mine now."

"Why did she give her to you?"

"My parents died" I say softly.

"Mine did too… last year," he says. What? His file did *not* mention that.

"I'm so sorry," I say, and mean it. "Mine passed fifteen years ago, but I still miss them every day." Why did I say that? He definitely doesn't care about his kidnapper's sob story.

"You don't have to talk about it if you don't want to, but, what happened?" He almost sounds like he cares. He's definitely just trying to find enough information on me to manipulate me later. It's what I would do if I was in his position. But I can't help but use any excuse I can find to talk about my parents.

"The Fire Dominion attacked this castle fifteen years ago and they both died trying to defend it. Which is ironic, considering my dad used to be the general for the Fire Dominion and they killed him just the same," I shake my head at the memory. I miss them so much it hurts. They were one of the few people who knew the real me.

"Shit."

"Yeah, shit is right. I was ten years old, and they managed to hide me and Fluffy in the dungeon. She was all I had with me that night." I look back at Fluffy's sweet face. You'd never know what a fierce protector she is.

"Why were you in the dungeon?"

"Why would the Fire Dominion ever think the Ice Dominion would put a noble in the dirtiest, most dangerous part of the castle?"

"I guess that makes sense."

I shake my head as I say, "Except, they did find me. How they knew where to look is beyond me, but they went all the way through the dungeon, to the last cell, as if they knew exactly where I was hiding. I was cornered, scared to death, and only ten. I thought for sure I was a goner. But, Fluffy attacked one of them and as she fought back something came over me and I threw all my magic at the other two. I don't know how, but it was enough to push them back into a cell and lock them inside."

Over the course of recounting my memory, I realize Aiden has sunk to the floor on his knees.

I take a deep breath and continue. "Fluffy had incapacitated the third soldier enough for me to drag him into another empty cell and lock it before he could fight back. Magic doesn't work when our cell doors are locked so they were powerless. When it came to their sentence, the queen let me decide. I thought an eternity in our worst prison in the Ailec Woods was a fate worse than death. And fifteen years later, they're still wasting away in there like the rot they are." I look at him sitting on the ground with a hand covering his mouth.

He removes his hand from his mouth. "My parents passed away in a car accident. You do know what a car is, right?" He tries to cover up his sadness with his little quip at the end. I get not wanting to talk about it, though. I do the same thing.

"Yes, I know what a car is," I say, rolling my eyes. "Our magic never required us to develop transportation vehicles like that." I look up at him. It is evident how much he cared for his parents and fuck, if it doesn't pull at my heart. "I guess we do have something in common."

"I guess so."

Trying to change the subject, he asks, "So if Fluffy was

your mom's and she died ten years ago, how old is she? She looks and acts like a baby."

"Foxes in Tirlun are almost as immortal as we are," I say, smiling.

"I'm sorry, immortal?" he practically yells.

"Did I not mention that? Humans here are essentially immortal. We do age, just very slowly. Most decide to release themselves back to the Mother after a couple thousand years, but they could theoretically live longer." Only, my parents got less than a thousand years. And I only got ten with them. Sometimes the Mother is cruel.

"But you're only twenty-five?" he asks.

"Yeah, very young. In fact, I'm the youngest captain in the queen's guard history," I say as I cross my arms over my chest.

"By centuries, it sounds like."

"A traumatic life moment really ages you."

His eyes soften. I did not mean for this conversation to get off track like this. My friends and I have dealt with more tragedy than most, even in Tirlun. But, somehow, without even trying, Aiden understands without me needing to say the words as he asks me another question to distract me. "So, you're a captain, huh?"

"Yes, I'm in charge of several squadrons of soldiers. For the most part, I'm assigned smaller, more critical missions that are just me and my team."

"Your team... your friends I've met?"

Fluffy comes to sit on my lap and I pet her as I explain. "They're my friends and my family and there's no one else I would trust with my life. I'm the captain, Del handles all our political dealings, Aneira does strategy and training, and Idris is in charge of spying and recon."

Aiden scoots himself closer to me and also starts to pet Fluffy. "Based on the little I've seen of them, that all makes sense to me except for Delwyn."

A small laugh escapes my mouth. "Yeah, he doesn't seem like he would be politically astute. That's why he's the best."

Aiden gives me a warm smile in response. And it does things to me I'd rather not acknowledge.

He keeps stroking Fluffy and she chitters with happiness at all the attention. "You never said how old Fluffy was."

"My dad gave my mom Fluffy as a wedding gift three hundred years ago."

"Fluffy is three hundred years old?"

"Yes, and that's not all." I look down at Fluffy. "Fluffy, please show Aiden here your outfit for the Fire Dominion." In the blink of an eye, Fluffy's fur turns from bright white to a fiery red. Aiden's eyes widen in shock, and I can't help but laugh.

"Foxes in Tirlun are prized animals because they're able to live in both dominions. Most animals can only survive one of our extreme temperatures. But since my father came from the Fire Dominion, he wanted my mother to have a pet that she could bring everywhere."

"That's actually very romantic."

"Yeah, they really loved each other even though it started as an arranged marriage."

"Arranged?"

"Aneira has been lacking in her history lessons, I see." Aneira filled me in on what she told Aiden after I went to my tent last night. I guess she didn't want to overwhelm him with information. Not that he believes any of it anyway. "After the war she told you about, as part of the peace agreement, many arranged marriages between the two dominions took place to prevent further conflict. My father, being the general of the Fire Dominion, was married to my mother, the sister to the queen of the Ice Dominion. It was probably the most important political marriage that came out of the war and took the Fire Dominion's best general into the Ice Dominion." And brought my father to my mother, which may turn out to be the worst decision the leaders of Tirlun ever made.

"Wow, so you really are a princess," he says.

"Hardly. If anything, princess adjacent." This may be the most pleasant conversation we've had since our first night. But, I can't keep talking about the past. I'll get lost there.

"Anyway, back to the task at hand. My bathroom is over there." I wave an arm in the direction of the bathroom door. "That other door on the other side of my bed is my closet. And that's everything in here."

"Wait, wait, wait. I think you missed a door," he says, pointing to the door I tried very hard to ignore.

"You don't get to see what's in that door."

"No?"

"No. That's a privilege you have yet to earn," I say, getting up from my bed and leaving the room, Fluffy close on my tail. He'll never see what's behind that door if I can help it. It's the tools, balms, and poultices to help me manage my pain. That's a weakness he can never know.

Aiden follows me back into the main living space. "That door next to the entry doors is my library. And that door by the windows is your room," I say walking towards it. When I lived here with my parents, this was my suite, but has since turned into a guest room after I moved into theirs. It has a matching bedspread to mine, on a slightly smaller bed. There's a small dresser and desk in matching wood, a closet, a private balcony, and a private bathroom.

He looks around. "This is actually pretty nice."

"Only the best for my prisoners," I say, smirking at him. "I had sent your measurements ahead to the royal tailor, so there should be enough clothes in here for your entire wardrobe."

"How do you have my measurements?"

I slowly look him up and down. "Let's just say I'm a very good judge of men and their proportions." More like I used Del as a model and made some slight adjustments. But, it's much more fun to make him think I studied his body so closely. Especially when that adorable blush comes over his cheeks.

He awkwardly chuckles. "Uhh—"

I save him from responding; I guess I'm feeling generous today. "You can take a shower or a bath and nap. I'll have food brought up into my living room. The party starts promptly at eight, so I'll meet you in the main space then at the latest. And in case it hasn't already been made abundantly clear, please do not try to escape. We're on the third floor of the castle, plus there are soldiers constantly patrolling. The last thing we need is for you to break your bones before the party tonight."

His eyes take in the room as I take him in. His pupils are dilated and his hands clench by his sides, but I can't think of anything to say to calm him. I've never been good at that. But the truth is, we need him. I need him, as much as I hate to admit it.

He shocks me by thanking me. I think that's the first time he's said that to me. I can't help but give him a genuine smile as I leave his room and shut the door. Taking a deep breath, I pad across the communal space back into my room. I can't wait for this fucking bath.

Chapter Eight

Aiden

I check the clock that's on top of the dresser in my room. 7:30. Perfect timing. I'm shocked at how luxurious this place is. Considering how our journey started, and how wherever we are must be in the middle of nowhere, I can't believe this city has all these amenities. That shower was one of the best I've ever had. The water pressure was amazing and there was every kind of shampoo and body soap. I spent way too long in there, but I felt nasty after being in the woods for two days straight. I haven't felt that dirty since I went camping with my parents over twenty years ago.

I open the closet to investigate my clothing options. I have no clue how Sage knew my measurements. She's surprised me since we've gotten to this castle. There's no way I could've been drugged again since this morning. So, whatever this place is, it's real. I can't figure out why they felt the need to convince me of magic and nobles. It's unnecessary. Maybe what they actually need me for is going to be so horrible it was better to come up with some outlandish story to tell me instead.

If being positive was effective at helping me move on from my parents' deaths, it should be able to get me through this. The festival tonight will be my best chance to escape; if I miss it, I'll be here for the foreseeable future. I'm going to need to play my part perfectly to have any chance of getting out of here.

I select a light blue tunic-style shirt. I've been told that this color compliments my skin tone and brings out my eyes, and Sage must agree. There are multiple pants options ranging in thickness, color, and material, so I select black slacks that feel like sweatpants but look like something I would wear to a meeting. I was worried my choices would be stiff and awkward based on the clothes Sage gave me on the way here, but these are comfortable and stylish in their own way. I grab a black coat as well since it's perpetually cold in the "Ice Dominion," and put on black leather boots that fit like they've been molded to my feet. Goddamn.

The only way for Sage to have gotten the fit of all these clothes so well is if she measured my body in my sleep. The thought brings a shock of electricity up my spine and a slight blush to my cheeks, but it's her fault I'm in this mess in the first place.

How she managed to get them sent here and had clothes made before we arrived is a mystery.

I check my outfit one last time in the mirror that hangs on the back of the bathroom door, fix a few stray strands of my hair, and step out into the common space.

My limbs refuse to move from my doorway. She hasn't seen me yet. Sage stands by the open balcony doors with her back to me. She's fucking stunning, wearing an emerald green floor length gown. The back of the gown is completely open and hugs her ass so perfectly. The silk looks buttery smooth, and my hand involuntarily moves towards her as if to touch it. I quickly pull it back to my side before I clear my throat.

"Oh, I know you've been standing there. I wanted to see how long you were going to stare before you decided to speak." She looks at me from over her shoulder.

Her face is glowing. She lined her eyes in black, which only makes them pop more, and with lips that look like a juicy peach that I would die to bite. Her hair fell over her shoulder as she looked at me and her auburn waves are perfect, layered with pearls and emeralds scattered through-out. If I didn't know better, I would've assumed she was the princess of this dominion. Minus the color of the dress, she certainly looks the part.

"You'll let flies into your mouth if you keep it hanging open any longer," she winks as she walks towards the dining room table.

I blush and snap my mouth shut as I move to sit down across from her at the table. "Sorry, you just... You look... Well, you look incredible."

"Is that a compliment, Aiden? I didn't know you had those in you when it came to me." This may be one of the first times she's called me Aiden and not Pretty Boy or *shifrah*, whatever that means, and it's doing things to me that I'd rather not focus on while I'm trying to escape.

"Yes, well, for the last several days we've all been in thick layers and pants, so who knew what you would look like in a dress? But I would assume it took you the entire time getting ready to end up like this." She sends a quick glare my way through her full eyelashes, and even though she looks deadly, I can only think about how beautiful she is. And how gorgeous those eyes would look staring up at me with her mouth around my cock. Fuck. No. Not tonight.

I get hard at the thought so I look for something to distract me. Serving myself some food, I have to get out of my seat to reach some of the veggies, and too late I realize that my erection is above the table. I quickly sit back down.

"You're not the only one who's giving me a compliment tonight," she says as her eyes look down at my pants. Shit. She did see that.

"Yes, well you know that I find you attractive. Unfortunately, my body is struggling to control itself."

Her smile is dangerous, but before she can respond, Delwyn, Idris, and Aneira burst through Sage's doors, talking over each other. Aneira is in a yellow and brown dress that flows perfectly around her toned body. The warm dress brings out the warmth in her dark skin and somehow also in her blue eyes. Delwyn's wearing a royal suit — blue and silver lapels framed by gold trim and straight-legged navy pants. The gold buttons are polished to perfection, and he even has a small gold and silver crown sitting on top of his white hair. Idris is in a purple and pink velvet dress, which makes her look more feminine than I've ever seen her.

"I can't wait for the ice show!" Aneira exclaims.

"I can't wait for the dragon battle," Delwyn says.

"Dragon battle?" I ask. "Please don't tell me you guys have dragons too."

"Not in the literal sense. Though I wish," Delwyn says.

"Some of our best artisans craft these massive dragons out of ice and work with expert spell-casters to make them as life-like as possible. I think they would be, maybe like, robots in your world? Anyway, then there's a giant battle in the sky and the last dragon standing wins a huge prize!"

"Delwyn can't help himself when it comes to anything violent," Idris butts in from where she's sitting on the couch.

The constant bickering between these people is more like siblings than a group of soldiers for a kingdom.

"What can I say, I live for the thrill," he grins.

"This is a little large for a celebration just because of a successful mission," I say. I didn't think there would be performances and shows. I was just picturing lots of food and maybe some music.

"What you don't know, Pretty Boy," Sage waves her fork in the air, "is that your entire bloodline was nobles of the highest caliber. Besides your ability to retrieve the lost weapon, most of our citizens believe it is a positive omen from Mother Nature that you have returned to Tirlun just as tensions are increasing again with the Fire Dominion. In fact, most people have no idea there even *is* a weapon and assume we were just bringing you home."

"No pressure or anything. Does this mean I'm considered a noble here?" My legs involuntarily shake under the table.

"Indeed," Delwyn answers. "And Mother knows, we need some fresh blood at this stuffy noble event," he says as he makes a plate piled high with food.

"Why do you keep saying "Mother"? Is this more of your culty nonsense?" I'm still reeling from the revelation that I'm a literal noble, but I can't keep ignoring the way they constantly say that word in such a reverential way.

"I got this one," Idris says from the couch.

My eyebrows raise; she's by far the quietest out of their little group and doesn't speak unless absolutely necessary or to make a little quip to one of her friends.

"Mother Nature is our god, or the closest thing to a god, but none of us would ever define her so restrictively. She is who we pray to, thank, and look to for guidance. The Mother rules over all living things and therefore influences fate and the way of the world. In that respect, I suppose nature is our religion, but none of us would ever classify it as such."

I have so many questions, but Idris is almost musical in the way she speaks, so I bite my tongue and wait for her to finish.

"We thank the ground and the world for our lives and are secure in the fact that we will return to it when our time is up." She finishes speaking and there's a hush over the entire room. The way Idris speaks, I wouldn't be surprised if she was secretly a priestess of this so-called not religion.

As Idris' comments sink in, Aneira stops snacking on some of the vegetables. "It's why, if you haven't been able to tell so far, we are so respectful of nature and do as little to harm Tirlun as possible. Even when we're on Earth, we try to make as little impact as we can. It's also why our world has never developed those horrible factories churning out chemicals or industrial farms. In that regard, you may view us as less developed than you, but we could never imagine developing to the detriment of the Mother."

This makes more sense than most religions. "I actually really respect that," I say and Aneira beams at me like I just told her she won the lottery. Her smile can make even the grumpiest person grin and I can't help but give one back.

"Okay everyone, class is over. Let's party," Sage says to us all, looking like trouble. Based on everyone else's ensuing grins, I'm in for quite a night. As long as I can keep my wits about me, this could be the perfect opportunity for escape.

Chapter Nine

Sage

We head down as a group back to the throne room. I don't think Aiden will be stupid enough to try to escape again, but if there's any time to try, it would be tonight in the craziness of the celebration. It's why I had a meeting with the city's guards to be extra diligent to make sure he doesn't leave.

I can't help but laugh at his little comment that it took me the entire afternoon to get ready. He has no idea what I did while he was in his room; I spoke to all the soldiers, had a private meeting with the queen to give her a formal update, went to the massage therapist, did some yoga to stretch out my joints, bathed, *and* got ready. He would be shocked that it only took me a half hour to get ready. Benefits of magic and my amazing servants, I suppose.

I think back to my conversation with the queen. After updating her on the details of our past couple of days, she was quiet for a few moments. Then she said, "Sage, this mission is critical for our dominion. I won't lie to you — I have a feeling we will need to use the weapon. Those Fire Dominion kings will do anything to exert more power."

It took everything in me not to snort at that. *She's* the one on the hunt for the strongest weapon ever made; it's her that wants more power. Then again, she's always been excellent at twisting the truth. I had to learn it from somewhere.

There must be some spell surrounding the weapon, preventing anyone from remembering what it really is. While most people still alive from that time were too young to fight, you'd still think that a weapon as infamous as this one would have more details.

Is it a sword? A talisman? A monster?

If my mission is a success, I guess I'm going to find out.

We have a map of where the Ice Dominion believes the weapon was left at the end of the war, but it only provides a vague location. Whatever magic surrounds the weapon must cloak both what and where it is, making this mission our hardest yet.

Aiden's bloodline is the only one that can use the weapon, so I can only pray to the Mother that it will call to him when we reach it.

Before we enter the throne room, the soldiers guarding the door stop us. Apparently Queen Neve has demanded a formal announcement of our presence. I get why, I just wasn't prepared for it, and if there's anything I hate, it's being unprepared and uninformed.

A herald silences the crowd and says, "Citizens of the Ice Dominion. May we announce the return of Prince Delwyn, Captain Sage, Miss Aneira, Miss Idris Fintan, and returning to Tirlun after centuries, Lord Aiden Columben of the Columben noble line!"

Delwyn and I enter the room first, arm in arm, followed by Idris and Aneira, and Aiden in the back. It's deathly silent as we enter, which gives me time to survey the room before having to make small talk.

Each marble column bordering the dance floor is woven with blue, white, and lavender ribbons. Upside down white peonies, bluebells, and more wisteria than I thought possible hang from the ceiling. Several drink stations line the edges of the room with castle servants standing at attention to help the guests. I don't see any food, so it's a good thing we ate before. I'm sure once we go into town we can grab food at a snack cart, but who knows what time it'll be before we make it down there.

Lord Boann approaches us as soon as we walk into the room. As one of Queen Neve's closest advisors, it makes sense he will try to congratulate us first — but it doesn't change the fact that I can't stand him.

"Prince Delwyn, Captain Sage," he says bowing to us. "I want to congratulate you both on an extremely successful mission. If we are able to find and utilize this weapon, it will be a huge advantage in the upcoming war."

"You say that like war is certain," I say.

I fear Lord Boann and some of the others in the queen's council want the war — they see it as a power grab and a chance to hurt those in the Fire Dominion. "The whole point of this mission is to access the weapon so we *don't* have to use it," I add.

"Of course, Captain. Or do you prefer to go by Lady when we're at court?" It takes everything in me not to roll my eyes at his jab. Some of the nobles don't think it's appropriate that a lady of my status is the captain of the queen's guard. But of course, if I was a man, it wouldn't be questioned. I like to think Tirlun is much more progressive than Earth when it comes to these things, but then men like Lord Boann prove me wrong.

"Captain is more than fine," I say through clenched teeth.

His eyes roam up and down my body as hunger fills his eyes. "It's just... How are you expected to find a husband if you are constantly on missions and leading soldiers?"

Like all I'm good for is getting married off to some noble?

"Queen Neve finds my skills on the battlefield to be more important than my skills in producing an heir. Are you disagreeing with the queen in her decision to have me be a captain?"

Lord Boann cringes and puts his hands out in supplication.

He's been trying to arrange a marriage between me and his eldest son, Roman, from the moment it was appropriate to do so. If he didn't have a wife already, I'm sure he would be trying to arrange it with himself. Roman may be even more insufferable than his father — so self-important, obnoxious, and somehow a bigger flirt than me. And not in a fun way.

Before things can get more heated between Lord Boann and me, Delwyn thanks him for his congratulations and leads us towards a drink table. "It's like you're looking to get into arguments wherever you go."

"I can't help it that every single noble makes me want to rip my hair out," I smile at him sweetly.

"You can't hold them off forever. Many lords and their sons are in the army *and* married."

"Oh yeah, so where's your wife?"

"Lucky for me, that decision is taking the queen a lot longer to make." Delwyn wants to get married as much as I do, which is to say, not at all. As the prince, his marriage has to be extremely strategic. I'd guess that Queen Neve is waiting for things with the Fire Dominion to play out in case a political marriage between the two courts is necessary — like the marriage between my parents.

The herald quiets the crowd again as he says, "And now, Queen Neve and Princess Dahlia!"

We turn towards the doors as Delwyn's mom and sister enter the room. "Shouldn't you have entered with them? Or at the very least, be waiting by the dais?" I say, nudging him with my elbow.

"Probably," he shrugs. "But mom is going to yell at me no matter what I do, so I might as well have fun hanging out with my cousin first," he says as he puts an arm around me. I swear, he looks for any opportunity to act like he's not royalty.

Queen Neve and Dahlia enter looking like ice themselves. Dahlia stayed in her dress from earlier, but the queen has certainly dressed up for the celebration; compared to the simple yet elegant sky-blue dress she wore when we saw her in the throne room earlier, she now truly encapsulates an Ice Queen.

Her entire dress is white and covered in white stones that shine in the light. The high neckline ends in lace shaped like snowflakes, and the sleeves billow out into a pattern that looks like waves. The skirt of the dress has the same pattern, and since the entire dress is white, it looks like sea foam is escaping snow. Her crown is just as intricate, entirely made of diamonds, with three distinct points, each being a snowflake. The middle and largest snowflake has a massive opal on the top and the entire look creates the perfect portrait of ice royalty.

The two of them strut up onto the dais and the queen searches the crowd for Delwyn. While I was studying her stunning dress, Delwyn snuck around the edges of the room and managed to get onto the stage slightly after them. Queen Neve gives him a quick glare, but the entire court is watching, so she can't yell at him until later.

"Thank you all so much for being here to celebrate this momentous occasion," Queen Neve begins. "We are truly blessed that my son, Prince Delwyn, and my niece, Captain Sage, were successful in their mission to bring the Columben line back to Tirlun."

It was *my* mission, not Del's and mine, but sure, let's give my cousin half the credit because of his royal title.

The entire crowd cheers and all eyes are on me from where I stand alone by the drinks table. I look over to where Aneira, Idris, and Aiden are standing together still by the doors. Aneira is probably bursting at the seams to mingle but was too nice to leave Idris and Aiden alone together.

I doubt Idris would say much to him and I have no clue what Aiden is feeling.

"In a few days, they will take off again to go retrieve the weapon that has been missing for three hundred years. With this weapon, we will hopefully have the deterrence necessary to prevent another war with the Fire Dominion. My sincere hope is that we will not have to use it, but as your queen, it is my duty to protect you from any threats we may face. For now, let us rejoice in their successes and send them off with a smile. Please, relax, enjoy, and celebrate the glory of the Ice Dominion."

I guess we're no longer keeping the second part of our mission under wraps. The nobles here tonight aren't likely to talk to anyone outside of this room, but the servants will. Since we're leaving in a few days, hopefully we'll be able to stay ahead of the gossip. The more people that are aware we're hunting for the weapon, the more likely Fire Dominion citizens will find out. And that means it's much more likely we'll face mercenaries and other interested parties trying to get the weapon for themselves.

"The glory of the Ice Dominion!" The entire room shouts in response. With that, the band plays music and couples dance.

I walk over to my friends and Aiden and look at Idris and Aneira. "Go ahead and enjoy the party, I'll watch him for the night."

"Thank you so much!" Aneira exclaims, kissing my cheek and running off to do whatever it is she does at these events.

"Thank the Mother," Idris says as she saunters off. I expected at least a little resistance from Aneira, but she must be really eager to socialize tonight.

"Wow, I really didn't expect them to run away so quickly. You must smell," I say as I turn to Aiden.

I do a double take. I didn't notice it in my room, but he's absolutely stunning. Surrounded by white and blue matching his light blue shirt, he almost looks magical. His dark caramel skin glows, surrounded by all the lighter colors, and his eyes sparkle. And fuck, he does smell — he smells like frost and sugar.

It's like the servants purposely stocked that bathroom

with delicious scents. Knowing them, they probably did. And somehow, this sweet smell only makes him even more manly.

"If I smell, it's only because you made me smell," he says.

I forgot I had even said anything to him because I was so distracted staring at him. "So, what do you want to do at your first party?"

"It's not like I have many options." I look around; he's right. The nobles' portion of the party usually consists of dancing, drinking, and playing political mind games. That's why my friends and I try to leave as quickly as possible and go to the parties in town.

"Do you dance?" I ask.

"You want to dance with me?"

"Why not? It's better than talking to anyone here." My eyes roam over the room. There are very few nobles I can actually tolerate. Most of them are so pretentious it takes all of my restraint not to yell or fight them.

"I dance, although I can't promise I'll know any of the dances here."

"Come on, I'll teach you." We walk towards the center of the room where several couples are already dancing. As a noble, I've been forced to learn all these formal dances. They're so stuffy and uptight, so I send a wind message over to the conductor asking for a simpler song. We make eye contact over the crowd, and he gives me a nod.

I take Aiden's hand and place my other on his shoulder. He's so tall, my arm is fully extended. He pauses, but then places his other hand on my hip. The music starts, and it's a fucking slow song. I look at the conductor and he gives me a guilty smile. Asshole.

The couples on the dance floor get closer to each other as

the intimate song demands. Aiden looks around. "Did we accidentally pick the most romantic song to start dancing?"

"It was no accident." I can practically feel his brain racing as his hands tighten on my body. "Oh, don't worry, it wasn't my doing."

His hands loosen around me as his face relaxes, but now there's a furrow in his brow. "I've grown up going to a million formal events and this band always plays. I've become friendly with the members and conductor, and I sent him a message to play a simple song for your sake, but he likes to meddle in my life and decided that the simple song needed to be a love song." I'd be lying if I said I wasn't secretly glad to be in Aiden's arms like this.

"A commoner meddling in a noble's life?" he asks with mock shock.

I lightly shove his shoulder. "I hope at this point you've realized that we're not crazy, or at least, not crazy to the extent you think we are. Don't get me wrong, I love having power over others. But I'm an equal opportunity power-grabber. I think everyone should have a chance to be as authoritative as me no matter how they were born."

"How egalitarian of you."

Over the course of this conversation, we inched closer together and are swaying to the music. It's oddly comfortable, like we were made to fit together. We sway in silence for a little and I'm strangely content in a way I rarely feel. The song ends and there's a tap at my shoulder. I turn around and Roman is standing in front of me.

"Lady Sage," he says, bowing to me.

"You know I prefer to go by Captain."

"But dressed like that, you can't be anything other than a

lady," he says as he obviously looks up and down my body. Just like his father.

Aiden shifts behind me, grabbing Roman's attention. "Ah, yes, you must be the famous Columben descendant. How are you liking Tirlun so far?"

"Besides being kidnapped and taken from everything I know, splendid," Aiden says.

Roman's laugh is sharp, cutting, and definitely fake. How his father could ever think I would marry him is beyond me. "Lady Sage, may I have this dance?"

I can't turn him down in such a public place. But I can't leave Aiden alone. Everyone besides the queen's council thinks he's here willingly and won't prevent him from leaving should he try to escape.

I turn to Aiden. "Why don't you go get a drink and I'll meet you over there after this song?" He nods, gives Roman a once-over, and heads off the dance floor.

I send a wind message to my friends that Aiden is unattended and someone needs to go guard him. I hope one of them isn't distracted enough to hear me.

My eyes quickly scan the crowd, trying to find one of my friends to make eye contact with, but Roman grabs my waist and pulls me unnecessarily close to him. As the music starts, he leans down to whisper in my ear. "You look ravishing tonight, Sage. Not that your dress leaves much to the imagination, but I bet you look even more delectable with it off."

His light scruff scrapes my neck as he speaks, and I can't help but let a small shudder run through my body. He probably thinks it's because of what he said, but the truth is, if I was back on Earth, it still wouldn't be far enough away. I try to pull away from him, but he's holding onto my waist too tightly to move anywhere.

I glower at him and say, "That may be true, but you'll certainly never find out."

He leers down at me. "I always get what I want, Sagey." My nickname sounds like poison coming from him. "And what I want is to marry you. I will do whatever it takes to make that happen. Your resistance will only make the inevitable that much sweeter."

"While I commend your confidence, I can assure you, we will never be married. I don't care what political games you and your father may play, but I am the only one that decides my fate. And I have already decided you will never be a part of it."

"I do love a girl with fire in her veins. And you certainly have more than most. Literally," he says.

From where my hands are clasped around his neck, I involuntarily let some flames release and lick up the sides. It's only the cold in his veins that prevents him from getting burned. I pull my hands off him and douse the fire.

"Yes, well, sometimes I miss letting my hellacious side out. And you give me a perfect reason."

He chuckles before responding. "Your periodic visits to your *uncles* in the Fire Dominion aren't enough to release your volatile tendencies?" He tsks. "Maybe they're getting soft across the mountains."

The impertinence in calling the Kings of the Fire Dominion my uncles makes me clench my fists. Even though both dominions are aware of how close I am to the men who were like brothers to my father, *I'm* the only one that calls them "uncle." And Roman knows that.

As the captain of the queen's guard in the Ice Dominion, I'm not often allowed to go on unwarranted trips to the Fire Dominion, but as they're not technically our enemies yet, I can often finagle vague political reasons to visit besides our annual summit of dominions.

But it's not enough. The Fire Dominion holds half of my heart. But since the attack on the Ice Dominion, that half has been left to shrink.

And if my aunt had it her way, that half would completely disappear.

Slowly placing my hands back onto Roman's shoulders, I snort. "Don't worry about them going soft over there. In fact, I learned some new tricks on my last visit. Care to see?"

I let my flames dance in my eyes and very slowly let a fire build and snake between Roman's legs.

He looks down and his face goes white. "That's alright," he says, trying to muster his confidence.

At the end of the day, he knows his power is no match for mine. I say nothing in response and we dance in silence until the song ends.

Bowing to me again, Roman says, "And with that, my dear, I will leave you to babysit the boy." A scowl passes over his face as he leaves the dance floor, likely looking for someone else to torture.

I head off the dance floor in the direction I saw Aiden leave before the dance. I can't see him, but I spot Aneira talking to a group of people. This woman attracts others like moths to a flame. Her energy is contagious, and it always brings a smile to my face to see her fitting in so well in the palace. It also doesn't hurt that her dress is the color of a sunflower and layered like petals. She's literally a beacon of sunlight in the otherwise cool-toned space.

I walk up to her and ask if she's seen Aiden.

"Sorry, no," she says, placing her hand on my arm. "Do you want me to help you look for him?"

"No, no, don't worry about it. I'm sure I just lost him in the crowd. Enjoy your night," I say, kissing her on the cheek and leaving her group to keep searching.

I walk the entire perimeter of the room and can't find him anywhere. A small wave of panic comes over me but I force myself to relax. It's a big crowd; I probably missed him.

I slowly approach the dais and walk up to Delwyn's throne. He's doing his best to not look bored out of his mind, but it's so obvious that he hates these things.

"Del, have you seen Aiden from up here?" He whips his head to where I'm standing slightly behind his throne.

"No. Please don't tell me you lost him."

"It's not my fault! That dickwad Roman interrupted us dancing. I did wind message everyone, but you all must have been too distracted to hear it," I say.

"Wait, wait, wait, you were dancing with Aiden?"

"Del — focus, please. I really didn't think he would be stupid enough to try to escape *again*, especially now that we're in Bruma. Ugh, now we have to spend our one night relaxing searching for the idiot." The farthest Aiden will get without being stopped is the gates, but I'll still be annoyed if I have to spend the rest of my night stopping at *all* the gates trying to find him.

"Hey, any excuse to get me off this stupid stage, I'll take it." Del walks up to his mother's throne, and whispers in her ear. She casually turns back to me, giving a curt nod to not alarm anyone who may be watching our exchange. To anyone else watching, Delwyn was asking his mother for permission to leave the dais and spend the rest of the evening with me — and it wouldn't be the first time.

We leave the room through the back entrance, trying to draw as little attention as possible. I send a wind message to Idris and Aneira telling them to meet us in town in about an hour. Hopefully we'll have found Aiden at that point and maybe we can salvage what's left of the night. We exit the front gates of the palace and check in with any guards stationed along the way.

Not a single one has seen Aiden. Incompetent fools. I'm going to give them shit for this tomorrow morning. I call for Blizzard, and he and Bluebell storm through the gates. Delwyn and I hop onto their backs and run through the streets. Luckily, Blizzard has already smelled Aiden which will make it easier to pick up his scent.

We get to the largest town square and are forced to dismount as the massive amounts of citizens celebrating in the streets makes it impossible to travel in any way but on foot. We leave Blizzard and Bluebell in a small stable on the outskirts of the square and weave our way through the crowd.

Music comes from multiple directions; a small band plays on the edge of the square fountain and several bands can be heard from the open windows of several taverns and shops bordering the square.

The square itself is filled to the brim — parents trying to corral their children as they weave between stalls, couples strolling arm in arm, and groups of friends drinking and laughing together. If I wasn't so stressed, I would be observing all of this with a sense of contentment. Instead, I can't help but think about how difficult it will be to find Aiden within this crowd.

Not to mention the fact that Delwyn is not particularly inconspicuous. With his massive frame and royal clothes, he's very obviously the prince. And Delwyn being Delwyn, he's incapable of saying no to any of the citizens as they all approach to shake his hand and give their congratulations on our mission. They give me respectful looks as well, but I've never been known for my skills in small talk.

Let alone the fact that it was really *my* mission, not ours.

Delwyn notices my strained body at this interruption to our search. "Go on ahead. I'll find you when I'm done here."

I give him a grateful smile and push my way through the crowd more aggressively.

Most people quickly move out of my way as I plow through the square. My eyes scan for any head that's raised above the crowd, since Aiden is one of the tallest individuals I've ever met. As I pass through the stalls, the merchants try to sell me ice cream or spelled fire-breathing toys and I have to shrug them all off.

One particularly pushy seller follows me on my walk so I'm forced to stop, turn to him, and holding two fireballs in my hands, I growl, "Back the fuck off. I'm not interested."

His face turns white with fear as the fire reflects in his eyes. "S-s-sorry, I didn't recognize you in the dress, Captain Sage." I shove past him, not bothering to respond.

Aiden's clearly not in this square. What if he got himself in trouble? Not everyone in Bruma will recognize him. And with no magic...

I head back to Blizzard as I try to brainstorm where else he could be. There are five major squares in this city and in order to leave through the main gates, he would have to go through at least one of them. There are smaller exits out of the city walls, but there's no way he would be able to find any of those right now. He's smart, so he has to assume that I told all the soldiers to be on the lookout for him, even if they think he's here willingly. Maybe he'd try to find a disguise, but how many people would be leaving the city on a festival night?

As I try to think, I get back onto Blizzard and have him walk slowly through the streets, working to pick up Aiden's scent. His ears perk.

"Do you smell something, Blizz?"

He runs down a street, getting faster and faster as he gets more confident in his path. He turns a corner and skids to a stop. Aiden is sitting on a curb, his head in his hands. He hears Blizzard walking towards him, and we make eye contact. His eyes are red and his hair is a disheveled mess. A rush of relief runs through my body; at least he's safe.

What happened? I look around the street and notice a street sign sprayed with ice.

That's odd.

I scan the rest of the road; there are several doors that have been sprayed erratically. I follow the path of ice shards to a frozen rat, tipped over mid-scurry. Shit. Aiden's powers must have been triggered by his entrance into Tirlun. I didn't expect it to happen so quickly.

"You didn't drug me, did you," he says resignedly.

Chapter Ten

Aiden

I watch as Sage dances with that asshole; she looks miserable and I feel a little guilty, but this is the best chance I have to escape.

Moving to the edge of the ballroom, I stand as innocuously as possibly. After being formally announced, everyone here knows who I am. But I'm hoping they don't know why and won't try to stop me from leaving.

Sage's friends are all otherwise occupied; Aneira is in the center of a group of twenty, speaking animatedly with everyone's rapt attention, Idris is nowhere to be seen, and Delwyn is sitting on the dais, but looks unimaginably bored as he tries to look anywhere but at the people who are working up the courage to speak to him and the rest of his family.

The back doors of the ballroom beckon and with one more quick glance, I sneak out.

There are soldiers standing guard outside the doors, but giving them a tight smile I walk with purpose down the hall. I keep my back as straight as possible and my strides slow and take a deep breath as I turn a corner without them shouting at me to stop.

Every turn I take reveals more guards and more servants, but no one prevents me from leaving.

"Excuse me," I say to a woman carrying several coats in her arms. "Which way to the entrance of the palace?"

She glances around as if surprised I'm speaking to her. With no one else in the hallway, she looks back up at me and her cheeks redden.

"Um —"

Uh oh, maybe she was told not to let me leave. But if her cheeks reddened, maybe she's nervous to tell a "nobleman" what to do as a servant. I hate this weird society and their old-fashioned social strata, but maybe in this moment I can use it to my advantage.

So many maybes, but it's the best I can do.

I clear my throat. "It's just, it's my first formal affairs like this and I'm a little overwhelmed. I could use some fresh air." I flash her my most charming smile that I thought worked on Sage when we first met.

She smiles in response. "Sure, of course. It's just down this hall, make a right, and then your second left."

"Thank you," I say as I turn to go.

"Wa-wait." I look back at her and she hands me one of the coats. "It's cold out there."

I don't want her to get in trouble for helping me. "Are you sure?" These coats have to belong to some of the nobles in the ballroom and I'd have to imagine they'd be upset.

"Oh, yes, yes. These are the palace employees' coats and we have plenty of extras."

I look back down at the coat she handed me; it's one of the nicest pieces of clothing I've ever personally touched. And this is what their employees wear?

All I can say is, "thank you," and follow her instructions out of the palace.

I make my way through their city, but it's dark and somehow in the middle of nowhere they managed to hide this massive, developed civilization. The roads are paved, the buildings architecturally intricate, and there are massive amounts of people out and about at restaurants, bars, and shops.

They all smile at me, but it's in friendliness and not recognition thankfully.

I approach a square that is filled with people laughing and dancing to music. Everyone seems to be celebrating my return and yet, don't know who I am.

That is, until I see a group of soldiers enter the square, clearly searching for someone.

Shit.

I back out of the square and turn into a smaller alleyway. The soldiers' boots echo in the distance so I'm forced to move deeper through the quieter streets and I quickly get lost.

Suddenly, I'm all alone and it's too silent. The only sound is my footsteps as I walk.

I'm wandering through unknown streets, lost and tired, when a screech sounds to my right. My hands stick out in alarm and a cold sensation runs through my entire body and exits through my hands.

In front of me is a rat, frozen mid-scurry. Weird. I'm

about to keep moving when another creak sounds from behind me. I spin and the same sensation moves through my body. And just like the rat, there's a shop sign that is now frozen mid-swing.

This can't be real.

But just in case it is, I shove my hands out in front of me and try to bring out the fear I felt. And again, a cold wave rushes through my body and ice suddenly appears everywhere I direct my hands.

I sit down on the curb and put my head in my hands and slowly allow the insane truth to settle in.

I haven't been hallucinating. Wherever I am, this place is real. And so is magic, apparently.

Once I accept that, my entire body relaxes, almost as if it's been waiting for my mind to catch up with what it already knew.

I'm sitting in this random alleyway for who knows how long until Sage comes riding along on Blizzard's back.

I look up at her from my spot on the ground. "You didn't drug me, did you?"

"I tried to tell you." Sage looks down at me from Blizzard's back.

So, yeah. Magic is real.

And I guess that means everything else Sage and her friends have told me is true too. I'm not sure how, but this isn't exactly how I wanted her to find me.

"I guess it took it happening with my own hands to believe it," I say. To my surprise, she gets off Blizzard and sits on the curb next to me. "Aren't you going to dirty your dress?"

"Everyone already saw how gorgeous I looked." She says it so seriously, but there's a teasing glimmer in her eyes.

"So, what now?" I heave a sigh.

"Now we celebrate. You might as well enjoy the festival, because after tonight we're back in mission mode. Come on, the rest of the crew is going to meet us in the main square."

Sage acts as if I'm going to go along with everything now that I know they're not lying. "You still kidnapped me."

She glances over at me. "And?"

"And? And just because I believe in magic doesn't mean I'm okay with the fact that you kidnapped me." Did she assume everything would be cool and I would forget about the events preceding this night?

She rolls her eyes. Somehow she looks sexy while being annoyed, but I'm the one who should be annoyed.

"*Shifrah*, don't you see? You have magic. You belong here. I may have kidnapped you, but I brought you home. If anything, you should be thanking me."

I can't help the snort that escapes my mouth. This fucking woman. Unfortunately, she's right. That feeling I thought was pulling me to Colorado was really pulling me here. Whether or not I want to admit it, my heart knows this is where I'm meant to be. And I can't lie, learning how to use magic sounds pretty fucking cool.

Sage stands up and offers me her hand; she's full of surprises tonight.

We hop back on Blizzard, and he's almost happy to see me; he gives me a little nuzzle with his snout before I climb on his back. The street is quiet as we make our way to the main square.

Sage takes a deep breath. "How are you feeling?" she asks.

"Scared," I admit.

She quickly glances at me before turning back to face the road. It's almost like she can't bear to look at me as she says, "It's terrifying when things change. Especially when they change in ways you could never begin to prepare for. It's how you handle the changes that determine who you are."

I lightly squeeze her shoulder. "I agree. And I also know that it's okay to be vulnerable and not always in control."

Sage whips her head back to look at me before turning forward once again. "What's that supposed to mean?"

"It means, I may not know you well, but I can already tell you struggle to allow others to help you." Her shoulders tense up so I quickly add, "With planning and organizing your missions."

She shakes her head but remains silent.

Blizzard moves us through the streets until noise reaches my ears as we approach the festival.

We make our way to a square that looks vaguely familiar, except now it's been transformed. Lights of every color of the rainbow float in the air above everyone's heads, the fountain in the center is made of ice that still somehow flows like water, and stalls sell everything from ice cream to a snack that looks like cake on a stick.

Children run through the street playing with stuffed animals that have actual fire coming out of them. Without bursting into flames.

Magic. Damn, this is going to take some getting used to.

From Blizzard's back, it's easy to spot Delwyn towering over the crowd. Sage must use her magic to send him a message because Delwyn turns to us, grinning with all his teeth and eagerly waving.

At the same time, two people on either side of him also turn around. Aneira jumps up and down smiling and Idris gives a smug grin. I wonder how much Sage told them and if they know I tried to escape.

Sage and I hop down from Blizzard's back and make our way to her friends. As I walk behind her, I can't help but notice how everyone's eyes are drawn to her. She's receiving stares and confidently looks back at the people we pass.

If I had to guess, she thinks they're looking at her because she's Captain Sage. But it's obvious to me they're all looking at her for the same reason I am — she's the most beautiful woman here.

Her auburn hair shines under the lights and gives her an ethereal glow, and her dress hugs her curves so perfectly she looks like a woman who could tempt even the holiest of men. And I am far from holy.

Aneira hugs me once we reach her and the others and cheerily says, "I heard you tried to escape, but instead accessed your powers. What an exciting turn of events!"

I normally would assume that was sarcasm, but I don't think Aneira's capable of being anything other than sincere. I've never once seen her be rude or mean. Idris, on the other hand, crosses her arms over her chest. Her golden arms resting on her pink and purple dress make her look like the sunset personified.

Delwyn slaps me on the back. "Welcome to the squad."

"Woah, woah, woah," I say. "Just because I believe you

now about magic, and I guess this secret weapon, doesn't mean I'm okay with you all kidnapping me and taking me from everything I've ever known. I get that I can't go home, but that doesn't mean we're all going to become buddy-buddy." Honestly, we probably will. I've gotten comfortable around them so quickly. But I can't give in that easily.

"Of course," Aneira says, softening her gaze. She's so nice. I have no clue how she became friends with the rest of them.

"In the meantime," Sage says, gesturing to a spot separated from the rest of the festival, "you might as well enjoy the celebration. The dragon battle is going to start soon, and we have to place our bets before it begins."

"Bets?" I ask.

"That's the best part!" Delwyn says with a gleam in his eyes. "We all bet on which dragon will stay in the sky the longest. There are always ten dragons, and as a rule, none of us can pick the same one. We only bet between the four of us — five now, including you— because we can get kind of competitive. Come on, let's go scope out the fighters." I've got to get used to this new culture I've been thrown into, so I nod and follow him.

We walk over to a sectioned off part of the square where ten people are speaking to themselves. Sage did the same thing in the tent and it created that weird air bubble that I now know is real, so maybe these people are doing something similar to send the dragons into the sky. It's going to take a while to get used to all this magic stuff being real.

The four of them chat with the competitors and I stay near Sage. She's very polite and inquisitive, asking each fighter very specific questions about their magic and ice formations.

After they finish talking, we head over to the viewing area, and they huddle together. Sage immediately says, "I call Charles."

"No. Not fair. You always get Charles," Idris says. My eyes look between Sage and Idris, trying to keep up with their constant back and forth.

"Yeah, because Charles' dragon always wins." She flips her hair and a cocky smile forms on her face.

"Exactly!"

Aneira butts in. "Why don't we let Aiden pick first?"

"Oh, no, that's okay," I say. "You're all a lot more invested in this than I could ever be." And I don't want to become a part of every little fight that merges between this group of friends. It all seems like it's in good fun, but I have no idea when it can turn for the worst and I'm not willing to risk getting caught in the crosshairs. Especially with magic now involved.

"Nah, Aneira's right," Delwyn says. "You should pick your fighter first."

On the other hand, I can't miss an opportunity to rile up Sage. My people-pleasing mask completely disappears around her and I'm still upset by the way she went about kidnapping me.

"Well if you insist... I pick Charles," I say, pasting an obnoxious grin on my face and staring straight at Sage. If her eyes weren't so piercing green, I would swear that they were on fire.

With her gaze not leaving mine, she says, "Fine. I'll take

Maureen." Everyone else selects their fighters and we get ready to watch the show.

All the surrounding music stops and an announcer comes to the center of the platform. "Citizens of the Ice Dominion, it is my pleasure to announce the dragon battle. Fighters are only allowed to imbue their dragons with an initial spell and then can no longer interfere. The last dragon flying wins. Players, commence your spells!"

Ten dragons instantly appear in the air. Delwyn wasn't kidding. They range in size from ten feet to forty. Some of them have colors and detailed scales while others are just ice in the vague form of a dragon. It's clear that some of the spells are more defensive while others selected a more offensive positioning.

Very quickly, five dragons drop to the ground and Aneira groans. "I always lose first."

"That's because you always pick the newbie," Sage says to her with a smile.

"They need someone to support them!"

After another fifteen minutes of fighting, only three dragons are left, and they happen to be mine, Sage's, and Idris'. I don't think Idris has ever been so expressive. She's standing and screaming at her dragon, pumping her arms in the air every time it has a successful attack and shaking her head when it fails.

Eventually, Idris' dragon falls, and she mumbles that she's going to get a drink.

It's come down to Sage's dragon and mine. Why am I not surprised?

She stares so intently at the sky, watching every move between the two ice dragons. But I can't drag my eyes from her. The concentration on her face is mesmerizing; the juxtaposition of her caring so much about a silly little game while dressed like a queen is hypnotic. Every movement of the two dragons is reflected on her face — a wince when hers is hit, a sparkle in her eye when it strikes well. I have no idea how much time passes until she finally looks over at me like she won the lottery.

"Hah! I win! Guess you should make your own decisions, Pretty Boy." I can't care that I lost when her eyes sparkle like gemstones.

I can't fake my happiness at her joy. "I guess you're right."

"I always am."

The rest of the night passes in a blur. There's a lot of alcohol consumed, a lot of games played, and a whole lot of laughter. Now that I'm not trying to actively run away, these people aren't all that bad. Even Sage.

We pile onto Blizzard to head back to the castle because Delwyn drunkenly sent Bluebell home without thinking it through. We're squished together with Sage in the front and me directly behind her. I may use the excuse of us being so close to wrap my arms around her waist. Her warmth protects against the cold wind on my arms as we make our way back to the castle. I swear she leans her back into my chest a little more than necessary. Not that I'm complaining. My anger at her actions does not translate to anger at her body. And my alcohol-riddled brain can't muster the desire to care.

We say goodnight to the rest of the group and Sage and I

walk into her room. She goes over to the dining room table where there's a fresh carafe of water and... pizza?

"Care to join me?" she asks as she plops into a chair.

"Is that pizza?" The smell draws me closer and makes my mouth water.

"Oh yeah, whenever we come back from a night out the servants leave some form of carbs in all our rooms. It's better for everyone come morning." I chuckle, snatch the slice out of her hands, and sit in the chair next to her. "Hey! I was literally about to take a bite!"

"Your slice looked like the best one." I can't stop myself from doing whatever I can to get a reaction out of her. It's odd because I've always tried to be non-confrontational — it's probably just because I've been kidnapped and my body's in fight or flight.

"Dick." She rolls her eyes, but a small smile crosses her face.

I pour us glasses of water and we sit in comfortable silence eating the pizza. "So, what happens now?" I ask.

"What do you mean?"

"I mean, now that I'm not trying to escape, what's the plan?" Maybe now they'll all be more forthcoming with information. I still have so many questions about this world, its magic, and this mystery weapon I'm supposed to be able to find.

"Oh, right. We'll spend another day here preparing for the journey. That means getting supplies, finishing research, resting up, and so on."

"And then?"

"And then we begin our trek through the Ice Dominion. It should take a few weeks on our ursas to the border. That's where we believe the weapon is. Hidden in the cave system under the mountains on the border with the Fire Dominion." She talks about this journey like I've been here before. These words are meaningless to me without any context.

"A few weeks? That's a long time."

"Well, normally we could reach the spot in under a week with our vehicles, but I don't want us taking them."

"Right, why would we not make the journey easier for ourselves?" My brain is racing a million miles a minute trying to imagine what a journey in this place would look like. The alcohol is not helping.

Sage devours her slice of pizza and takes a giant sip of water before responding. "Our vehicles run on our magic and our magic is not endless. Maybe in the beginning of the journey we won't need to reserve our power, but as we get closer to the border, who knows what we'll face. So, instead of trading out our vehicles for random ursas and horses halfway along the journey, we'll take ours the entire way." I briefly remember her talking about their version of cars, but I'm way too drunk to think about this further tonight.

"Anything else?" she asks, taking another sip of water.

"I have a million other questions, but seeing as it's almost four in the morning, I figure it's best to save those until tomorrow."

"Good idea, I'm zonked."

I choke on my water. "Zonked? Who says that?" What a silly word to come out of an otherwise serious mouth. The more time I spend around Sage, the more I'm realizing there's way more to her than meets the eye.

"Me. I say that," Sage says with a small smile on her face.

"Well then, I hope your zonkiness is gone in the morning." She giggles. I didn't think a sound that light and inno-cent could come out of her mouth. Goosebumps cover my body.

Her eyes laser in on them. "What?"

"Nothing. Good night, Sage," I say. Shaking off any lingering goosebumps, I head to my door as I shove my warmth towards her out of my body. She has no regard for me or my feelings and I need to keep reminding myself of that fact.

"Good night Aiden."

Chapter Eleven

Sage

Something is smothering my face. I shoot out of bed, which is followed by a loud yelp.

"Sorry Fluffy!" Fluffy lightly growls before jumping back onto the bed to receive her apology pets. As I scratch behind her ears, I'm surprised at how good I feel after our very late night. Maybe it's because I won't constantly have to be worried about Aiden running away.

I stretch, get out of bed, and open my bedroom door. I'm surprised to see Aiden sitting at the table, looking ready to go.

"You're not even dressed?"

I look down at my light blue two-piece sleep set. "Does it look like I am?"

He crosses his arms over his chest. I can't help it — it's too easy to rile him up.

Without responding, I shrug and head back to my room to get ready.

The sound of his footsteps follows behind me, and I wait until he's in my room before I turn around. I take a moment to appreciate his figure. I did a fantastic job with his measurements; all the clothes he's worn so far fit him like a glove. This outfit is no different, but it's definitely more of an "Earth" outfit. But damn, does he look good.

"So, what's the plan?"

"We're going to do final research and preparations before we leave for the journey tomorrow. Think you can handle that?"

"Do you need to be so condescending all the time? This is all very new to me."

I turn towards my closet so he can't see me cringe. I always do this. I'm blunt and short in the way I speak, and everyone always thinks I'm being rude. I can't add Aiden to that list. As I take a deep breath, I grab whatever clothes I can find so it looks like I was doing something.

I turn back to him and say, "You're right, I'm sorry. I can be grumpy in the mornings before my coffee."

His stance relaxes. "I'm not sure I've ever heard you apologize. But you're forgiven."

I try to give him a warm smile, but it comes out like a grimace. In an attempt to regain control of the situation, I saunter over to him until I have to crane my neck to make eye contact.

"Well Pretty Boy, while I appreciate your forgiveness, you're going to need to leave my room so I can get ready. Unless you would like to join?"

To my surprise, he looks down at me and lightly grabs my chin. He stares at me for a moment before he leans down and softly says, "Oh Princess, if I joined you, we would never leave this room."

I can't help the shudder that runs through my body at the thought. He definitely feels it, as his smile widens and he scans the length of my body. I reach up and tug his hair until we're breathing the same breath. His frost and sugar scent fills my nostrils and I greedily inhale the smell.

"You couldn't handle an entire day in this room with me, Pretty Boy."

"Perhaps we should find out," Aiden says, staring deeply into my eyes.

Before I can respond, Delwyn speaks from behind Aiden, "Sorry if I'm interrupting," clearly not sorry at all, "but we've got a full day of prep ahead of us, so we should get going."

I nod and head into my bathroom, not even bothering to look at Aiden. The door shuts as I lean against it and I take a few deep breaths. I look down at my hands, realize that I grabbed two shirts, and throw them on my bathroom floor. Hopefully a very cold shower will do me good.

We're sitting around my table — Aneira joined the men while I was showering — drinking coffee, when Idris stumbles in, dressed but disheveled.

"Someone had a fun night," Delwyn says, wiggling his eyebrows. Idris just glares at him. Aneira is unusually quiet.

As Idris fixes her hair with her reflection in my window, she asks, "What's the plan today, boss?"

"I need to go to the library and copy down any notes we

can find regarding the weapon. Anything we find could help us down the line. Aiden, you'll join me for that," I say.

He doesn't argue and gives me a nod in confirmation.

"Aneira and Del, I need you to gather our supplies and make sure we have three other ursas ready for the journey. And Idris, I need you to talk to your network and make sure there aren't any unexpected surprises waiting for us along the way." And all of our Fire Dominion sources are up to date — but that's best left unspoken; you never know who's listening in a palace.

"Unexpected surprises?" Aiden asks.

"Since tensions have been increasing between the two dominions, it's rare, but possible, that a small Fire Dominion force will be doing some recon or spying in Ice Dominion territory. Especially the closer we get to the border," Delwyn says, licking his fingers clean of his breakfast.

Both dominions have been sending more of their soldiers into the other's territory. It'll make the fact that we're going on a mission to the border less conspicuous, but will more than likely lead to more altercations. Especially with my track record.

"We obviously will avoid them if we get wind of any troops, but we'll fight if necessary," I add. "Which is why, Aiden, you will continue to train with Delwyn in both combat and magic so you're not a liability should conflict arise." Now that he's accepted the truth, I'm excited to see what he can do with his magic.

Delwyn flashes his signature giant grin at Aiden. "This is going to be fun."

"Preparations first. Training after lunch," I remind Del.

"Sir, yes, sir." Mother, give me strength.

I open the massive dark purple doors to the royal library and take a deep breath. The smell of books is always soothing to me. I look down the center of the library where the front desk is followed by rows of study tables with cozy chairs that are scattered with royal scholars and librarians doing research.

On either side of the center section are endless three-story stacks of books ranging from everything to Tirlun history and politics, spells and magic, religion, philosophy, and fiction novels for entertainment and enjoyment. There's even a small section of Earth literature that we've managed to smuggle back over the years of our few Earth-located missions.

This is one of my favorite places in the entire palace. Not only does it provide my main source of entertainment, but it's also a place for me to gain a political edge over the vultures of this court. They're all so conceited that they never even consider the fact that knowledge can be more powerful than any sword.

The head librarian looks up from where she's sitting behind the front desk, giving me a small smile. "Ah, Sage. Glad you made it back safely from your mission." Looking over at Aiden she adds, "You must be our famous Columben descendent."

"The one and only," Aiden says, a little more confidently than he was yesterday speaking to the lords at the celebration.

"Wonderful. Follow me and I will show you what I've gathered for you."

We walk behind her as she winds through the maze of books. Further back are more private study spaces with couches and lamps for a more relaxed setting. She leads us to my favorite alcove — all the couches and chairs are made of the softest coffee brown fabric, and three beautiful stained-glass lamps surround the seating. I often come here when I need to breathe and escape the political machinations of the court.

Spread out on the massive table in the middle are books, scrolls, and random single pieces of parchment. "Anything I could find mentioning the weapon, especially anything written around the time of its disappearance, has been pulled from our archives," the librarian says. "Additionally, I grabbed the history of the Columben family and their magic in case it could help him with what to look for within himself."

"Thank you so much," I say. "This is amazing and will save us so much time."

She smiles. "I'll leave you both to it. Please let me know if there's anything else I can help with."

"Thank you," Aiden says. She gives a small bow and walks back to the front of the library.

"I think you should start going through your family's information," I say. "We aren't sure where the weapon is exactly, or even what it is. So, we're going to be relying on your blood and magic to call to it and lead us to it."

"Sounds easy enough." His voice is dripping in sarcasm.

I stifle the eye roll that's beginning to emerge. I don't think I ever said this would be easy? I hold onto this annoyance; it's good. It'll keep me from feeling the attraction I'm trying so hard to bury down.

"We have a general vicinity and will search as long as it takes to find it. However, it'll be much faster and easier for all of us if you can help guide us to it. Anything you learn about how your spell and blood magic works as well as your family in general could be helpful. We won't know what we need to know until we need to know it."

Aiden grabs the largest tome closest to him. "I guess I better get started."

Chapter Twelve

Aiden

S age and I do research in the library all morning while the rest of the group does other necessary preparations. So far, the information gathered about this secret weapon can be summarized into about five points.

- The weapon has immense power
- It's hidden somewhere in the mountains on the border between the Fire and Ice Dominions
- Only someone of the Columben bloodline can use the weapon
- I should be able to "feel" the weapon as we get closer to it (whatever that means)
- No one knows what the weapon is or what it does

According to the maps and history of the original war, there's a region of the mountains that's believed to be the general vicinity of the weapon, so that's the direction we'll go. But, otherwise, everything else is a mystery.

Sage claims it's because of the spells and magic surrounding this weapon, cursing everyone to forget what and where it is. It's just too simple of an explanation.

I look at her now, concentrating on whatever she's reading. Her face is scrunched in focus and she's wearing leggings with a light blue sweater. Her hair is pulled up in a clip and she still somehow looks as gorgeous as she did yesterday in a full gown and makeup. Whatever happened between us last night has made her more relaxed around me today.

She walks around like she doesn't need anyone and is unbreakable and infallible, strutting around the castle like she's the princess that I call her. But maybe now she's beginning to trust me. And maybe I want that.

She must sense me staring at her because she looks up. "How's your research going?"

"Nothing new."

"Yeah, me neither."

"What's next?"

"You're going to train with Del this afternoon. I need to do some stuff alone. Aneira and Idris are gathering the rest of our supplies and checking status reports for the journey. How are you doing?"

"Terrified," I say honestly.

"That makes sense," she says, trying to give a reassuring smile. "Remember, you're traveling with the strongest warrior in all of Tirlun."

Her smirk makes it impossible for me not to taunt back. "Delwyn?"

"Ha, ha, very funny. Keep that attitude up and I'll tell Del that you need to be trained twice as hard."

"If it means I can finally start using my magic, I'll do it," I say seriously.

She nods. "It'll come when it's ready. Magic is alive, to a certain extent. Until you fully accept what it means for you to be here, it'll be hesitant to emerge. While you think you've accepted your role in Tirlun, it doesn't agree. You have to figure out the truth of this place for *you*, and the magic will follow."

"Easier said than done." I've been trying to accept everything here, but at every turn there's something new for me to process. I pride myself on being a fairly easy-going guy, but this world is threatening that hard-earned title.

"I'm confident you can do it."

"That might be the nicest thing you've ever said to me."

Sage stands up to stretch. "Alright, I think we've earned a lunch break."

"Thank god, my stomach has been growling for the last hour." She chuckles as she leads me out of the library.

Chapter Thirteen

Sage

I might've heard those growls. And I might've ignored them. Keeping him unhappy will make it easier for me to be annoyed at him. It's much better to be annoyed than simpering like a love-sick girl.

I lead us out of the library and walk to the kitchens.

"Where are we going?" Aiden asks.

"We're going to the kitchens. I try to avoid formal meals as much as possible. All the queen's political advisors are there and then I'm forced to speak to them and field their endless questions and marriage proposals."

"Ah yes, like that lovely gentleman at the party last night." I snort. Gentle will never be a word used to describe Roman.

"Roman has been trying to win my hand in marriage for the last ten years."

"Ten! And you're what— twenty-five?" His shock is palpable.

"Yup." I stifle my disgust at that fact.

"This man has been trying to marry you since you were fifteen?"

"Yes, but luckily my parents were dead so they couldn't agree to it without my consent." Aiden's face looks comical as his jaw drops and eyebrows raise in shock. I can't help but chuckle. "I'm kidding. They never would've forced me into a marriage I didn't want. But, until I turned twenty — that's technically when we become adults — my guardian would've had control over that decision."

"Who was your guardian?"

"The queen." She luckily had other things to concern herself with than my nuptials.

Aiden stops short and his hand flies to his chest. "The queen?" he sputters.

"Yes. She is my aunt. After my parents passed, she took responsibility for me and raised me alongside Del and Dahlia. Thankfully, she gave me my space to make my own decisions. When I became captain of her guard, it became clear to everyone that I wasn't interested in a political marriage. At least in the near future. But that hasn't stopped the lords and ladies from trying anyway." And every time they try another scheme to get me to agree, it makes me hate this court and its nobles a little bit more.

Several palace workers scurry out of my way as we make our way down the hall. One, a man wearing a kitchen uniform, nervously twiddles his hands as he waits for us in the hall.

I slow down until we stop in front of him. "What is it?" His skin is almost as pale as mine, so his blush is immediately visible. I can't feel guilt when they're still terrified to speak to me after so long. They allow my reputation to cloud how they view me instead of seeing me.

"I-I wanted to ask what food you need prepared for your journey?" Seriously? They ask us this question every single time we go on a mission. And the answer never changes.

"Didn't one of the others tell you?"

His eyes roam the hallway, as if trying to find someone else to finish this conversation. "They told me I should ask you."

"Well, I'm on my way to the kitchens right now. You couldn't have waited until I got there?" I'd think that if the workers were as terrified as me as they act, they'd actually remember what I say before every mission.

He grimaces. "I was on my way to the market, so they told me to catch you on the way. I'm sorry if I interrupted."

"Okay, well we need the usual stuff, but with enough dried meat to last several weeks." We'll do a little hunting as we make our way to the border, but it's always good to have enough food in case meat is scarce.

"Yes, Captain." And just because I can, I toss a fireball in my hand. He somehow gets smaller, trying to pretend like he's not scared of a little fire.

The rumors of how I use my fire to train the queen's guard must've made its way through the entire palace. I do work the queen's guards very hard, but if any of them actually tried to get to know me, they would realize I'm not that bad. Not that I make it easy..

"Well, off you go." He bows before trying not to sprint past us towards the palace entrance.

"What did you do to make them so scared of you?" Aiden asks.

I scoff. "Why do you assume *I* did anything?"

"Because I've met you."

"Yes, for all of the three days that you've known me, you know exactly who I am and what I do." I thought he was different; not one to make immediate assumptions based on outward appearances, but maybe I was wrong.

"I've seen enough that I can make a strong assumption." I can't help the pang of sadness that courses through my body at that statement.

"You should know better than most that things aren't always as they seem."

"Alright," he says, raising his hands up innocently. "But was it really necessary to scare him with that fireball?"

I toss the fireball between my hands a few more times before extinguishing it. "If all it takes for him to be scared is a little fire, we've already lost any potential conflict with the Fire Dominion." Aiden quirks his head down at me, studying my face. Before he can look too closely, I turn my head back towards the hallway.

The way to the kitchens is a gradual decline to the ground floor, with the paintings and decor on the walls slowly disappearing. It's always frustrated me that whichever monarch decorated this castle didn't deem the servants worthy of beautiful things. Even though we've come a long way since then, some things still haven't changed. And Queen Neve doesn't want them to.

After a few moments of silence, Aiden must realize I'm done talking about the servants and my magic because he asks, "So, back to the arranged marriages — You're saying you've had to fend off these advances for ten years?"

Grateful for the change in subject, I say, "Yes. That's why

I always volunteer myself to go on any mission that involves me leaving the capital. Over time, it became clear I was the best at these missions anyway, but at first it was a welcome escape from the torment of court." And the constant reminder of my parents' deaths.

"So you volunteered for the mission to kidnap me?" I make eye contact with two servants we pass, and they scurry past us. The last thing I need is for the more unsavory details of this mission to make its way out to the public.

"No, actually. Queen Neve hand-picked me and my team for this mission. She believed we were the best equipped — and we were."

"Team. Don't you mean friends?"

"Both, which I did say earlier." Doesn't he listen? I guess I'll cut him a break since he's been bombarded with new information. "As a captain, I'm required to have my own private squad that comes with me on smaller missions as well as lead larger battalions. Most captains' squads are around seven or eight soldiers, but the three others and I work better than a larger team would. For larger missions we usually take a squadron, which is twenty soldiers. Another reason why the queen chose us — a smaller group is much less conspicuous."

"How is that possible?" he asks as we wind closer to the kitchens. The smells of fresh baked bread wafts towards me and it takes all my energy not to sprint the rest of the way. He must notice a change on my face because he says, "Come on. Let's get our food before you collapse and then you can finish telling me."

We sit down at my go-to picnic table, which is covered in plates of bread, chicken, vegetables, fruit, and some divine looking pastries. Del and Aneira are already there eating, and Idris comes into the kitchen shortly after us.

The kitchen staff is used to us invading their space, so they aren't afraid of yelling at us if we get in their way — they're some of the only few — being that they need to cook for the entire castle. Someone does just that as Idris makes her way to our table, almost spilling a bowl of a delicious looking sauce.

"Genie!" Del yells, getting up to give the royal chef a fat kiss on her cheek. Everyone hugs and kisses her, even Idris, who has learned it's easier to give in than to fight it.

"My name is Genevieve, but everyone calls me Genie," she says to Aiden, shaking his hand.

"Genie is the best chef in all of Tirlun," Aneira adds eagerly.

Aiden says, "Well Genie, it's very nice to meet you. Where did the nickname come from?"

"She's a magician with her food. She always knows what you need, even if you don't. And it's always delicious," I pipe in.

Genie gives me a warm smile; she's always been a beacon of light in this castle whenever I needed motherly affection after my parents died. She's basically acted as a pseudo-grandmother to almost all of us; even Del, who often needed more attention than his busy queen-mother could give.

And she's never been afraid of me. I can count on one hand the amount of people I can say that about.

"So, it looks like your mission was a success. When are you all heading back out?"

"Tomorrow," Idris says.

"So soon?"

"We can't risk any Fire Dominion spies beating us to the weapon."

"Oh, you kids and all your scheming. I'm too old for all the political nonsense. Don't forget to say goodbye before you leave and I'll give you some treats for the road," Genie says as she walks back into the main part of the kitchen.

"Bye, Genie! Thank you!" We all say, even Aiden to my slight surprise.

After we all have our plates made and dig in, Aiden turns to me. "Okay, back to our conversation from earlier."

I groan. "Can't this wait until after we've finished eating?" I didn't realize how hungry I was until we sat down.

"I think you're capable of multitasking."

Aneira giggles across the bench. She's not the one who can't eat because of his request.

"Fine. What specifically would you like to know?"

"How the four of you manage to be a better fighting squadron than those double your size?" Aiden asks. "If I'm really about to enter more unknown territory with complete strangers, I would like to make sure I'm properly protected."

Delwyn bellows a laugh. "Don't you worry your pretty little head. You're the most protected you possibly could be." Guess I'm not the only one who thinks Aiden is pretty.

"How is that possible?"

"Who would like to begin?" I ask begrudgingly. I eye them, making it evident that I would rather not be the one to start this conversation.

"I'll start!" Aneira says, practically jumping off the bench. She clears her throat and sits up straight. She looks each one of us in the eye before stopping on Aiden. So dramatic.

"My first — and favorite — reason why we're the best is because we've grown up training together. We've been friends since the Fire Dominion attack fifteen years ago and have been training as a unit ever since. We know each other's strengths and weaknesses and can complement each other's fighting styles without even trying. Our bond and silent communication aren't something that can be imitated in any other squadron; it was built into us as we grew, and we made each other stronger in turn." She finishes her mini speech with a proud smile, then leans back and continues to dig into her makeshift sandwich she was working on.

Delwyn opens his mouth to talk but is interrupted by Aiden. "Hold up — you said that Idris was originally a member of the Fire Dominion, so why were you all friends *after* the Fire Dominion attack?"

We all look at one another, debating whether it was time to share this with Aiden. I turn to Idris. "It's up to you."

She nods and begins in her quiet but confident voice. "I know you were given a brief summary of what happened fifteen years ago. I was with my parents here on a diplomatic mission, so we were staying in the castle's guest chambers. When the Fire Dominion soldiers attacked, my family was not a part of it. Of course, the Ice Soldiers didn't know that."

Aiden is on the edge of his seat as he listens with rapt attention.

"They stormed into our room in the middle of the night and murdered both of my parents sleeping in their bed." She takes a deep breath before continuing and sips some water. I give her another nod of approval to share what is about to come out of her mouth.

"I was awake. The noise of the attack woke me up. I was about to wake up my parents when the soldiers stormed into the room, so I hid under their bed. I heard them kill my parents and then say, 'They brought their daughter. She must be in here too.' And then they began searching for me." Even though I know this story, and well, am a part of it, it still fills me with rage every time I hear it. I look at Aiden and the rage is on his face as well; so much so, he's too absorbed to interrupt like he so often does.

"I was terrified, shaking, trying to keep as quiet as possible under the bed. After what felt like hours, I thought they were getting ready to leave when all of a sudden they looked under the bed. I was screwed. Except it was like they didn't see me. They stared right through me, got up, and then left the room. I didn't know what happened and I stayed under that bed until I heard Sage come in and call for me. We were always friendly whenever one of us visited the other at court."

She looks down at her plate. "I heard her scream when she saw my parents dead on the bed, so I decided to run out from under the bed to finally see what happened. I was standing right next to her, but she didn't say anything. Then she shrieked like I appeared out of nowhere." She stops to take another sip of water.

Aiden watches her, then politely asks, "What happened next?"

Idris grimaces. "Well, in that moment, it became clear that I was invisible." Aiden gasps. "The fear and trauma of the night must've triggered the dormant power in my body, and it saved me from the Ice Soldiers. So, I was left stranded in the Ice Dominion. Queen Neve decided to keep me as 'collateral' after the attack, since I was a child of an important noble Fire Dominion family. But Sage and Delwyn refused to let me be treated like a prisoner," she says, giving the two of us a grateful smile.

That one small, easy decision, led to a loyal friend for life. If anything, it should be me giving her a grateful smile.

"They made sure I was allowed to be tutored alongside them and train with them as well. Since Sage had fire powers too, we were allowed to practice and strengthen our fire powers together. Under their watchful gaze," Idris says with a twinkle in her eye.

"Eventually it became clear that there was more for me in the Ice Dominion than there would be if I decided to go back to the Fire Dominion. So, I pledged my allegiance to Queen Neve. Once she discovered my invisibility, she began to send me on spy missions. Which I guess brings us to another reason why our squad is so strong; my invisibility gives us a huge advantage over other groups when it comes to scouting and planning surprise attacks." Without waiting for any of us to respond, she gives us all a curt nod and leaves the table.

"Damn," Aiden says. "Where is she going?"

"I'm not sure she's ever shared that story in its entirety to someone," I say. "Idris doesn't share a lot with others, so whenever she does, it can be hard for her to process her emotions. We just need to give her space for a few hours, and she'll be okay." I don't either; it's one of the reasons Idris and I get along so well. We both respect and understand the way the other processes their feelings.

"Sheesh, I-I-I'm sorry," Aiden stutters. "I didn't realize

that my question would lead to all of this. I wouldn't have asked."

Del says, "No, it's good you asked. If you're to become an official member of our group, it's important you know everything, the good and the bad."

Aiden takes a deep breath. "So, are all of you invisible?"

Aneira decides to answer. After all, she's done the most research on how our magic works. "Besides your standard ice and fire powers that every member of the dominions has, most have the ability to wield basic spells. That typically means enchanting an item to stay cold, or hot if you're Sage and Idris, for an indefinite period of time, sending messages on the wind, or using the elements for various purposes. However, certain individuals or families can be gifted with special powers. Your family had an affinity for blood magic and Idris can turn invisible. It's very rare though and very coveted."

"I'm scared to ask now, but I'm already in this deep. What else?" Aiden asks.

Del smiles at Aiden. "You may have heard us bragging about how strong our magic is, but it's true. With the exception of my mother, and maybe Dahlia — although if you ask me, she doesn't train enough — Sage and I are the strongest magic wielders in the Ice Dominion. We've been training our skills since before we could walk. Literally. I remember the first time my ice came out — I was in my crib crying, and next thing I knew, there were beautiful snowflakes drifting around me."

Lucky Del. I interrupt him. "My first encounter with my magic was not as peaceful. My parents were giving me a bath — I was maybe two? I guess I was unhappy with something they were doing, because next thing we know, the entire pipe system in the bathroom explodes. Shit goes flying everywhere — sewage, piss, toilet paper, and actual shit." I can already hear the beginning of Del's belly laugh, but this moment will haunt me for my entire life.

"We all get covered in it. And of course that didn't make me any calmer. So, my baby anger managed to literally inflame all the sewage. On top of being *covered* in sewage and shit, we were smelling sewage and shit on fire. Let me tell you, I may have been a child, but I still remember that smell to this very day." I shudder with the memory.

"I totally forgot about that!" Delwyn says, tears streaming down his face from laughter.

"Yes, well, it's kind of hard for me to forget." Aneira laughs so hard she snorts food out of her mouth which makes the three of them break down hysterically all over again. I pout and impatiently wait for them to settle down.

Aiden turns to Aneira and asks, "What was your first experience like?"

Before she can begin talking, I grab her hand. "Please, let me." She gives me a grateful smile and a peck on the cheek and tells us she's going to the training yard.

"Fuck, did I say something bad *again*?"

I chuckle. "No one said our story was a happy one. After all, what better way to bring a group of friends together than traumatic events?"

While we've been mostly ignored by the kitchen staff over the course of this conversation, some workers tend to mill around our table to try to hear our usual chaotic stories or just to stare at us. I make sure no one is nearby as I begin this part of the story. Aneira claims she doesn't mind how many people know about her past, but the fact that she preferred for me to tell Aiden proves how much it still bothers her.

"Aneira has very little elemental magic," I say. "Aneira's story might be the saddest, which makes it even more astounding that she's by far the most positive out of all of us. None of us are super clear about her life before we met her, but it wasn't good. Del and I met her when they were both eight and I was five. We were in our ursa riding lessons, except that particular day was the safety lessons. And we were bored. Our teacher at the time was this annoying, mean woman. Earlier that day, we had a potions and spells class, and our teacher taught us how to make a sleeping draught. Personally, I can't believe they thought that was appropriate for us to learn, but whatever."

Del piles his now empty plate with pastries. "I think you complained about nightmares and not wanting to wake up your parents."

"Oh yeah! He was always super gullible." Good times. Some of the few before my life turned upside down.

"And scared that we would complain about him to our parents," he says before he stuffs his face.

"True! Anyway, we decided to sneak some of the draught into our teacher's coffee and after about fifteen minutes, she was dead asleep. Del and I took our ursas out and decided to go to the main square. Turns out that safety lesson probably would've been helpful, because it was a busy day and the ursas had not yet learned how to maneuver through a thick crowd."

"I did think it was crazy how those giant animals could weave through everything like that," Aiden says.

With crumbs and sugar falling out of his mouth, Del says,

"Yeah, we kind of didn't give them any other choice after that day."

I fling a napkin in Del's direction. "As I was saying, we were trying to reach a barn where we could leave them while we explored but we couldn't make our way there. We started panicking until this cute little girl with big poofy black high pigtails came up next to us bouncing and smiling and told us she could get us to the barn if we bought her lunch. I don't think she knew who we were at the time, but she was skinny, with barely a rag on her body, and most likely starving, so we said yes."

I pause to take a bite of my sandwich and Aiden immediately asks, "What happened next?"

"I've barely eaten my lunch!"

"I'll take it from here," Del says.

My eyes widen as I realize his plate is practically licked clean. He eats more than anyone I've ever met and with that giant sweet tooth, it's astonishing to me that he has no fat on his body.

"Aneira successfully guided our ursas into a barn and we began walking with her into the town square. It was clear to both of us that she was poor, but we were kids, and she was nice, and those things never mattered back then. As we were about to enter this amazing bakery — it was one of our favorite spots whenever we went into the main part of the city — we were suddenly swarmed by a gang of street urchins."

Aiden laughs. "Street urchins? Seriously?"

"There's literally no other way to put it. Our kingdom does its best with the poor and homeless populations—through free education, housing, and job training, but a lot of the orphans skip out on their lessons to try to steal in the streets. The problem has gotten much better since then, but it was a problem." Del taps his finger against his lips. "Come to think of it, I would bet this incident sparked my mother's increased efforts in helping the poor and orphaned communities."

"Nothing like the prince complaining to solve a problem that should've already been fixed," Aiden says.

I stop eating for a moment as I get frustrated by Aiden's comment. "It's not like your world is perfect. So, yes, unfortunately it sometimes takes the elites having a close encounter to truly work on solving the problem. Why do you think we always like to go on missions out of the capital city? It's important to understand what's actually happening in the land instead of staying in our ivory tower." I take a huge bite of meat and bread, turn to Delwyn with my mouth full, and say, "Please, continue."

"We were surrounded by street urchins," Del says. "Apparently, our little Aneira owed them some money. They saw our nicely made clothes and assumed we were wealthy merchants' kids, not royals. They told Aneira we could pay her debt if she wanted us to. Sage and I had been working on our powers a lot, but they weren't very controlled. Our parents also had not yet given us the go ahead to use them without supervision." He pauses. "Not that we ever listened."

Aiden smiles. Del has always been a natural storyteller; he spreads his hands out on the table in anticipation and continues. "We were prepared to fight them, but before we got the chance, Aneira pushed us behind her, puffed up her chest, and said to the group of four large boys, 'I, nor them, will be paying you anything.'" Del and I both can't help the smiles that come with this memory.

"They started laughing, but before they could even do anything, Aneira moved so fast, attacking them before they saw it coming. The girl had learned some moves on those streets. In a matter of minutes, they were all on the ground, bloody and bruised. Aneira turned her back to them, not a scratch on her, smiled at us and said, 'How about that lunch?'"

Aiden chuckles. "Wow, I can't imagine Aneira hurting a fly."

I quickly add, "Aneira will go to extreme lengths to avoid causing harm to others. But if she must, she'll attack harder and fiercer than any of us."

Del picks up where he left off. "We take her to lunch and start talking to her. We were right, of course. She was an orphan, living on the streets. But she was so nice to us. She clearly could've robbed or hurt us at any point and never did. She was polite and treated us like regular kids — being royal children, it was not something we often got. It was so refreshing to just be kids with her, without our stuffy titles." Now it's my turn to stuff my plate with pastries as Del finishes this story.

"As we were finishing our lunch, royal guards swarmed the café — they had found our knocked-out teacher and came to find us. They were about to take us back to the palace and Sage told them she refused to move unless we brought Aneira." Aiden turns to me.

I quickly swallow the pastry I was thoroughly enjoying and shrug. "I'd never had any real friends in court besides Del and Dahlia. Every other child in the palace was nice to me out of obligation. They also were all little shits. Aneira was the first genuine friend I ever had, so I made the guards take her back to the palace with us. I brought her to my parents and told them I wanted her to live with us. They were shocked at first, but quickly warmed up to her. I mean, you've met her, how could you not? She's been with us ever since."

"So, what about her powers?" Aiden asks. "Does she not have any?"

"We're not really sure. She doesn't remember her parents, so there's nothing in her history. She does have some ice magic, and she can send us wind messages, but that's the extent of what we've seen. Her spells are incredibly strong, which doesn't make sense because all of our magic comes from the same source. It may develop later, but it's not likely at this point. But because of that, she's trained harder physically than the rest of us." I'm about to eat my second pastry when Aiden waves his hand at me to continue.

I really want another pastry, but I graciously continue. "Her street days taught her how to fight fast and dirty, and then she began her formal fighting training in the palace. I think she felt obligated to protect us after we took her in. Whatever the reason, she's become the best fighter in the history of the Ice Soldiers. Even without her magic, she can beat almost anyone in a one-on-one battle with her skills alone."

"Damn."

"Yeah. Damn indeed." Finally. Pastry time.

"So that's another reason why we're the best squad," Del says. "We have the best magic wielders *and* physical fighters.

And there are spells to weaken magic, so having a fighter that won't be affected by those things is invaluable."

"She also forces us to train harder than any other soldiers," I grumble. "I let her lead my soldiers in their daily training exercises. She's not only a better teacher, but her positive attitude makes them actually want to try. Speaking of, I'm going to go meet her in the training yard. You guys should join when you're done eating," I say as I finish off my pastry.

I lied. I'm not going to the training yard, but I did not want to have that conversation with Aiden. I walk through the silver gilded hallways to enter the healing wing. I'm here way too often.

Thank the Mother for Sana, who manages to do a magical job of covering up why I'm always there. I mean, how would it sound if other people found out one of the queen's highest-ranking guards has a chronic illness? They probably wouldn't even know what that is. I certainly didn't.

We can get injured and can die from our injuries, but other than that and old age (which takes thousands of years), we don't die. So how can I possibly have an illness, let alone a chronic one?

It all started about five years ago. I would get random pain in my joints, throbbing headaches, and intense fatigue for no reason. At first, I brushed it off as exhaustion from working too hard. I had been going on a lot of missions and training with my soldiers. But, even when I would stay in the castle for extended periods of time, it kept happening. I went to Sana for help, and she said she'd never seen anything like it in her close to a thousand years. We consulted the queen, and she reluctantly suggested I go to Earth for answers.

Earth? Their healing methods are so far behind ours that I thought there was no way they'd be able to help. But we were out of options. My squad and I went out under the guise of a mission.

I saw a "doctor." That was fun, trying to explain my symptoms without using any of our terminology. Apparently this was a fairly common occurrence on Earth, chronic illnesses. I did as much research as I could, because I didn't want to have to go back any more than necessary.

According to them, the only fix was medicine that would never make its way through the portal, so I asked for as many natural remedies as possible. Recommendations included cold therapy, acupuncture, medical massage, compression, and a lot of rest. So now here I am, walking to Sana's room, to try to get the whole gambit in before I'm gone.

My friends, the queen, and Sana are the only ones who know.

But there's no one here to make me feel less alone. I wish I had someone to share the weight with, someone who I would let make me feel safe. To sit with me in silence and stroke my skin and not say everything will be alright. Because it won't. But who will be with me no matter what, to make me present when I can't get outside of my own head? Who, instead, fills my head with thoughts of love and pleasure, instead of fear and pain?

I knock on Sana's door, but she's been expecting me, so it opens right up. "Ah, Sage, dear."

"Hello, Sana," I say, kissing her cheeks.

She's been like a mother to me since mine passed away.

"Are you ready for your journey?"

"As ready as I can be."

"Remember, cold therapy every night and morning, have Aneira or Idris give you massages as frequently as possible, and please for the love of the Mother, try not to overexert yourself unless *absolutely* necessary."

I do have a problem with pushing myself too hard and immediately regretting it.

As I sit on her table to receive my compression and massage, I can't help but think about the last few times I overexerted myself while on a mission. I laugh to myself. It must be loud enough that Sana looks at me and asks why I'm laughing.

"The soldiers think I have prophetic powers."

"Really," she says, sounding unconvinced.

"Well, there've been a few times that I may have overexerted myself on a mission." That earns me an eyebrow raise. "So, I've forced them to stop in place for a few days. And coincidentally, there's almost always an event that would have crossed our paths had we kept moving."

"Please elaborate," Sana says as she's working on rubbing oil into my legs.

"One time, after stopping for two days, we stumbled upon a massive avalanche that was two days old. It would've taken all our magic together to stop it from crushing us."

"Interesting."

"Another time, we were walking and realized we were right behind a massive snowstorm. Had we kept going, we would've been directly in the middle of it."

"Hm, maybe you do have prophetic powers." She moves up to my arms.

"Ha. People love to explain the unexplainable. But maybe that's why the Mother decided to curse me with this illness; to be able to rally our soldiers behind me even more fiercely."

Sana stops what she's doing and grabs my chin to force eye contact. "Sage, you're not cursed. Don't ever lose your spark that you keep dimmed more than necessary."

"How do you know I dim my spark?"

"I'm a healer, remember dear?"

Healers have an extraordinarily unique ability to access any magic in the world that has potential healing abilities. As my flames and heat can be used for various purposes, and Sana doesn't have any fire powers of her own, she can sense and use mine. Only for healing purposes, but still, an insane gift of magic.

"Yes, well, I think it's for the best to keep my fire dimmed while in the Ice Dominion," I say. "You never know who will want to throw it in my face, especially with tensions between the two dominions increasing." Tensions that are increasing so much that I fear obtaining this weapon won't be enough to prevent an all-out war and thousands of deaths.

"I have a feeling you'll change your tune."

"Oh? Are you the one with the prophetic powers now?"

"Maybe," Sana says with a light smile. "I'm going to start compression, so remember it feels a little weird at first when I pull your magic out."

It's like a tingle in my soul as she tugs on my fire magic. She swirls it with her ice magic, creating mini hurricanes on every major joint. She heats up water in the air next to already cold water in the air, pushing the cold air downward. As the pressure chamber spins, she physically moves the hurricanes over my joints, increasing and decreasing the pressure depending on where she places each one. Sana manages about ten of these at a time. I allow myself to relax into the table, the pressure relieving the pain in my joints.

She does this for about an hour, and when she's done, I'm feeling a million times better.

"Thank you, Sana. I don't know what I'm going to do without you for a few weeks."

"Sage, my girl, you will be perfect." She takes my hands in hers. "I'm not sure what this is, and while it causes pain, it has made you stronger than anyone I've ever known. It has made you compassionate and understanding, and the Sage of five years ago would never have been the captain you are today."

My throat feels heavy, and tears begin to form in the corners of my eyes. I can't cry. Sana has seen me cry too many times from pain, she doesn't deserve it now.

As if sensing where my thoughts are going, she says, "It's okay to be sad. It's okay to be frustrated at the cards you've been dealt. But never, for one moment, believe you are cursed. You are brave and strong and fierce. And to those who don't know you, you may seem like a bitch," I smile at that, "but that doesn't mean you are one. You are one of the most loving people I've ever met."

I take a deep breath, pushing my emotions down. "Thank you, Sana. I'm not sure what's to come in the next few months with the conflict between the two dominions, but wherever I am, you'll always be safe."

She pats my hands. "Don't worry about me, love. I'll be fine."

My heart races. I didn't realize how concerned I am for her well-being until the truth of the next few months slams into my gut.

"You don't understand. I don't think this mission will be the end of the conflict."

"Oh, I understand just fine, my dear." She gives me a knowing look.

How could she know?

She says, "But what I understand even better is who you are. You are a born leader, a kind friend, and most importantly, a protector of the innocent. Never forget it."

I give her something I give so few others — a hug. She startles at first, but then wraps her arms around me. I breathe in her eucalyptus and mint scent.

"I love you, Sana."

"I love you too, Sage. Remember, your strength comes from so much more than your magic. It comes from your heart."

Every day I'm scared to die. And I don't think there's another human in Tirlun that can say that — let alone at twenty-five. Who knows what will happen to me? With this illness, with my life and my choices. It's impossible to predict when things will take a turn. And maybe that should make me reckless. But I think I'm just bitter. Bitter at those who don't have to worry about their life turning on its head with a snap of their fingers. Those who get to live in blissful ignorance to the pain and suffering I experience every day.

And so, I become mean. And cold. And distant. Because it's easier to be angry than sad.

I weave through the gardens, preparing myself for something I both love and dread. I make sure anyone who sees me leaves me alone; anyone who dares to make eye contact gets a wave of hot air sent their way. It's more than enough warning for them to look away — everyone avoids me when I bring my fire side out to play.

Even Lord Boann, who's walking through the gardens with another advisor, likely plotting ways to starve the poor, takes one look at me, gives me a tight smile and a small bow, and quickly walks in the other direction.

With the help of ice on my feet, I move past the ice rink, and melt the ice as I reach the gates of the cemetery. This is the royal cemetery, reserved only for royals and their family.

The ground is sacred — the Mother blessed it to never freeze, even here. It's one of the only places in the Ice Dominion that stays green year-round. Between the soft tufts of grass that grow over the newly tilled soil and the oaks that guard the borders of the cemetery standing strong and proud as they shield any visitors from the elements, it's a sanctuary in the strongest of terms.

I approach my parents' graves, and I can't help the lurch in my stomach. As much as I believe in the Mother, it's difficult for me to truly believe that there's some part of my parents still alive. I try to feel them through the things I do and hope it makes them proud. Would they be proud of who I've become? They always told me to stay true to myself, but how can I be myself when she's buried underneath the weight of everyone's expectations?

Plants that are spelled to have their names written on

their stems mark their graves. I rub the petals of my mom's peony bush as I whisper, "I'm scared."

The words fall out of my mouth, and like a storm suddenly breaking, I fall to my knees as sobs rack through my body. Other than my bedroom, this is the only place I allow myself to cry. And now, with Aiden, I can't risk him hearing me through my bedroom doors.

I cry. I cry for my parents. For my loneliness. For the secrets that weigh on my soul. For the comfort I wish I had the strength to ask for.

My life is full of contradictions. I'm touch starved but afraid of affection. I'm drowning in fears but can't share them. I wish for a long life, but I'm scared to grow old. I'm terrified of my future but can never stay present. I'm in constant pain but never let anyone help. I have so many hopes, but I dread making them come true.

I feel nothing. I feel everything.

I wipe my tears on the back of my sleeve as I look at my father's firebirds, their orange and red petals spiked and out of place.

I talk softly to my parents' plants. "I may not be able to visit for a while. Not that you're actually even here." I take a deep breath to settle my shaking soul.

Grief is both a blessing and a curse; to grieve means you've loved so deeply that their soul has left a mark on you that will never disappear, but the pain of that disappearance can be unbearable.

What a gift to miss someone this much. But, Mother, it fucking hurts.

"One breath, one step," I say as I rise and shake the grass of my pants. I pray it's not a coincidence that a warm breeze wraps around me the moment I speak the words they taught me to give me strength.

"One breath, one step."

I'm still weighed down from my visit as I make my way back to my room. I turn a corner and run straight into a servant. "Watch where you're going," I growl before I realize it's one of the bushy-tailed new girls. Great.

I'm about to apologize when I look behind her to Aiden at the door of my room. He stares at me like I'm nothing but the dirt under his shoes. There's no way I'm apologizing in front of him. The girl stammers apologies as I brush past her and reach Aiden frozen at the door.

"Are you going to get in my way too?" I ask. He opens the door wider and steps to the side, saying nothing.

Chapter Fourteen

Aiden

I follow Sage into her rooms and stand in shock in the living room. She slams her door, spends about two minutes doing something, opens it, glares at me, and then leaves the suite. I don't know what I witnessed between her and the servant, but her eyes looked haunted when they met mine. From everything I've seen, she's rough around the edges, but never outwardly cruel. I'm not sure where she was, but it must've deeply unsettled her.

My afternoon felt weird without Sage here, not that I would ever tell her that. Delwyn trained me after lunch and I barely produced snowflakes. I think Delwyn is getting more frustrated with my lack of magic than I am because we end up focusing more on physical combat for our lesson. I'm more comfortable with that anyway — it reminds me of my old lacrosse days. I try to explain lacrosse to Delwyn, but he doesn't understand the point. They have sports here, but they mostly involve swords or bows and arrows. The only sport that sounds anything like what we have on Earth sounded way too complicated and I zoned out very quickly.

Sage hasn't returned from wherever she went. After showering, I decide to explore more of the castle by myself before dinner. It's massive; everything is made of silver and marble, making you feel like you're literally in a castle made of ice. The entire kingdom, castle included, has a slight chill, but it's surprisingly not as cold as I envisioned an "Ice Dominion" being.

The servants are well taken care of and enjoy their jobs enough. Everyone I walk past smiles and acts friendly; they all know who I am at this point, but I have no actual authority over them, so they don't fix themselves and bow like they do for Delwyn or Sage. I prefer it that way.

I turn a corner to where I thought the direction of the library was, but I slam straight into someone's body.

"Oh, geez, I'm so sorry!" I say before realizing who's standing directly in front of me.

Roman gives me a foxlike sneer. "Look at you, wandering the halls all by himself. Where are your babysitters?" he asks, looking around.

"I am a fully capable human being." I may puff out my chest, just a little bit.

"But you're not truly a human from Tirlun. In fact, I can't see a single trait in you that makes you equal to any of us, let alone me," he scoffs.

God, this guy is a dick.

"Sage didn't mind the first night we met." I immediately regret it as soon as the words come out of my mouth.

Roman nostrils flare before quickly recovering. "What's that supposed to mean?"

I need to find a way out of this without throwing Sage under the bus. She doesn't deserve any more attention from this asshole. "I mean she's not nearly as judgmental as you, and from what I understand, she's closer to royalty than you'll ever be."

I think I recovered well. I'm not suited for politics.

"Hm. Well, we'll see about that. Don't forget why you're here. To get that weapon and bring it back for *our* use."

I mock salute at him.

His face gets red, something I didn't believe possible with all the ice in his veins.

He whispers, "You're going to regret making an enemy of me," before stalking off around the corner.

How did Sage manage to attract the biggest jerk in this massive palace? I shake my head and keep making my way down the hall. I'm not in the library's hallway, but there's a beautifully carved wooden door. It's covered in flowers and forest animals. Curious, I open the doors.

It's like I'm transported into another world, suddenly surrounded by color. Thousands of flowers hang from the ceiling in every shade. A small path is barely visible through the thick green foliage, and as I walk it, every step shows a new and exotic plant. There are some flowers I recognize — giant blue hydrangeas, violets, bluebells, daisies — but even more that I don't. Along with the flowers are herbs and vegetables. I keep walking, not sure where to look. This must be a greenhouse, but I can't see the walls or windows to be sure.

Taking a deep breath, my nose is filled with every fragrance, but one sticks out. Where have I smelled it before?

I try following my nose, but it's difficult when there are different scents coming from every direction.

I weave my way through the garden and turn a corner to a fountain with two benches. Sage sits on one of the benches, smelling the plant to her left. She hasn't noticed me yet, but she looks at peace in a way I've never seen before.

I clear my throat so as not to startle her.

This time she didn't know I was here. She must've been more distracted than I thought. Sage looks up from the plant. "I'm surprised to see you here."

"Why? I'm allowed to walk around without an escort, aren't I?"

"Relax. That's not what I meant. I didn't have you pegged as a garden guy."

I take a deep breath. Sage always makes my blood boil and all my politeness fly out the window.

"Sorry. I'm a little on edge, I guess."

"Why?"

"I had a lovely run in with Roman on the way over here," I say, approaching her bench.

"Ah, that'll do it."

As I get closer, I realize why the smell is so familiar. It's her. I look at the flowers and back at her. "This is you."

"I'm sorry, what? Yes, I'm right here. Are you alright?"

"No, no, no, that's not what I meant. This flower smells like you. What is it?"

"It's a peony. I didn't realize you paid such close attention to my scent."

"I can't get it out of my head." My body lurches forward like the words were pulled out of me and I couldn't have stopped them even if I wanted to.

She tilts her head at me but doesn't comment as she plays with one of the creamy white petals.

She's contemplative as she says, "I've always loved peonies. They can survive cold winters but still blossom when the heat finally comes. Their buds are very small, but when they bloom, they explode to many times their original size. The smell reminds me of my mother. She always kept fresh cut peonies on her bedside and made sure her perfumes always contained at least a little. After she passed, I stole most of her perfumes, so that's probably why I smell like that."

I sit down next to her and take a deep breath of both her and the flowers. "It's more than peony with you though. There's something almost spicy in you as well."

Like I'm in a trance, I involuntarily move closer to her. She's frozen in place. I slowly move my head to the crook of her neck and smell.

I lightly breathe out onto her neck and whisper, "It's the most intoxicating combination. You're fire and ice wrapped in a stunning package." Something about the sadness I witnessed in her eyes earlier today makes me want to do whatever it takes to get her mind off of everything that could've caused it.

I watch as her chest moves up and down rapidly beneath my body and I can't pull myself back. She doesn't seem to be able to move either, though she could move either of us if she really wanted to.

We're frozen, breathing each other in like a drug. I can't help myself from inching my lips closer to her neck and placing a soft kiss right beneath her jaw. She shudders from my touch.

This woman undoes me without any effort.

Before it can go any further, someone clears their throat, and we jump apart. Sage pats down her hair and outfit to make sure nothing is out of place.

I look up to Idris staring at us. "Lovebirds, it's dinner time. I knew I would find Sage here, but what a lovely surprise to find Aiden as well." Idris smirks at me before wrapping her arm around Sage's as she stands up. "Let's go. Queen Neve will be in an even worse mood than usual if we're late."

I walk behind the two of them to give myself a few moments alone to compose myself.

Chapter Fifteen

Sage

Of course I'm sitting next to Roman. How does he always manage to get as close to me as physically possible? Del is on his other side, thank the Mother. He will hopefully keep Roman distracted as long as possible. Aiden is on my left, followed by Dahlia and then Queen Neve at the head of the table. There's a total of twenty nobles at this table and about fifteen too many if you ask me. I love to play the politics game when it suits me, but right now there's nothing more I'd rather do than be playing with Fluffy in the gardens.

Roman leans over to whisper in my ear, "You look ravishing as always."

He's not wrong — I'm wearing one of my favorite deep violet dresses with a fitted corset and loose sheer sleeves. I grabbed the dress and got ready in Idris' room after my unfortunate encounter with Aiden.

Unfortunate in my room. The encounter in the greenhouse was... less so.

But, if I was going to be forced to sit through this wretched dinner, I may as well look gorgeous while doing it. That doesn't mean I'm looking for compliments from Rancid Roman.

"Thank you," I say, giving him a tight smile.

Thankfully, the queen gathers everyone's attention before this conversation can continue. "Dearest members of my beloved court, I want to offer my gratitude to you all for joining us for this celebratory dinner. My son, along with my niece and the rest of their excellent team, will be leaving tomorrow morning for what may be the most important mission in the Ice Dominion's history. They will be retrieving our greatest weapon, the one that ended that horrible war so many centuries ago. With this weapon, which we will hopefully never have to wield, we can once again bring peace to Tirlun. So please, raise your glasses in a toast to our fearsome soldiers."

A "Here, here!" raises up from the rest of the nobles as they all take sips of their champagne. If there's one thing my aunt is good at, it's a rallying speech. She makes our mission sound like a noble quest that's sure to be a success. Forget the fact that we don't know where the weapon is, what it is, and if we'll even be able to bring it back *if* we find it. But, you know, here, here!

The rest of the meal goes as smoothly as expected. Besides a few more lewd comments from Roman, it's just regular court politics. Which means nobles scheming to get more power, suck up to my aunt, and leverage themselves for more control should the war come.

Aiden's certainly enjoying himself, talking the night away with Dahlia. They would look gorgeous together. She's nicer than me; more graceful, less damaged. Not that it matters. We're leaving tomorrow, and Queen Neve would never approve that courtship. Never mind the fact that the thought of them together makes my blood literally boil.

I send a wave of frost through my insides to cool it down. I've gotten too good at hiding what I'm feeling — both physically and mentally — that the neutrality on my face masks anything inside. Thank the Mother for that; otherwise, all these politicians would know too much. Aiden would know too much.

I'm still in my head, so I don't notice Roman scooching his chair closer to mine. "It doesn't appear you're eating your dessert. Want me to feed it to you?"

My nose involuntarily wrinkles and my eyes narrow as I stare at him in disgust. I can't be as rude as I would like to him, but that doesn't mean I need to let him speak to me this way.

"I would rather eat glass," I say with the sweetest smile I can muster.

His laugh shakes all the nearby plates and glasses and almost everyone looks up from their private conversations to see what caused him to make so much noise.

"Oh, Sage, when we're married, you're going to eat whatever I tell you to."

"I'd like to see you try."

A flash of anger — ah, there he is. Beneath his handsome and faux-charming veneer, I can see the monster inside. He tries to hide it from everyone, but he can't hide it from me. I know what it's like to hide a monster within.

He gets as close as physically possible and through clenched teeth whispers in my ear, "You're going to regret every snide comment you've ever made to me once the queen approves our marriage."

"She'll never approve of it." I take a big sip of my wine. She will *never* approve of it.

"I wouldn't be too sure about that."

I almost choke on my wine.

"What's that supposed to mean?"

"It means, according to my father, once your little scavenger hunt is done, the queen is most likely going to agree to my proposal. Finally."

A wave of ice floods through my body. I'm hot and cold at the same time. My hands release small flames that I need to quickly douse before anyone notices.

There's no way my aunt would agree to that. There would be no need. If we have the weapon, she'll be satisfied. She won't need any more power plays to win favor within the court nobles. Right? Shit. Maybe I misjudged her ambition.

Well, if all goes to *my* plan, it won't matter what she wants anyway.

I've managed to calm myself down within a matter of seconds, but Aiden still manages to notice, because he turns from his conversation with Dahlia to speak to Roman with me sandwiched in between. "I've only known Sage for a few days, but I can already tell you that you'll never get her to do something unless *she* wants to."

Roman's nostrils flare and he clenches his jaw before asking, "Aiden, you've only just joined our lovely realm. So, I would suggest not getting involved in matters beyond your understanding."

"It's *my* understanding that you've been harassing our lovely Sage all night. And she responded in probably the politest way I've ever heard her speak," Aiden starts. Had he been paying that close attention all night? "Before her already shockingly long-lasting patience finally disintegrates and you see the ire I know she has, *I* would suggest you back the fuck off."

I can't lie, that was hot. But pissing Roman off is not a good idea. He pushes off his chair to stand over both Aiden and me.

"You're going to regret saying any of that," Roman says through clenched teeth.

Aiden stands up in response. Now we have the entire tables' attention, even the queen's. We'll see how long it takes for her to interfere. She lets the nobles squabble every now and then as she believes it makes them less likely to be mad at her.

Aiden's taller than Roman — I can tell from my angle underneath both of them. I push my chair back so I'm no longer sitting in between very tense males.

Roman collects ice in his hands. Fuck, Aiden hasn't been able to produce any magic since that first night. I'm about to get involved when Aiden physically shoves Roman back about five feet. I can't help the laugh that escapes my mouth before I cover it with my hand to muffle the sounds; people here are so used to fighting primarily with magic that they forget physical force can be as effective. Roman looks angrier than ever, while Aiden's hiding a laugh himself.

Roman turns back to Aiden, about to shoot some spikes at

him when the queen stands up from her chair and says, "Enough."

Both men freeze and everyone turns their attention from them to the queen.

"While I appreciate the passion expressed when it comes to my niece, we cannot afford any injuries or delays to their mission. So, I will ask for both of you to back down. I believe this is as good a time as any to end this meal. Thank you all for coming, and once again, we wish our soldiers luck on their journey."

She leaves the table and walks out of the throne room before anyone can even respond. She's not entirely unaffected by what happened and a small trail of ice follows her footsteps.

Del comes up to me and says, "Let's go back to your chambers."

Aneira grabs Aiden and Idris follows behind. The five of us leave the room before anything more disastrous can occur.

Chapter Sixteen

Aiden

Sage looks so beautiful tonight. Her purple dress makes her auburn hair shine brighter and her green eyes somehow greener. I was listening to Roman taunt and tease her all night at dinner, and I couldn't take it in the end. It wasn't the smartest decision, considering most nobles have very strong magic, but my reaction was involuntary.

Sage probably thought I wasn't paying attention, especially as my back was turned to her for most of the meal when I was talking to Dahlia.

Dahlia's lovely — sweet, kind, caring, and of course, beautiful. But no matter how hard I tried, my attention was never wholly focused on her. I couldn't stop myself from being aware of Sage's every slight body adjustment or response to Roman.

I was shocked that she let him speak to her like that. She takes zero shit from anyone. It must be some court politics that I don't understand. But at the end I exploded. Thankfully the queen interfered when she did because that would've ended very ugly for me. None of them have mentioned the incident since we've been back in Sage's living room. Just lots of laughs.

As soon as we entered Sage's room, she heads off into her bedroom before I can say anything. Especially because at the moment, Delwyn is telling some ridiculous story of Idris getting trapped in the attic of a bar on a mission. "And then we all met at the inn, and we couldn't find her. Sage tried to send her a wind message, but there must have been some spells blocking communication because they couldn't break through. We were about to go back to find her when we all saw tavern-tall flames. Turns out Idris' solution for getting out of a trapped attic was to burn it all down!" I have no clue what a fucking wind message is, but regardless, Idris' response is extreme.

Idris, trying to justify her actions, adds, "The magic block only worked from the outside in. It didn't stop magic use on the inside. And I couldn't let myself be found! I had important information!"

"That's why," Aneira giggles. "Not because you didn't want to be rescued by a locksmith."

There's a knock at the door, which is surprising because as far as I know, Sage's friends never knock. And, all her friends are already in her room.

"Come in," I say as the door opens and a petite elderly

woman with the longest white hair I've ever seen walks in. She's only slightly taller than Sage and her hair almost reaches the floor. Her skin is a similar shade of bronze as mine, and she has bright blue eyes like everyone else here but Sage.

"Hello, dear. I'm Sana. You must be Aiden. Is Sage in her room?"

"I-I believe so, yes. May I ask, what are you doing here?"

I glance at the rest of Sage's friends to gauge their reactions and they're all as calm as can be.

Her crow's feet multiply as she chuckles. "Of course, how rude! I am the royal healer and physician. If you have any major injuries," she says, looking over my bruised skin, "I would be more than happy to help you. But light scrapes and bruises are best left to time or one of your own spells."

Not even addressing the spell comment, I say, "I see. Well then, why are you treating Sage? She's to be in even better shape than I am after today." Why am I the only one talking right now?

The rest of Sage's friends are busying themselves around the room and Aneira runs off into the library, leaving me to fend for myself.

Her eyes darken and she gives me a clipped frown. Shit, that was rude. Who am I to ask questions from the royal healer? "I sincerely apologize if that was rude, I probably have no right to ask that."

Her face smooths out to its previously less wrinkled visage. "I think it's for the best if you direct these questions to Sage. She can decide whether or not she wishes to share those details with you."

I give her a nod and she turns towards Sage's room, carrying a giant medicine bag that looks way too heavy for a woman of her age and stature to be carrying with such ease.

As I turn back to Sage's friends, Delwyn is doing a terrible job pretending to look out at the stars. The terrace door isn't even open.

"Delwyn, what's going on? Why hasn't Sage left her room?"

Delwyn clasps his hands behind his back as he turns to me. "I think those questions are best left for Sage to answer."

"Or not," Idris says, her nose in a book, clearly pretending to read.

"Seriously? No one's going to tell me anything?" I thought after I gave into their little schemes, they would be done hiding secrets from me. Apparently not.

Idris shrugs. "You might as well find something to entertain yourself with. They're usually in there for about an hour." She looks back down at her book and actually starts reading.

Delwyn walks over to Sage's library to join Aneira.

I'm not going to get anything else out of them until Sage comes back out, so I pick up the research I gathered earlier today in the library and flip through it.

I read through the notes for the hour while Sana is in Sage's room.

But, I can't stop thinking about what Sana said. Sage doesn't seem like the type of person who would ask for excessive help. In fact, from everything I've seen, it's almost a struggle for her to ask for any help at all. I would ask her myself, except every time I think I'm getting let in, she shuts down.

It took several days for her to decide that I got to learn about Idris' invisibility. For whatever reason, she decided at lunch today I earned the right to know. Although, if you ask me, it should've been Idris' decision. They're obviously hiding more secrets from me, and if I ever want to feel like I truly belong here, I'm going to need to trust those around me.

Aneira leaves the library and flits over to the couch and looks over my shoulder to see what I've been reading. "Oh, how lovely! You're learning more about your family!"

"Trying to, anyway," I say. "There are a shit ton of family trees, but not a lot of information about my magic or this weapon."

"That's probably because they wanted to keep it a secret. Nobles in Tirlun can be very weird with sharing information about their powers. They probably assumed your parents would teach you... unfortunately."

"Great, more secrets."

"Don't worry! We'll all help you!" Aneira adds cheerfully. I appreciate her optimism, but it doesn't change my frustration at the situation.

Sage and Sana step out of her room as they speak in hushed tones. "I know, Sana, I'll be careful," I manage to hear Sage whisper. Sana pats her arm, turns to us all with a smile, and heads out the door.

Sage flops down on the couch next to me. "How's the reading going, *shifrah*?"

"Not great, considering everyone here loves to keep secrets."

"What's that supposed to mean?"

"Only that you're all so hesitant to share things with me." I look at them in turn. "It took you days to tell me about Idris' powers and there's clearly more you're keeping from me. How am I supposed to work with you all and go on this most likely fatal journey if I'm being kept in the dark?"

Sage looks at me with zero emotion. "First off, you thought we were all crazy in the beginning, so why would we have given you more fuel for that fire? Second, anything we're not telling you isn't critical to the mission and therefore isn't relevant to you. Trust goes both ways — you don't get to learn all our secrets just because we're going on this mission together."

I've been getting whiplash from all these literal life-shattering revelations. I would rather know everything upfront and deal with it at once instead of truth-bomb after truth-bomb. But, it's clear I'm losing this battle, at least for now.

I have to stay positive and trust everything will work out. It usually does.

"Fine. Keep your secrets. Just promise me you'll share anything about me and my magic."

"Deal!" Delwyn shouts before Sage can say anything snarky back.

Idris stands near Sage's bar cart. "Anyone want a drink?"

The alcohol helps ease my frustration at my lack of answers.

After we all have our drinks, Sage asks, "Is everyone ready for tomorrow?"

"Bags are packed and waiting by the ursas and horses," Aneira says.

"Ursas *and* horses?" I ask. I'd assumed I was going to have to figure out how to ride one of those massive beasts. I hope one of the horses is for me.

"We figured you would be more comfortable riding a horse." Phew. "And Idris will never admit it, but she's scared of ursas," Delwyn mock-whispers to me.

Idris lightly slaps his arm. "I am *not* afraid of ursas. They sense my fire and don't like me very much."

"Sure."

Idris turns back to Sage. "All our intelligence suggests our route should be clear. We've already sent messages to the inn we plan on stopping at along the way, and should anything change, I'll keep you updated." Wow. She's been hard at work in the last twenty-four hours.

Before Sage answers, a look passes between the two of them that I can't read. "Excellent," Sage says. "Del?"

"I've informed any squadrons out on missions in the field to be expecting surprise check-ins from us," he says.

"Perfect. Sounds like we're all set. Any questions?" Sage looks at each of us, ending on me.

I say, "Considering I didn't know this realm existed a week ago, I don't think I have a right to question any of your preparations."

"Of course you do, you're part of the team," Aneira says gently.

I give her a grateful smile. "I trust you all. At least, to get me through this alive, if only for your sakes. So, I'm good."

Aneira claps her hands. "Ooh, I'm so excited! It's been so long since we've been on a real adventure!"

"How about the last time we were sent to the border and had to fight off two Fire Dominion squadrons? Alone?" Idris questions.

"Nah, that doesn't count. The battle only lasted an hour," Sage says.

I choke on my water. "How many soldiers are in a squadron again?"

"About twenty," Delwyn says.

"So, you're telling me the four of you fought off forty soldiers and won in only an hour?"

"Yup." Delwyn flashes his giant smile at me. "I told you, we're the best." Every story proves their cockiness right. It's still astounding to me how fierce they are, especially when they act like toddlers interacting with each other.

"What he's forgetting to mention is that he almost lost his leg in the process," Sage adds.

Delwyn scoffs. "No one needs to know those details."

"*And* Aneira was stabbed in the gut!"

"Yeah, but since then, no one's ever gotten close to my gut!" Aneira cheerfully says.

We all hang out in Sage's room, laughing and chatting. And they make me comfortable enough to be myself too. Even Sage, whose face can brighten like the sun and then darken like smoldering flames in the span of ten minutes. She may be hesitant to talk about her feelings, but they're clear as day on her face. At least, around her friends.

Still, I was worried she would judge me the most out of

all of them, but no matter what I say, there's never any judgment, just sass and opinions.

It's surprisingly refreshing. I'm so used to trying to be a certain type of person, especially around girls. It's nice to let my guard down. I've only known this group of people for a few days, but I'm more comfortable around them than I've been with some friends for years. Maybe I really do feel at home. Whatever it is, I'm not complaining. I'm going to need their friendship if this journey is going to be as difficult as it seems.

After another couple hours of drinking and laughing, everyone leaves to go back to their own rooms until it's only Sage and me.

I shut the door behind Aneira and turn to Sage frozen at the table. She's staring into space and most likely has completely forgotten I'm even here. I debate getting her attention when she shudders and comes back to herself. She blinks a few times before looking up at me with wide eyes. I have no idea what just happened, but whatever came over her has her spooked.

"Are you alright?" I ask.

She attempts to quickly cover up her emotions. "Yeah, why wouldn't I be?"

I stare down at her. "Sage, I saw you. It looks like you saw a ghost. Come on, talk to me."

She shakes her head, already preparing to shut me down. Again. But instead, she takes a deep breath and sits down at the table. I follow suit, not wanting to spook her into changing her mind.

"I'm nervous about this mission," she says. "I don't want to scare you because you're kind of our only hope. But I guess everything kind of came rushing into me. All the risks and dangers and the slim possibility of us even finding this weapon. There's a lot at stake."

Her gaze is angled downward and her fingers fiddle with the edge of the table. I wasn't even sure she was capable of acting nervous, always so confident and sure of herself. I scramble, thinking of anything I can say that would stop that heartbreaking look on her face. I don't even know why I care, but I would do just about anything to bring that light back into her eyes.

"Sage," I start. She looks up at me, and it's a good thing I'm sitting down because that gaze would have brought me to my knees. "I know that a lot has happened over the last few days, and that there's a lot I still don't understand about this world and my role in it. But what I *do* know for certain is that you can push through unspeakable odds."

A small smile forms on her face, so I keep going, trying so hard to earn that full grin she gives to so few individuals. "Just think — you managed to seduce, kidnap, and trick me, and I'm still here of my own free will. *You*, Sage, have convinced me of the importance of this mission and my purpose here. Whether or not you've realized it, you've given me something worth fighting for."

I don't get the smile I was hoping for, but she tilts her head a little like a bird assessing its prey. "Did you not have something worth fighting for before this?"

I smile softly. "I know you're trying to change the subject, but I'll allow it." I take a deep breath. "Ever since my parents died, my life has been muted, colorless. Dating, my job, even my friends have stopped having meaning. I realized that none of the other relationships in my life were ever that important to me compared to the one I had with my parents."

I nervously rub my hands along my thighs. "And so, as much as I was pissed that you kidnapped me, there was a part of me that was also relieved. It gave me an excuse to leave a version of myself behind. A version that I think I no longer was, but who everyone still expected me to be. The last few days here I've felt more myself than I have in *years*. So even if I never go back to Earth, I think I'm okay with that. Maybe you'll even find yourself with a new member of your squad." My heart races when I realize what I blurted out. "I-I-I mean, if you'll have me."

Sage gives me the huge, genuine grin I had been hoping for. "Aiden," she says, her soft, low voice singing my name. "It would be an honor for you to join my squad. As long as you think you'll be able to handle my bitchy self."

"I've handled it pretty well so far."

"You have."

A peaceful quiet settles over us as we finish our glasses.

"You didn't have to protect me at dinner," Sage says quietly. "I can handle myself."

"Oh, trust me, I know," I say. "But just because you can, doesn't mean you should."

She slowly shakes her head. "I didn't even realize you were listening."

"I couldn't help myself." Her eyes widen as I try to recover. "It's just that Roman is so obnoxiously loud."

"Either way, you're way too nice to me. I kidnapped you for fuck's sake! You got over that fact so quickly, and I get why you're nice to everyone else — they were following my orders — but fuck, stop being nice to me!"

Is she mad at me for being nice to her?

"I'm sorry, are you... mad at me for being nice to you?"

She puts her drink down on the table and starts to pace around her room. "No, of course I'm not *mad*. But, I don't understand. I get that you kind of had no choice but to accept things, but you still could be furious. I would be."

"I was mad at first. But everyday I'm starting to under-stand why you did what you did. So, I understand. It's not your fault." I had no idea she was holding all of this emotion inside of her.

"Of course it is! It was my idea! I took you from everyone and everything you knew! I brought you to another fucking realm!"

She's madder at herself than I ever even was. I didn't realize she felt so much guilt for what she did.

I walk over to her and place my hands on her arms to get her to stop pacing. I look down into her swirling green eyes. "Sage, I forgive you."

"Wha- What?"

"I said, I forgive you. For kidnapping me, for tricking me, even for drugging me," I say trying to put a smile on her face.

She starts to calm down and my heart warms a little at the thought that I was the one to calm her down.

I add, "Now that that's out of the way, can we agree to no more hating each other? We need to work together to complete this mission, and I'd much rather have you with me than against me."

"I never hated you," she says, looking down at the floor.

Before I can respond, Fluffy bounds out of her room and jumps into my arms. She nuzzles into me asking for pets. Sage smiles at us. "She likes you."

"What's not to like?"

She rolls her eyes like I knew she would. "Alright, Pretty Boy, I'm going to bed, and you should too. One last sleep in a real bed before we're back to sleeping on cold, hard ground."

"Don't remind me."

"Goodnight, Aiden," she says as she walks into her room. My name sounds like a caress coming out of her soft lips. It's a caress I'd let hold me forever.

Chapter Seventeen

Sage

Sadly, we wake up bright and early. I'm not a morning creature, but Queen Neve and Dahlia meet us at the palace entrance to say goodbye.

I saddle onto Blizzard when Aneira walks out of the stables with the largest ursa I've ever seen. I thought Blizzard was big, but this ursa is probably fifty percent larger.

"Aneira, are you sure you're going to be able to control that massive animal?" I ask.

"Of course, he's a sweetheart. Aren't you, Barbarian?" she asks, scratching under his chin. He nuzzles up against her head.

"Its name is *Barbarian?*" Aiden asks as he's saddling his horse.

We decided against ursas for Aiden and Idris. Idris doesn't get along particularly well with the creatures and although I'm sure Aiden will also never admit it, they make him nervous as well.

"Yes, but he's a big softie. I think everyone was scared of him," Aneira says as she continues to pet the ursa.

Aiden's tightening his saddle as he calmly and smoothly checks his horse. I realized I had assumed he knew how to ride, since everyone in Tirlun can, but being from Earth, it may not be so common.

"I'm glad you're comfortable around horses," I say.

"Yeah. My family and I rode in Colorado whenever we visited in the summers. But I have to ask, you guys don't have cars or anything that can get us there more comfortably?"

"Aiden, I already explained this." The amount of times I've had to repeat myself over the last four days... "First of all, think about how horrible the cars in your world are for your planet. Second of all, we do have vehicles that can move significantly faster across the snow, but we use our magic to power them. We thought it was best to save our magic should we run into any trouble along the journey. Just because we're strong, doesn't mean we're infallible."

And if this mission goes how I expect it to, we're going to need all the help we can get.

He slightly shakes his head. "Just thought I'd ask again."

He hops onto his horse, and I can't help but notice the way his muscles are visible through his leather pants as his thighs clench from the exertion. My mind involuntarily thinks about what those powerful thighs would feel like underneath my hands as I hold them while I suck-

"Sage?"

"Sorry, what?"

"I asked if everything's okay?" Aiden asks.

I realize I've been staring at his legs for the last however many minutes. "Yeah, all good. Just wanted to make sure everything was secure!" I pat his horse then head over to Blizzard.

I pass Idris on her horse, and she comments, "You must *really* care about Aiden's safety, huh. Especially the safety of those legs."

"Shut up." My control over my face and emotions evaporates around this man.

"I don't blame you. I'd also love to see what those things could do."

"Idris!" She smirks and moves her horse towards the castle gates.

Delwyn leads us out while I take up the rear. As we head out of the castle gates, I realize the entire city's population is lining our path out. They cheer and throw flowers as we pass. I look at the citizens, every shape and size, every skin tone, and eyes different shades of blue. There are occasional hazel or the very rare violet or green eyes like mine, but those are hard to spot.

As we reach the main gates, I spot amber gold eyes. We make eye contact, and the man nods then hops off the roof where he was perched.

A small part of me is infuriated at this display; I've told the queen several times that this mission needs to be low-key. It didn't need to be a secret, but we also shouldn't be shouting it from the rooftops.

For our safety. For the safety of the weapon. For the safety of the Mother-forsaken realm!

But no, she had to use it as an opportunity to gain more favor with the populace.

As soon as we cross the city gates, we pick up the pace, and our animals trot through the Ailec Woods. The wool cape I put on this morning flaps in the wind behind me as I speed up and I can't help but smile.

There's something so freeing about being on the back of an animal, in tune with nature, feeling the Mother all around you — in the wind, the air, the birds that flee as we race past them. I send this freedom through my bond with Blizzard, and he looks back at me, giving his version of a smile before removing himself from our line and weaving through the trees.

The massive and magical forest bisects the entire Ice Dominion and will be where we spend most of our journey. Not that I'm complaining — this forest has been my home almost as much as the palace in Bruma. There are no real roads, as we didn't want to have to cut down any of the trees to clear the way. But from the millions of people that have traveled these woods, certain paths have become informal routes.

We'll travel slightly away from these informal roads. Between wanting to keep our exact location a secret in case of ambushes, to the annoying business of getting stopped by citizens wanting to greet their prince, it'll be much better for everyone if we stay to ourselves.

Blizzard and I catch up to Idris in front of us on her horse and I send her a warm breeze as she smiles at us. Next is Aneira, who's having a serious conversation with Barbarian, so she doesn't even notice us passing. I slow Blizzard briefly so I can study Aiden on his horse without him noticing. He looks comfortable enough but turns his head from side to side like an owl while looking at the forest around him.

I try to see it through his eyes. It looks similar enough to any forest in Colorado, but everything is more vibrant. The colors, the smells, even the air.

I send him a wind message, *Isn't it gorgeous?*

He jumps out of his saddle, eyes wide as he looks at me.

Shit. I totally forgot to explain wind messages. Did we not teach him? Oops.

Try sending one back — I can't hear you from this far away. He stares blankly back.

Guess he's not very intuitive. *Imagine the individual you want to speak to. Sometimes it helps speaking the words out loud. Eventually you won't need to; you can just think them. But picture your words being carried on the wings of a bird flying straight into my ear.*

A dimple appears on his face. I never noticed it before. It makes him look boyish in a very attractive way that I don't care to admit.

How very poetic, I hear in his deep, slightly gravelly voice in my right ear. I beam a smile in his direction.

Well, I've been told I'm a poet. I signal Blizzard to pick up his pace again until I'm riding side by side with Aiden.

"Look at you, picking up our texting system!"

He laughs, the gravel in his voice present, and it sends a shock of heat through my core, so I look away in case the sensation is at all visible on my face.

I turn back to him and add, "Don't think this means you can send me dirty messages at all hours of the night."

He scoffs. "You wish."

I flick a tiny snowball at him.

"Hey!"

"Del told me you were able to make some snow. So, fight back!" I say with a mischievous grin.

He bites his lip as he stares intently at his hands; then, he lifts one from his reins. A few flurries of snow build in his hand before collapsing onto his legs.

"Why is this so hard?"

"To be fair, we've had our magic running through our veins our entire lives. It's only now reawakening within you. It may take a little while for your body to come back into harmony. Besides, we don't know how much the "Earth" in your blood will affect your magic. It may be very weak because of that."

I sure as fuck hope not. The more confidence I portray, the more he's likely to believe it.

"Great."

"You're so positive about everything else. Why is this making you so frustrated?" I ask. He's one of the most positive people I've ever met. Even Aneira, who's always so optimistic, is not quite as positive. It's a different way of looking at things. Not necessarily expecting everything to work out, but managing things as they come into the most beneficial light.

"I've always been competitive. I played sports in college, did my best as an employee until I created my own very successful company. So, when it comes to things that are required of me, I don't like to fail those around me." There goes another pang of guilt at taking him away from his life.

"I'm the same."

Failure is weakness. And weakness is death.

"I could also tell." I frown as I lean back on Blizzard until I'm completely horizontal on his back. "Throwing fire above your city to beat Delwyn and prove you're the best?"

That's what he considers competitive? That's just a Tuesday.

"I have nothing to prove. I *am* the best. But, I have to make sure everyone else never forgets."

"Of course."

I really don't have anything to prove. To anyone else, anyway.

We trot through the forest in comfortable silence for a little longer and I play with my magic to keep myself occupied, shooting up sprays of water only to evaporate them with a rush of heat. I test how many I can juggle at one time successfully — I make it to about five before a water spurt falls to the pine needle-coated forest floor below. Blizzard glances at the water as it falls and looks back at me as if to ask, *Seriously?*

"What?" I ask. "I'm bored, I need to do something to occupy myself."

"Are you talking to me?" Aiden turns from his horse to make eye contact with me.

A spark of electricity shoots through me as his piercing blue eyes connect with my green ones. Almost like the tug of my magic with the way his eyes draw me towards him.

"No. Blizzard."

He shakes his head. "I'll never get used to that."

"Spend more time with your horse — her name is Ginger, by the way — and maybe you can communicate with her too."

"Ginger? Hey, Ginger," he says, patting her neck. She chuffs and shakes out her mane. "Can you tell what she's feeling?" he asks.

"Sort of. It's almost a relief. Maybe she's happy she can finally convey her emotions to you." Blizzard agrees with me based on the feelings he sends my way. I stroke his back as I watch Aiden.

"Is that right, girl?"

It's very endearing how he wants to communicate with her. He's so naive to our ways. I keep forgetting he wasn't born here; he's fitting in so seamlessly in so many ways. Although, he just seems like that — able to get along with anyone and be at ease anywhere.

We stop for lunch along a river. We can't help but sneak some of Genie's treats, even though they're spelled to last us the entire journey. I take the time off Blizzard to really stretch and get my blood flowing.

The ursas and horses huddle in their own groups. They tolerate each other's presence but are definitely wary of one another. Not that I blame them. If I was a horse, I would be wary of a giant omnivorous beast. The ursas, on the other hand, are secretly big scaredy cats.

Idris left our lunch spot to scout ahead. We're going to have to camp in the Ailec tonight since the next village is still another day away. If we were traveling in vehicles like we would on a typical mission, we would have gotten there in only a day, but it's worth the extended journey to reserve our magic.

Just in case.

If a war comes, the nobles in both Dominions will use it as an excuse to grab more power. I wouldn't be surprised if they go so far as to dispatch their own soldiers to try to trigger the war that I'm trying so hard to prevent. The Kings in the Fire Dominion may be a couple of the only elites in our world that I know for certain do not want another war. They lost too much in the last one.

My magic stirs inside of me. I've barely used any the past few days — I'm worried I won't be able to contain everything I'm trying to conserve. I'm going to have to release some of it along the way, while still making sure my levels remain high.

Aneira sits next to me while Del and Aiden practice sword skills. It's admirable that he wants to learn how to defend himself and not rely on us. Del slows the movements of his arms, showing Aiden each step in an effective sword swing. Aiden furrows his brow in concentration and slowly repeats Delwyn's movements.

The slowness of his motions only makes his muscles more defined. The veins in his forearms and hands are pronounced as he twists them to properly hold his sword. The muscles in his arms ripple with the exertion as he focuses on mimicking Del. And it's perfect; it may take him one or two tries, but he picks up the proper form astonishingly quickly.

Aneira must have noticed me staring quietly. "So, when are you going to do something about this sexual tension of yours?" she asks.

I look back at her. "What are you talking about?"

"Don't play dumb, Sage. Everyone can see it. Skies, everyone can *smell* it."

"It's not that simple."

It's not nerves, it's guilt. But if I show guilt, then I show weakness.

"I think it is."

"It's not, Aneira. I literally kidnapped him. He may be attracted to me, but it doesn't change what I did or who I am.

I'm sure he wants nothing to do with me in that way. It's just a physical reaction. Chemical."

Aneira shakes her head, her dark ringlets bouncing with the movement. "It is not chemical. Whether either of you cares to admit it, you want each other. You'd have to be blind not to see it."

I put my head in my hands. She'll never understand the conflict that rages in my soul. "I'm not denying that I wouldn't love to rip off his clothes right now. I wouldn't do that to him. Now that he knows who I am, what I can do, he most certainly doesn't want me."

Aneira places a hand on my arm. "You're not a monster, Sage."

"Oh, no? A monster doesn't steal a man from his home with no remorse? A monster doesn't have a scary amount of power? A monster isn't cursed with an illness as punishment for everything she's done?" I hiss my last question.

"Sage, that's not what I meant. You know-" I can't listen to her platitudes anymore.

"Enough," I say, standing up and storming off deeper into the woods to cool myself off.

I pace back and forth. One foot leaves a trail of ice and the other a trail of fire. I have trouble controlling my power when my emotions run high. It can be hard containing it all inside of me; I restrain myself every single day from showing off my true strength. If my family only knew the monster that's underneath my skin, they would never treat me the same.

Delwyn thinks his powers are stronger than mine because I let him. Even though the queen is my aunt, she's still the leader of the Ice Dominion. If she knew how much power really ran through my veins, she would see me as a threat. And I know how she treats threats to her rule.

When my powers started coming in full force at around five years of age, my parents quickly realized how strong I was. I trained with my cousins in public, with my dad less frequently, but still, times when others knew. But every night, when everyone went back to their chambers, I had extra lessons with my parents. They knew that there was no stopping the power within me, so instead they taught me how to control it. They let me use as much of my power on them as I needed to in order to keep my true strength under wraps and taught me how to hide who I fully was.

But even now, all these years later, when my emotions run high, I sometimes involuntarily loosen the leash I keep on my powers. No one besides my parents knew the true extent of my powers. I suppose Sana can when she borrows my fire to heal, but even she doesn't know how hot my fire burns.

The flame she claims I dim. She's right, I do dim it, but she has no idea; part of my training with my parents included shielding the strength from anyone with the power to feel it.

I run my hands through my hair as I pace back and forth. My squad always tries to remind me that I'm good, even when I murder and scheme and fight. At the end of each mission, it gets harder and harder to believe them. This last mission especially.

And if they truly knew who I was and how much I actually scheme, they would hate me. Most citizens in the Ice Dominion fear me, at least a little. *They* don't — it's one of the reasons why I love them all so fiercely. They've always embraced all of me; or at least, the all of me that I show them.

I'm terrified that if they knew the true me, what I do to protect them, they would fear me like everyone else.

I create a wind field around my little clearing in the woods so they can't hear me from where they are by the river and scream as I spray flames into the sky. The wind catches the flames and spins them around me like a tornado. I make sure none of the flames touch the trees as I release the cap on my powers.

I shoot ice into the tornado of fire in sharp daggers, funneling my power into immense focus as I force the wind to spin the fire faster. I force myself to think about this moment and this moment only, pretending the flames are enemies.

I form foot-long daggers of ice with spikes coming out of the ends as I shoot them at each section of the flames. I create a wind seal around the entire section of the forest, so no one can hear my magic. It's a bubble of power with me at the center.

I scream, letting this moment be a release for my pain, sadness, and anger.

All of my power gets shoved into this vortex. No one needs to know. I'll make sure it doesn't happen again. Fuck. This was supposed to be a release and now I'm spiraling again about what comes next.

I shove as much energy as I can into my magic and slowly, too slowly, the flames begin to die. After about ten minutes, I allow the wind to settle around me and I flop to the forest floor on my back, exhausted and spent. So much for preserving my magic.

I hear a whistle and slow clapping from behind me. I sit

up quickly and turn behind me to Aiden leaning cockily against a tree about ten feet away.

"You weren't supposed to see that," I say from where I'm still sitting on the cold ground. Shit. Shit. Shit. What if he tells my family? They'll be terrified.

"Why not? It was amazing," he says, looking down at me as he pushes off the tree and approaches me. More like amazingly horrifying.

"It didn't scare you?"

"What scared me was I wasn't sure how you would come out of that unscathed. I thought I was going to have to carry you back to where we made camp. No offense, Sage, but for a tiny woman, you've got some weight to you."

A snort escapes my mouth. "Don't worry about me, I can handle myself."

"Of that, I have no doubt." He pauses before continuing. "I've only been in Tirlun for a few days and have probably seen just a drop in the ocean of what the magic here can do, but that was like something out of a fairytale."

"Or a horror story," I murmur.

He shakes his head as he sits down next to me. "No, Sage, that was beautiful. Whatever you did, it was a display of beauty and control."

"Yeah, well, you're lucky you saw that display. I'm not even sure any of my friends have ever seen me do that." I still can't believe he saw that. My nerves are wrecked and it takes everything in me to stop my voice from shaking.

"Why not?"

I sigh. "For the same reason I got nervous that you saw it. I don't want them to be scared of me. And *they* give me space when I storm off. You didn't get that message." I give him a pointed look.

That earns me a little chuckle as he says, "You don't seem to mind everyone else being scared of you."

"Everyone else, no. My family, yes." He nods and looks at me like he understands. "Truth be told, I wouldn't blame you if you were scared of me. Not only because of this, but because of everything. Or maybe not scared, but angry, or furious really, or..." he cuts me off before I can continue spiraling.

He turns his whole body to face me, placing his hands on my arms. "Sage, I already told you. I'm not mad at you. Not anymore, anyway. I understand why you did what you did."

I shake my head as I look anywhere but at him. "How can you say that?"

He ducks his head so he can look into my eyes. Fuck. There's that electricity again.

"I can say that because I've been spending all my time with you and your friends for the last few days. I'm learning a lot, and while I'm sure I don't know everything, you wouldn't do anything without cause. And besides, I'm really an amazingly nice man." He gives me a small smile at the end, trying to lighten the mood.

I take a deep breath and give him a small smile back. "I'm sorry you had to see me like that. Come on, let's go back to the others." Anything to be done with this conversation. I start to stand up, but he pulls me back down.

He must've pulled harder than he intended because I end up on his lap. I'm about to move away when he grips my arms tighter. I freeze, feeling his heat through his clothes and his warm breath on my neck. We lock gazes.

"Never apologize for expressing yourself. You don't need to hide who you are."

I can barely breathe from the feel of him surrounding me, but I whisper, "Yes, I do." More than he could ever know.

"No. You don't. You can't scare me. No matter how hard you try."

"How can you say that? You barely even know me."

"I know enough." He moves one hand from my arm and tucks a tress of hair that had fallen out of my ponytail behind my ear. I can't stop a shudder from running through me. He smiles as he feels it. "I can see right through you, Sage."

His eyes have not strayed from mine for a moment, and I almost believe him. I want to believe him. But I can't let him get close. It'll only hurt us both.

"If you say so, Aiden."

I push off him and this time he lets me. I hold out my hands for him to grab as he stands up. Once we're both standing, he looks down at where our hands are still clasped. I let go of him like he burned me. He might as well have.

"Sage," the way he says my name causes a shudder to run through my spine, "you might've been the one to kidnap me, but I'm the one who's not going to let you go."

Chapter Eighteen

Aiden

Something has changed between Sage and I over the last couple of days. I'm not sure which moment it was — watching her with her friends, seeing her power, or her fear — but the disdain I felt when she kidnapped me is gone. If I'm being honest with myself, I haven't felt it for far longer than I care to admit. And now it's starting to dangerously turn into the opposite of that.

We pass very few other groups along the journey. Somehow I have a feeling that was Sage's doing. While there are no actual roads in this massive forest, it's clear there are commonly used trails. And we're barely on them.

After we travel for a few more hours, a giant stone structure appears out of nowhere. It practically blends in with the forest itself, covered in vines and flowers. The stone is a brown hue similar to the trees and if I wasn't following Sage, I would've ridden right past it.

"What is this place?" I ask as everyone dismounts off their animals.

"It's our prison," Idris replies.

I take my time climbing off of Ginger. "And why are we stopping at a prison?" Are we adding criminals to this already ruthless group?

Delwyn lightly slaps my back as he walks past me and adjusts his sword in its scabbard. "Because, Sage never misses an opportunity to torment her would-be murderers."

My head whips towards Sage's as a small smirk crosses her face. I do remember her telling me that story in her room, but I can't believe she voluntarily visits them. I study her closer; her hands shake as she tightens her various harnesses and holsters. Why would she choose to come here? And why do her friends let her?

Chapter Nineteen

Sage

I hate this prison. I prefer to torture my prisoners in a beautiful room where I can eat between sessions. The taunting of luxury and freedom is often more effective than the threat of dying in a cold, dark hole. Well, luxury and also pain. Most people, even soldiers, have a pathetically low pain tolerance.

I greet the soldiers guarding the main entrance with a curt nod and crossed arms. The sooner I get this over with, the sooner I can leave. I don't know why I always insist on visiting them. I think I need to prove to myself they can't hurt me anymore.

We walk down the musty staircase. The stone that makes up this prison was never finished so the walls are as rough as the criminals the stone holds. All that can be heard besides our footsteps is the dripping of water, and as we get closer to the bottom, moans and cries. Del leads the way down with me behind him, followed by Aiden and Aneira, and Idris bringing up the rear.

I look behind me as we approach the bottom of the staircase to Aiden's wide eyes and slightly shaking arms. His eyes meet mine. "Is this your jail?"

I make sure my face looks as bored as possible, keeping my eyes dull and mouth flat. I place my hands on my hips to stop them from shaking. "Yes. Are you scared? You can wait outside if you don't want to join."

He swallows so deeply his veins move with the motion. "No, no. I asked for you to share more of your secrets with me." Aiden takes a heaving breath. "Show me."

I take a step back and blink several times as I try to think of a response.

From behind him, Aneira asks, "Are you sure?" I think she's actually talking to me, but purposely directs the question at Aiden.

He nods, steeling himself. "I want to see what happens to those who don't agree with you." Delwyn looks back at him from where he's speaking to the soldiers on duty. Before he can answer his taunt, I grab Aiden's elbow to guide him down the hallway.

"Alright, Pretty Boy, but remember, this is only your fate if you're really, really bad," I say as I pout my lips and bat my eyelashes at him.

He allows me to guide him down the corridor. I make sure Aiden's distracted by my comment and looking forward as we walk past Delwyn, and I give him the smallest shake of my head. His eyes hold way too much sympathy as he speaks to the guards and everyone else turns to head back up the stairs. Aiden hears their fading footsteps and looks behind us before stopping short.

"What?" I ask, tapping my foot against the stone.

"Where are they going?" he asks. Anywhere is better than this Mother-forsaken place.

"Probably to rest. They don't take the same pleasure as I do out of these visits."

His eyes narrow as he walks back to where I'm standing. "Why did they leave us alone?"

"Why? Are you scared?" I am. But he'll sure as shit never know that.

"No." His voice shakes. I can't help the urge to grab one of the whips hanging next to the empty cell we stopped in front of and drag the whip behind me. His hands open and close rapidly at his sides. "But, you all do everything together. Why is this one thing suddenly different?"

I pull out my favorite dagger and drag it across the cell bars, causing a reverberation that can be heard throughout the entire dungeon. His pupils get even larger as he stares at me. Holding my weapon gives me some semblance of control.

"Because. This next location is best viewed with as few people as possible." I nod my head in the direction we were traveling. "Shall we?" Aiden takes a deep breath and nods.

I lead him down the hallway, holding the whip in one hand and dragging my dagger down the bars in the other. We pass the occupied cells, and I force my eyes to twinkle with malice and a close-lipped smile to emerge on my face. Most of the prisoners are curled into the back corners of their cells but the few audacious ones look up at us as we pass.

After a period of time that is somehow both seconds and

hours, we reach the end of the hall. At the end are three cells that form a semi-circle, sealing off the bottom floor of the prison. With only one small entrance, it's impossible to escape. This floor is reserved for our long-term residents — the worst of the worst.

And now I'm standing in front of the worst of them all.

I throw my flames into the torches lining the stalls and get ready to face my past.

"Hello, boys." I widen my grin to show my teeth. The clang of chains against the stone is the only response as three weak bodies take form in the dim lighting. Aiden takes a sharp intake of breath, but I can't afford to look at him right now.

The male in the center gets the closest, wrapping his bruised, veiny hands around the bars of his cell. "Hello, Sage." His eyes are as dark as I remember.

My mind wants to revert to the scared ten-year old I was when I first saw those coal-black eyes, but I refuse to allow it. "Hello, Cockroach."

"Cockroach?" Aiden asks from behind me, softer than I've ever heard it before.

"Oh, yes. Cockroach. Quite a fitting nickname considering he'll be spending the rest of his life trapped in a dark and dirty home." Cockroach tries to spit in my face, but I blast heat to evaporate it before it can even get close. I shove down the urge to shudder in fear and disgust. I need my mask of indifference now more than ever.

His voice is rough and scratchy from disuse. "My name is Cockroach because I was able to get into any place, any time, anywhere." He looks at Aiden standing behind me before his eyes meet mine again. "Sage certainly knows all about my skills, don't you?"

"Enough." I throw a band of ice around his mouth, freezing it shut. "Or did you forget? You may not be able to use magic within the cell, but I can most certainly use it out here." A glare is his only response.

I force a smug-sounding chuckle to come out of my mouth as I stroll to the cell to Cockroach's right. The burn marks are still stark against his inky black skin. They trace his fingers up to his shoulders in deep red and mottled purple, an involuntary tattoo that will always remind him and me of my strength.

"Aiden here is a newcomer to the Ice Dominion," I say. "And I thought to myself, well, why not show him the weak men that I managed to defeat when I was only ten?"

I turn back to Aiden as he processes my words. His jaw drops and he studies each prisoner again in their cells. Each one has burn marks that they stupidly thought they could defend against. Even then, my power was unmatched. It was the only time I've ever allowed the full strength of my fire to emerge. I've never permitted it since.

I sigh loudly. "I'm bored. Aiden, have you seen enough?" If I never came back down here, I will still have seen too much. And yet, I keep coming back.

Some would call that masochism.

I call it a reminder.

"Yes."

"Thank the Mother. Sorry boys, looks like you'll be without my fantastic company again." I look each of them in the eyes, their hatred shining through.

I walk back down the hall and flick my hand, removing the ice band from Cockroach's mouth. "I will get out of here, Sage," he says. "And when I do, you'll regret every snarky comment that has ever emerged out of that pretty little mouth of yours."

I don't turn around. "If you ever manage to escape, I'll look forward to our rematch. Maybe this time you'll have the courage to face me one on one." The cell bars rattle as he throws his hands against them. I grab Aiden's arm and squeeze it, if only to give my hands something to do so they don't have the chance to shake.

"Are you glad you came, *shifrah*?" I ask. I use his nickname as a way to settle my nerves. He looks at my hands wrapped around his bicep before looking back at me.

He gives me a clenched smile that looks way too much like pity as he asks, "What happened to you?" I've already told him more than most about my past. And he still has the nerve to ask me that?

"You don't get to judge who I've had to become." I hate pity.

Chapter Twenty

Aiden

Once again, the things that Sage has been through have struck me to my core. She tries so hard to cover her fear and sadness with anger and strength, but to me, it's just resilience. Her will to continuously go on dangerous missions even after all that's happened and still, she feels guilty for kidnapping me.

I glance over at her now; she's joking around with Delwyn like she doesn't have a care in the world. The best way to help her shake off the encounter is through banter and teasing, so I join in as best as I can as we continue on our way.

I sleep in Aneira's tent and Sage sleeps in Idris'. At first I thought it was something I did, but it was clear that Idris had asked to spend the night with Sage. I wonder if something is going on between them; they share this intensity that I don't understand. It may not be sexual in nature, but there's an unmistakable fire.

I'm worried that it's inappropriate for me to share a tent with Aneira. When I share my concerns with her, she laughs. To my surprise, she tells me that her and Delwyn have fucked. You would have no idea based on the familial bond between them. She's about to start talking about some incident with Sage before glancing at me and thinking better of it.

Sage can do whatever she wants. I can't deny that I notice some frost involuntarily coating my hands when Aneira mentions that. Of course, the one time I produce the most magic since my first incident is thinking about Sage having sex with someone else.

That can't continue. I need to figure out my magic on my own. Delwyn has given me some training sessions on physical fighting, but without me being able to produce any ice or water, he can't really teach me how to use it.

Over the next few days, we rarely cross paths with anyone else. Once, we travel past a farmer in one of those open sled vehicles I saw in the city, carrying some sort of produce. He comes to a screeching halt as he sees Sage on her ursa first. She keeps walking, not even bothering to greet him. Delwyn, however, hops off Bluebell to greet his citizen. The man's tanned skin turned almost white in his shock at meeting the prince. He gives the rest of us a respectful smile and nod of his head before continuing on his way.

This continues a few more times as we progress through

the forest. Sage ignores the citizens and Delwyn stops to greet them.

Now, at the end of our fourth day on the road, we amble into a little village. Idris supposedly already warned them of our arrival, but the faces of the villagers we pass suggest that even with notice, they're still shocked to see us. I'm not sure who their eyes go the widest for; Delwyn, their prince; me, the stranger; or Sage, their mysterious and beautiful warrior. Delwyn's drinking the attention up, smiling and waving, winking at any of the women who bat their lashes. Sage stares them all down as if they're enemies, each carefully shifting their gazes the second they make eye contact. The more cocky men maintain eye contact, clearly looking more for her beauty than for her reputation as a fighter. To them, she smirks, as if taunting them to approach her.

We walk through the main street of the village to an inn. It reminds me of a bed and breakfast; a cozy looking beige cottage with lattice walls and dark green ivy climbing up the sides. Two men, almost the size of Delwyn and I, come out through the front door to bring our ursas and horses to the stables. We hop off our animals, gather our belongings, and head towards the inn.

I turn to Delwyn as I ask, "We haven't passed any other permanent structures besides the prison in the last two days. Why is this village so small?"

Delwyn looks at our surroundings as if realizing their size for the first time. "We would never cut down trees to populate the land. This forest has been here longer than any written record and it happened to have a clearing large enough for a small village, so that's all that was built. We grow and develop *with* the Mother, not in competition, so even us royals need to learn to rough it," he says, giving me one of his signature grins.

"Is that why we've barely traveled on a road?"

"Exactly, my friend. Any roads have been made from consistent traveling through the same paths. We wouldn't want to accidentally harm the ground by placing foreign stones or other pavement on it."

I nod as we enter the inn. That makes sense based on Idris' speech about their relationship with the "Mother," but it's still such a shock in contrast to how humans live on Earth.

The main floor must serve as a restaurant. Scuffed wooden tables are scattered throughout and comfortable-looking brown leather booths line the walls.

At the back is a bar, and behind it, a man that looks like an old oak tree. I have yet to see anyone here that truly looks old; Sana was up in her years, but her eyes were still clear, and she moved with strength and grace. This guy, however, looks like he could drop dead at any moment.

"Ah, my favorite customers," he says as we approach the back. He comes out from behind the bar, hugging everyone like they're his grandchildren. Based on all the other interactions I've seen, I'm not shocked that he's so informal with his royalty. They all smile and hug him back. When he gets to me, however, I *am* shocked as he pulls me in for a hug. "And the mysterious Aiden."

I can't help but smile at his genuine kindness and warmth. He turns back to the rest of the group. "You must all be exhausted from two days on the road with no real beds or meals. I have the two rooms you requested ready for you upstairs and supper will be served in about an hour."

Idris says, "Sorry, but we asked for three rooms."

"Oh, did you? Oh, I'm so sorry. It must have slipped my brain. The rest of the rooms are booked for the night." He begins to twiddle his hands.

Delwyn claps him on the shoulder. "Don't worry about it, old pal. We can fit into two rooms."

The owner smiles in relief. "Dinner's on me for the mistake."

Sage looks at him. "You already spoil us enough. We can pay for our supper." Interesting. Royals staying in a local inn often enough that they can have this rapport with the owner. Granted, I'm not sure where else they would sleep when traveling through the woods.

"Sage, you always treat me so well, it would be my pleasure." He hands us the keys and adds, "you have the two rooms at the end of the hall."

Sage gives him a warm smile and we make our way up the stairs that are past the bar. As we approach the end of the hall, Aneira turns back to Sage and I and sweetly says, "Delwyn, Idris, and I will share this room. You two can get the other," motioning to the door past the one they stand in front of.

Sage and I are sharing a room... alone? I can't hide my excitement, but one look at Sage and my forming grin drops.

"Why are we not splitting up how we normally do with two rooms; Del alone — now with Aiden — and the three of us together?" Sage asks, with a slight whine to her voice. Does she really not want to share a room with me that badly?

"Because Sagey, we want to play before this mission gets

more intense," Delwyn says with a mischievous grin. Play? What could he possibly mean?

Sage grunts in displeasure as she grabs the second set of keys out of Idris' hand and walks to our room. She opens the door and I'm pleasantly surprised as a wave of something sweet hits my face.

I'm not even going to ask what that was about as long as it means we're sharing a room.

"Peonies?" I look at her.

She chuckles as she walks in and places her bags on the floor. To the right of the door is a small table with two chairs. On top of the table is a bouquet of fresh pink peonies.

"Everyone knows they're my favorite." It's the *only* thing anyone actually knows about her. That's real, anyway.

I walk over to the table to smell them. "I think they're starting to become mine too."

Sage turns towards the other half of the room. "Fuck, there's only one bed. Let me see if they'll switch rooms with us." Before I can respond, she must've sent a wind message to one of the others because I hear giggling through our shared wall and Sage's face gets red and scrunched.

"I'm assuming they said no to switching rooms?"

"They claimed they only have two beds and it's only fair they get that room since there are three of them."

"I mean, that does make sense." A thrill runs through me for what that means for Sage and I.

"Well, I hope you don't mind sharing a bed with me."

Don't mind? I can't wait.

"It's not like we haven't shared a tent before."

"Yeah, but that was different," she says, glancing over at the bed. It's small, but looks comfortable.

"Different because we were on bedrolls?" I'm trying to assess how she feels about us after that last couple of days. I can't deny that I want her anymore. She's much more hesitant to admit the truth that I feel deep in my bones.

"Yes, Aiden, obviously." Maybe she doesn't want me anymore and this really has turned into solely a mission for her.

"Sheesh, sorry. I just wanted to clarify. But, I mean, it's fine. It's just sleeping."

"Yeah you're right. I'm going to shower first if you don't mind. Then you can and we'll go down to dinner." Disappointment runs through me at her dismissal of anything more than sleep happening tonight. But I don't want to push her.

"Sounds good."

Sage opens the door to the bathroom with a wave of steam. Like a mirage, she walks towards me with one white towel around her hair and another around her body, pronouncing her curves.

"All yours," she says, stepping out of my way so I can enter the bathroom. As I step around her, I catch a whiff of her intoxicating scent — that fire and ice that's actually peony and cinnamon. I can't stop myself from taking a deep inhale before entering the bathroom and shutting the door.

In the bathroom is a toilet, sink, and shower. Only the shower doesn't look like any I've used before. The ones in the palace were like the ones used on Earth; a shower head with knobs to control the water temperature. This shower has a head and no handles or controls that I can see. I look around for several minutes trying to figure out how to turn it on before giving up and going to ask Sage.

I open the bathroom door to find Sage standing completely naked with her back to me; her creamy pale skin almost glows in the soft rays of the setting sun that shine through the tiny window. With her curves on full display, she looks so delectable that my mouth waters. She takes her hair out of her towel and damp auburn waves fall down her back to hit above her ass. I must make some sort of noise because she turns around to me standing in the doorway.

"Like what you see, Pretty Boy?" She's just standing there. Completely naked. Not one hint of embarrassment or shame on her face.

I can't help my eyes from trailing down and up her body. She has a couple bruises and scars on her legs that I can only imagine are from battles, but her soft belly is perfect. My eyes move up to her breasts; perfectly round, resting on her upper rib cage from their significant size. My mouth waters even more as I look at her hard, pink nipples. I gulp and move my gaze up her neck to finally rest back on her eyes.

When our eyes meet, a light pink flush covers her cheeks. She looks so perfect right now it's taking all my restraint not to take her right now.

"Sorry, I-I-I needed help figuring out how to turn on the shower."

She shakes her head like we're having a normal conversation and she's not standing in the middle of the room without a stitch of clothing on. "Right. I keep forgetting this whole realm is new to you." She pads past me and her stomach grazes against my hard cock. She looks up at me from under her lush lashes. "You must *really* like what you see."

She looks back down and stares at my very visible erection. I must be affecting her at least a little as her blush darkens as she looks down at my hard cock.

A blush is already forming on my cheeks, but trying to get some semblance of control back, I clear my throat. "You already know I've liked what I've seen since the moment I laid eyes on you." The left side of her mouth tilts up like she wants to say something snarky in response, but instead walks past me into the bathroom.

I follow her when she turns to me and says, "Right. So, some of the smaller villages don't have the plumbing to carry water into the shower. They spell the shower heads, and you need to trigger it with your ice magic."

"How am I supposed to do that?" And how am I supposed to concentrate when she's standing in front of me naked?

"I guess it's lesson time." She claps her hands together and her tits lightly bounce with the movement. I bite my lip to stifle my groan.

Sage watches me and licks her lips before speaking. "Everyone has the ability to do basic spell work. This is one of the simplest spells there is, since it only really relies on an expression of your ice magic. The spell itself in this instance has already been cast, it only needs activation. What you're going to do is find the source of your magic within yourself. It's different for everyone. Mine feels like a dragon curled around my heart."

I can't help but laugh. "I'm sorry, a dragon? I thought you said there were no dragons here?" Every second is a new fucking revelation. I'm trying to keep up, but it's a lot.

She slaps my arm. "Not anymore, but there used to be.

And I can't explain it, but if they still existed, that's what I would feel meeting one. Find that place within yourself and will the water to turn on." I'm no longer turned on because now I'm just fucking confused.

"That's it? I need to *will* it? That's too easy." Nothing since I've entered Tirlun has been easy.

"I told you; this is one of the easiest spells. More complicated spells require more complicated magic."

I take a deep breath. "Okay, find my source." I look inward, trying to find the calm I gain whenever I'm doing something that requires complete focus. I close my eyes and try not to notice how close Sage is standing to me. Her body radiates heat like a furnace; that, combined with her intoxicating scent, makes her unbelievably distracting.

Oddly, I begin to feel something within me as I focus on Sage. I don't question it and follow that thread within myself. And there, deep down, in what can only be described as my gut, is ice. The ice is formed in the shape of hands, almost like it's trying to reach out and soothe Sage's heat. I don't blame it — I'd like to do the same.

I open my eyes to find Sage smiling. "You found it, didn't you?"

"Yeah, I did." I smile back at the pride visible on her face.

"Good. Now take whatever it is and push it in your mind towards the shower head." I follow her instructions and try to imagine the hands moving towards the shower head. Involuntarily, they begin to drift towards Sage. I pull my focus back and push them forward instead. Just like that, the shower head turns on.

"You did it!"

I smile as I run my hand under the water and it's freezing. "Fuck. It's as cold as ice."

"No, duh, Aiden. You do have *ice* magic."

She's so sassy. I love it.

"So how do I warm it up?"

"The spell is adjusted to your personal temperature. Once you step in the shower, it'll automatically shift to your perfect temperature," she says as if everyone in the universe knows that.

"That's handy."

"Magic."

I shake my head. "Unless you would like to join me, I'm going to get naked now, so you might want to leave." She actually looks like she's contemplating it before stepping out of the bathroom.

Chapter Twenty-One

Sage

I need to get a grip. Why did I act like a giddy school girl because Aiden triggered the easiest spell? He's so positive and upbeat about everything — it's infectious. He's taken everything that's happened in the last week in stride. Every time something new is thrown at him, I'm once again shocked at his ability to adapt.

And the interaction before that. Fuck. Watching him get turned on simply by staring at my naked body was one of the hottest things I've ever seen. I'm used to being completely naked in front of countless men, but something about the way he looks at me sparks something deep.

Like he wants to devour me and save me all at once.

The inn's stairs creak as I make my way down to meet Del in

the restaurant. He's already sitting at our favorite table, chatting with the innkeeper.

I groan as I settle on the wooden bench across from him.

"How are you feeling?" he asks once the innkeeper has left our table.

"Ah, you know, the usual." I rotate my wrists and slowly massage my fingers. "Everything hurts and I feel like I was run over by an ursa. Just like any other day."

Del shakes his head in sympathy. "So, I've been planning out our next couple of days. Since my mother unilaterally decided that this mission would not be a secret, we don't need to avoid the major roads. But, there's still not many places for supplies, so we should grab anything we think we'll need for the next couple of days here."

"Yes, whatever Queen Neve decides is law," I say as I roll my eyes. I can't help but think about what Roman said to me at our last dinner. Did she really change her mind about my arranged marriage? I thought she cared about me more than that.

Del's chair groans under his weight as he scoots his chair closer to me. "Sagey, what's that supposed to mean?"

"It means that I understand she's our ruler, but does that equate to absolute authority over my entire life?"

My joints start beating in pain; stress always makes it worse. I start putting more pressure into my massage and of course my cousin notices.

"What's going on? What did I miss?" Del looks at me with such concern I almost pity him. Queen Neve may be my aunt, but she's his *mother*, I can only imagine what she has planned for him.

I take a deep breath before responding. "Before we left, Roman told me that once we return from this mission, your mother will approve our marriage."

Now it's Del's turn to start fidgeting; his snow white hair shakes in disbelief and his massive hands begin to fidget with his top. "No, no, she wouldn't do that to you."

He's always had a blind spot when it came to his mother, not that I can blame him. I probably would with mine as well if they were still alive.

"Why would Roman lie?"

"To get under your skin. Like he always tries to do," Delwyn says, nodding as if trying to convince himself.

I have no desire to continue hashing out my lack of agency over my marriage prospects. Besides, I have absolutely no intention of allowing my aunt to dictate my future anymore, but Del is not in the headspace to have *that* conversation yet.

"Let's just get back to planning the rest of this mission, yeah?"

He nods in agreement.

As we finalize our plans, the rest of the group comes down the stairs, with Aneira talking animatedly about something with Aiden. He looks genuinely interested, but it's Aneira. She could be that excited describing a flower she saw on the side of the road. "That's when Sage and Blizzard come flying down the side of the mountain. She turned the slope into ice so they could get down faster. Then she froze their feet to the ground so we could finish them off!"

"Aneira, what are you telling him?" I ask.

"The last time we were on the border! Remember?"

Ah, yes. I let my temper get the better of me during that fight. The Fire soldiers didn't have the courtesy to wait for me to begin attacking my friends, so I forced them to wait. That was fun, that ice slide. We should do that more often.

"Mhm, I remember."

"Why were you there that time?" Aiden asks.

"As we've said, both dominions often send small squadrons into each other's territory for recon. There's a lot of wilderness, so once you cross the border it's fairly easy to hide — if you know what you're doing. We have a squadron of our own on our side of the mountain range, but we got word they were going to try to overwhelm them, so the queen sent us to assist."

Idris snorts. "We didn't come soon enough. It was a slaughter. Those Ice soldiers were way too lax in their training." Yeah, because they weren't mine.

"Mountain Range?" Aiden asks.

"The border between the two dominions is a mountain range," Delwyn says. "There used to be three clear paths through. After the attack fifteen years ago, the Ice Dominion destroyed two of the paths, leaving only the middle one for transport. Easier to guard. Although, there's always other ways through the mountains if you're willing to risk it."

"Why have one at all? It seems like neither dominion wants anything to do with the other."

I tap my fingers on the table as I scan the inn for any potential eavesdroppers or other nuisances as I say, "The Fire Court itself never claimed responsibility for the attack. They swear it was a rogue group of soldiers. Since we couldn't prove it was them, we couldn't completely cut off ties. Also, as Del said, it is still possible to cross the mountains without the paths. Extremely dangerous, but possible. So, it only makes sense to have at least one formal route to cross; once a year, there's a meeting of the nobles at one of the courts. It alternates courts each year. It's probably the tensest time of the year; last year we hosted, and I think we killed like, thirty fire soldiers?"

"Something like that," Idris says with a sly smile.

It's simultaneously the most fun and the most tense time of the year. I still miss my Fire Dominion family and friends.

Queen Neve knows how much they all mean to me and doles out permission for me to visit very sparingly. Like it's something to be earned to visit what used to be half of my life.

Aneira's hands wave with excitement. "There's still some trade between the two dominions, which is also how many of the soldiers sneak over the borders. Thankfully for us, the mountains where we believe the weapon is hidden is on our side of the range, so we won't have to worry about sneaking across it."

"Wonderful," Aiden sarcastically chirps.

"Relax," I say. "Have our stories not told you enough? We're the best of the best."

A server comes over to take our dinner orders. I'm starving from our hard day of traveling.

"Whatever the special is tonight. It's always delicious," Del says.

"Del, anything you eat you think is delicious," I say.

"That's because it is!"

I turn to Aiden. "The specials here are always delicious.

While Del's palette leaves something to be desired, you can always trust mine."

"Oh, can I?"

"Yup." I may not be good at dealing with my emotions, but I'm excellent at eating through them. It creates a certain connoisseur.

Idris crosses her arms over her chest. "Sage is an elitist when it comes to food."

"I am not! Some of the best food I've eaten has been from food carts. I just *appreciate* good food." They laugh. Assholes.

Dinner is delicious, as always. I'm about five ciders in and definitely feeling it. Idris, Aneira, and Del are all very close to one another on one side of the table; Aiden and I a respectable distance on the other. Everyone's a little buzzed, but the three of them know exactly what they're doing. Nevertheless, I try to get them to switch rooms one more time.

"Del, are you sure you don't want to switch rooms so you don't have to sleep with the two snorers?" I ask. I'm not sure my willpower is strong enough to withstand a night alone with Aiden. Sharing a bed.

Del puts his arms around Aneira and Idris. "I don't think we'll be doing much sleeping." Aneira giggles.

Before I can protest again, Aneira mock bows as the three of them link arms and stumble up the stairs. "Goodnight, you two."

Once we can no longer see them, Aiden turns to me, eyes

wider than I've ever seen them. "Are they about to have a *threesome?*"

I can't help the cackle that escapes my mouth. "Yes, Aiden. They're about to have a *threesome.*" What an innocent man. Adorable.

"But you guys are like family. Doesn't that make things complicated?"

"It's only complicated if you make it complicated. The three of them are very clear with one another — just sex, no romance. Although, if you ask me, Aneira and Idris have been in love with each other for as long as I've known them. They're just too scared to admit it." I try not to listen to the hypocrisy in my own voice.

"So, what, Delwyn is their buffer?"

"Something like that. I'm pretty sure Del can tell they're in love too. But he loves sex too much to stop encouraging it."

"How often do they do this?"

"Never in Bruma. There are too many other options. But depending on how long the mission is, at least once." And then I'm left to fend for myself. Although, I can usually find *someone* to keep me company.

"Wow."

"What, you've never had a threesome?" The tease is involuntary. This is dangerous territory for me — talking about sex with a man that I'm desperately trying to convince myself I don't want to have sex with.

There's that blush that's somehow visible on his caramel skin. "I have, it's just never been so casual."

My core tightens at the thought of me and him together, along with a past lover. The image of him kissing me on the neck while another is lower down on my body. He suddenly gets jealous and growls as he forces the other person out of the room so he can have me all to himself. Then he takes me and...

"Have you?" His question thankfully interrupts my daydream before I go against my better judgement and bring him upstairs.

I ignore his question and return back to our earlier topic of conversation. I need to stop thinking about Aiden and threesomes. "We can live for thousands of years. Unless you find your soulmate, which is *extremely* rare, sex is inevitably going to be casual. Even though we're very young, it's the culture." I think back to my parents. The strongest soulmates I've ever seen. They couldn't even imagine touching another sexually, their hearts and bodies were reserved solely for one another. What I would give for a love like that.

"Who knows if Idris and Aneira are soulmates? They won't until they're willing to try. So, until then, it's casual sex. And the two of them never have sex alone — they're too scared of their feelings for that." Aiden shakes his head. "You're taking everything else in so well. This is what you're struggling to wrap your head around?" It's curious that this man who's been so flirty with me since we've met is so shocked at our culture of casual sex.

"I've always seen sex as something more intimate."

"So no casual sex for you?"

He shakes his head. "I only have sex with women I care about."

Why does that make my heart drop? He may be physically attracted to me, but he definitely doesn't *care* about me. "Right. Well, shall we go to bed?"

"Let's."

I wash up in the bathroom and change into my sleeping set and come out to Aiden sitting on the edge of the bed.

"You've got to be kidding me," he says.

"What?" I ask.

"*That's* what you're wearing to bed? Are you trying to torture me?"

I look down at my pajamas. They mostly cover everything, if barely. "I run hot. This keeps me cool."

"Trust me, I know."

"Do you?"

"Every time I'm near you, I feel like I need to take off at least a layer of clothing." I bite my lower lip at the thought of him naked.

"Are you sure that's why?"

He rolls his eyes at me as he gets off the bed. "Yes, Sage. Not everything is about sex." The way he walks to the bathroom like he's got something stiff in his pocket suggests otherwise.

"If you say so," I shout after him as he shuts the bathroom door.

I turn back to the bed and assess the situation. It's not as big as mine, but we should be able to sleep side by side with minimal touching. I get in on the left side as Aiden walks out of the bathroom. Now it's my turn to stare.

He's only wearing boxers. His very defined chest is on full display — it's like his abs were drawn on. His tattoos cover both arms and the top of his chest. It's hard to tell what they are — some sort of swirling pattern, but they're almost as mesmerizing as his muscles. He approaches the right side of the bed, and even if I wasn't watching him, the shift of the bed as he lies down is indication enough. With his massive frame the bed heavily favors his side.

"Could you possibly weigh any more?" I ask.

He moves to look at me. "What are you talking about?"

I gesture to our sleeping situation and say, "I'm practically raised a foot above you; you're weighing your side down so much."

"Don't be so dramatic, Sage."

"You're calling *me* dramatic? You're the one who freaked out over pajamas." Never mind the fact that I'm salivating over tattoos. I know how to hide my desire.

"Those are not pajamas. They're lingerie."

"If you say so, Pretty Boy. But you've clearly never seen real lingerie if this meets your definition."

"Ha. Very funny, Princess."

"Goodnight, Aiden. Try not to crush me in your sleep."

"Night, Princess."

We roll over so our backs are facing one another. As I'm trying to get comfortable, my knees decide to hurt like they've been stabbed with knives. I clench my jaw and grind my teeth together to stop from crying out in pain.

One breath, one step.

Aiden must have heard something because he murmurs, "Did you say something?"

Through clenched teeth, I try to take slow, deep breaths. "No, it must've been the sheets moving around."

Fuck, this hurts. I have some salve in my bag, but if I go get it, Aiden will know something is wrong. And I don't want to deal with that right now. I swallow the pain like I so often do and try to move my legs into a more comfortable position.

"Stop squirming," Aiden says.

"Don't tell me what to do," I say. Each minuscule movement sends another wave of bone-breaking pain through my body.

"When I finally thought you were being nice, Princess, you have to ruin it by being a menace to sleep with." Even though I'm in agony, I have enough anger to kick him under the sheets. "Hey!" I'll probably regret that tomorrow, but it feels so good right now.

I can feel him flip over to look at me, so I do the same. Our faces are only inches apart.

He stares into my soul as he asks, "Have you ever been peaceful for one day in your life?"

"How can I be, when there are people like you constantly pissing me off?" I stare right back. I wonder if he can see flames in my heart through my eyes.

It's easier to be angry.

He shakes his head and says with way too much compassion, "Sage, it's okay to not always be angry."

I guess he can. I quickly send ice through myself to cool off. I can't stand the way this man can see through my mask. "It's not anger, it's annoyance." It's not really annoyance either, but I'd rather him see any other emotion in me than the truth.

"If you say so." He moves his hands ever so slightly to graze my arms, causing goosebumps to rise.

My breath gets shallow; I can't stop myself from shifting my body closer to him. He involuntarily does the same. We take a moment, breathing the same air. Time has stopped and I can't help myself from breathing him in. He smells like frost and sugar. Why does this masculine man smell so sweet?

I have no idea what to say back, so I say nothing, closing my eyes and allowing myself to be soothed by his soft breath on my face. I can feel sleep approaching, and in the tiny part of my brain that's still awake, I can't help but think that falling asleep has never been this easy.

Chapter Twenty-Two

Aiden

I don't want to think about what it means that Sage fell asleep so quickly next to me. I also don't want to think about the fact that it was one of the most restful nights of sleep of my life. We get ready for our journey in comfortable silence, moving through the small room, collecting our things and getting dressed. After we finish loading up our packs, we meet up with everyone else downstairs for breakfast.

When I ask Sage what the pastry is that tastes like clouds and fruit, she responds, "Heaven." Not wrong, but also not helpful. Her and Delwyn have some of the largest sweet teeth I've ever seen.

We secure our items on our respective animals. Delwyn tells me lunch will be at a camp where some of the ice soldiers are stationed running training exercises. Hopefully that means I'll have time for some physical and magic training. I hate being the weakest member of the group. It's not something I'm used to, and I don't like the way it feels.

As we head out of the village, Aneira travels next to me on her massive ursa. "How did you sleep?" she asks.

"Great. And you?"

"Well, there wasn't too much sleeping, but when we did, it was great."

I still can't get over the fact that they had a threesome. Not because of the act itself, but they're a family. It's mind boggling that they can maintain their platonic relationships with one another after doing something like that.

"Ha. I heard about your little escapades."

"Sage told you?"

"Enough. Can I ask, does Sage ever partake in these… nights?" I can't stop myself from speaking the question out loud that's been running through my mind since last night.

"Are you asking if Sage sleeps with her cousin?" She giggles.

"No! No, that's not what I meant."

Aneira continues to giggle and says, "I'm being silly. I think Sage and Idris may have had a few wild nights in their youth, but after some experimenting, Sage realized she largely prefers males. Don't get me wrong, she has some wild nights, just not with us."

I clear my throat, trying to rid myself of that image. "Right. Of course. That makes sense."

She looks over at me with way too much understanding. "To be honest Aiden, I think she does it less for fun and more for escape."

"What do you mean?"

"Well, don't tell her I told you," she says, looking up ahead where Sage is talking to Delwyn, "but you only see a tiny portion of who Sage is. She keeps her cards very close to her chest. She's dealt with way more than anyone in her young life should. And she keeps it all inside. So, she often uses sex and men as a way to escape herself."

When we were back in the castle, I forgave Sage and I thought it was enough. But, maybe, the reason she hasn't been willing to give into this connection between us is because she still hasn't forgiven herself — for kidnapping me, or for something else in her past I don't know about. That can often be the hardest part.

I hum as I think about how I can help her so we can finally move on and focus on the future. There's no point in mulling over the past. The important thing is to learn from it and allow it to guide who you become.

Sage's slightly husky voice whispers in my ear, *Are you two talking about me?* I whip my head up ahead where Sage smirks back at us.

Aneira's eyes go round. "Sorry!"

A soft breeze smelling of peonies floats around me right as I hear her voice again. *Don't forget to talk about my sexy lingerie if you're going to continue to speak about me.*

I give her a look as I send a wind message back. *Trust me, Sage. The moment I see you in your version of lingerie, I'll shout it from the rooftops.*

After our morning of hard traveling, it's a welcome sight to see the military camp. We walk through semi-permanent structures, groups of soldiers eating around fires, and farther away, soldiers training, all woven through the spaces between the large trees of the forest.

We head towards the largest tent located directly in the middle of the camp and hand our horses and ursas off to soldiers who are waiting for our arrival. As we walk into the pale blue tent, I'm shocked by how furnished the inside is. In the center is a large table with weapons, cups, and maps strewn casually about. On the left-hand side is a bed and a stack of books, and on the right, a dining table covered in scraps of food and four chairs.

A hardened-looking woman gets up from one of the chairs. She's covered head to toe in weapons and the sides of her hair are shaved short with the top spiked like blonde-colored mountains. She's beautiful in the way everyone here is beautiful; and once again, there are those blue eyes. Only her blue eyes are so dark they're almost black, and as they make contact with mine, a shiver runs through my body.

She shakes hands with everyone else first, and as she gets to me she introduces herself as Elva, one of Queen Neve's generals.

"Aiden," I say as I shake her hand. It's rough with calluses and her firm grip tells me all I need to know about her skills with a sword.

"How are your training exercises?" Sage asks.

"To be expected," Elva says. "There's another camp stationed about ten miles east. We'll most likely run some battle plans against them in the coming days."

Wait, are they talking about fighting their own soldiers?

I must look as confused as I feel, because Delwyn leans over to explain. "The Ice Dominion is getting worried about the ever-looming threat of war. Especially now that we are after this weapon, the fear of retaliation is only growing. So, the training of our military has escalated. They won't kill each other, but injuries are allowed and encouraged. It's the only way they'll get better."

"Seems ruthless."

"War will be worse."

Elva walks us over to their canteen, chatting with Sage. Probably about torturing men and new magic attacks. We get stares from the other soldiers that I'm quickly growing accustomed to. They all give respectful bows or nods of the head to Delwyn and Sage and simply stare at the rest of us.

I wonder when I started considering myself part of "us."

After we eat a surprisingly satisfying lunch, Delwyn takes me to the training section of the camp. We run through swords and other hand-to-hand combat techniques we've already practiced. After an hour, I'm out of breath and exhausted.

Every time a new person comes near our training space they stop to bat their lashes and twirl their hair at Delwyn. He eats it up, giving them a big grin and a wink.

"Do you flirt with everyone?" I ask.

"Only when they flirt first," Delwyn says.

"So yes."

He laughs. "I guess so."

His mannerisms remind me so much of Sage, I can't help but laugh along with him.

Cooling down, Delwyn walks me around the training yard. We pass groups of two or three soldiers running laps or doing body weight exercises. They all stop what they're doing to give Delwyn a respectful bow as he passes. Small circles are drawn in the grass, with pairs of soldiers sparring one-on-one with both powers and traditional weapons.

In the distance is another large tent that I assume must

house all the weapons, as each soldier who walks out carries multiple spears, swords, bows and arrows, and other things I can't name and brings them to their respective training spaces. A space for archery has bullseyes set up farther than I could ever imagine hitting, and another area has dummies made of wood and straw that are being effectively torn to shreds by knives and swords.

There's even a small horse ring where both horses and ursas are being used to help the soldiers practice how to fight while riding them. However, the soldiers' main focus is on a giant ring in the center of the space. A crowd of soldiers surround the loosely constructed fence, shouting and cheering at whatever is happening in the middle.

Delwyn sees me staring and says, "Come on, you're going to want to watch this."

We head over to the ring and the soldiers clear a path for Delwyn so we can be right up against the fence. In the center of the ring is Sage. Or rather, Sage surrounded by five massive warriors, all wearing black training leathers and massive grins on their faces. Like they're enjoying this. But none of the grins are as intense as Sage's. Her canines somehow look sharper in this light and her hair is in a long braid with several wisps flying around her face. Streaks of dirt cover her cheeks, and a small trail of blood runs down her lips.

But, like there's a spell that I have no hope of breaking, my gaze finds its way back to her eyes, as always. The green looks like a fresh meadow on a spring day and the ferocity in her grin is somehow balanced by the peace in her eyes. She's at home in the ring, calm.

The other soldiers continue to circle Sage as she slowly spins her sword in her right hand. She fakes a yawn and says,

"I haven't got all day." She's as good at enraging these warriors as she is me, because they immediately attack. I involuntarily take a sharp breath in. I have no idea how this petite woman has any hope of coming out of this unscathed.

Delwyn must've heard me because he pats my forearm where it rests on the fence. "Don't worry. Sage has gone up against worse odds than this."

"How?"

He suddenly looks serious, a face I'm not sure he's ever worn. "She didn't have any other choice." I suddenly recall the comments she made in the prison. Delwyn shakes his head as if to erase whatever thought came over him, gives me a reassuring grin, and turns back to the fight. I can't even comprehend what that means for Sage because I'm captivated by her in the ring.

With her sword in her right hand, Sage parries against a literal mountain of a man. Simultaneously, she throws up a wall of fire to stop the three on her left from getting closer. They all try to use their ice powers to douse the flames, but her magic is stronger than the three combined. Holy shit, her magic must be strong.

The last woman slowly stalks her from behind, and Sage is so focused on what she's already doing that she doesn't notice her approach. I'm about to scream for Sage to turn when she drops her hand from maintaining the fire wall to grab a dagger out of her boot. With one smooth movement, she turns and throws the dagger straight at the female, who's forced to drop to the floor to avoid being hit.

I can't help the "whoop" that escapes my mouth. Sage whips her head to find me and gives me one of those gorgeous grins and a wink. She then builds a pillar of ice to lift herself ten feet off the ground. The others build their own pillars to reach her, but she melts them one by one so they have no chance of getting high enough.

All five fighters are getting frustrated, and she can tell. "Do you guys want to give up now or do I actually need to knock you all out?" They all give Sage a murderous glare, but she isn't even looking at them, just checking her nails.

Without waiting for them to respond, she quickly melts her pillar and lands back on the ground. Before anyone can even begin to approach her, she creates five ice balls that are each the size of a head. The soldiers she's fighting all smile — this must be a common fighting technique that they think they can defeat.

Sage slowly looks each of them in the eyes, like she knows what they're thinking. They all build their own ice balls, but before they can fully form, Sage surrounds each of her balls with a flame. The flame somehow doesn't touch the ice ball inside, but the heat warms me from here. I can only imagine how much skill and practice something like that must take.

The other fighters suddenly look worried, and with a small stomp of her foot, the five fire-ice balls shoot out like bullets straight into each of the soldiers' heads. One by one, they drop to the ground, knocked unconscious. A brief silence fills the air after the last drops, and then the entire crowd breaks out into cheers and shouts. Sage gives a casual bow and waves to her adoring fans. Delwyn hops over the fence to enter the ring and approaches Sage, so I follow.

He's about to give her a hug before she puts her hands out. "Please, don't. I'm filthy and sweaty and gross."

"That's never stopped me before," he says as he pulls her in for a bear hug. She practically disappears underneath his massive frame. I'm still shocked how someone this tiny managed to take out five individuals all twice her size.

They separate and I turn to her. "That was incredible. I thought there was no chance you would come out winning against those odds."

"Thanks so much for your confidence," Sage says.

Fuck. That came out wrong. "No, no. That's not what I meant. I meant- Well, that- You seemed so- What I'm trying to say-"

"Relax. I get what you're trying to say. And thank you — I am pretty amazing."

"Right, yeah. That's what I meant." Very smooth, Aiden.

"Come on, Pretty Boy. It's time for your training."

"You're going to train me? I thought Delwyn was supposed to. And aren't you exhausted from that fight?"

"I don't really think you'll be making me break a sweat, but I appreciate your concern."

"Don't we need to keep traveling?" I ask. I'm still trying to catch my breath from my workout and as much as I do want to work on my magic, I wouldn't mind a travel break.

"Not as much as you need to practice your magic."

"Why can't Delwyn train my magic?"

She waves her glove-covered hand in his direction. "Because Delwyn needs to talk to Elva about some things, so you're stuck with me."

She stretches and I can't help but look at her ridiculous curves as she moves and rotates various limbs. As I look around, I notice I'm not the only one staring. Men and women alike are frozen in place as Sage obliviously continues moving her body in provocative ways. I can't help the growl that escapes my throat. Sage looks over at me and gives one of her devilish grins. Maybe she's not so oblivious.

"Come on, Pretty Boy. Let's start training before you want to fight this entire camp."

We walk over to our designated space where Sage slams snowballs into my chest before I can even comprehend what's happening.

"Hey! I'm not ready!"

"Del might go easy on you, but I won't. Your enemies won't give you the chance to get ready in battle."

"I don't have any enemies. Unlike you." Our constant back and forth sets my blood on fire.

She scoffs. "Aiden, you're the one who wanted to be a part of our squad. Our enemies are your enemies. And trust me, we have a lot." I already admitted to myself that I'm part of their family, but I guess I never fully absorbed what that really meant.

"Fine. So how do I make sure I'm always ready?"

"Remember the source I taught you about last night? It always needs to be slightly active. You can never let it sleep completely. That's where your magic comes from, and it needs to be always accessible."

I look inward again and find my source more easily this time around. It allows me to quickly create snowballs that I throw towards Sage. She laughs. For someone on Earth, that was a fantastic throw. For Tirlun, it must've been weak.

"Okay, so you're using your magic to create weapons, which is good. But you also need to use your magic to make the weapons effective and deadly. It's not enough to create a snowball — the snowball needs to hurt or kill."

"How do I make a snowball kill someone?"

Sage turns towards a dummy that's at the edge of our circle, about fifty feet away. In a blink, she sends a snowball so fast through the air that it burns a hole through the head of the dummy. I look back at her with my jaw hanging open.

"Okay, so granted, that dummy is made of straw, so it would be a lot harder to burn through someone's head. But you get the idea."

"Teach me, please." I have no time to try to pretend I know what I'm doing. I just want to learn.

I spend the next hour training the hardest I ever have. Magic takes both a physical and mental strain and I'm more exhausted than I thought possible. Training with Sage is surprisingly fun; her exercises are all unique but easy to understand.

I create water in almost every form possible — snow, ice, water, mist, fog, rain, and more. She explains that while our magic naturally emerges as ice, by controlling the temperature within it, we can change the form it takes. She also teaches me basic offensive and defensive tactics within each form. While I certainly don't master any of them, she gives me a strong enough foundation so that even if Delwyn or Sage are not able to train me, I know enough to work on my magic alone.

After two hours, we say our goodbyes to Elva and head back on the road. I'm so tired that it's a struggle to keep my eyes open as the slow cadence of my horse lulls me to sleep.

I wake up with my cheek against something coarse. As I slowly blink, I realize I'm sitting behind someone on an ursa.

It's not Sage because I can't smell her intoxicating scent. I shift and my mouth is filled with tiny dark ringlets. Ah, Aneira.

She must have sensed me wake up because she turns back towards me and smiles. "You were falling asleep on your horse, so we decided to let you rest for a little and tied you to me. Barbarian has plenty of room," she says, lovingly patting Barbarian's back.

"Sorry about that," I say.

"Don't be! I'm sure Del and Sage worked you hard on our lunch break."

I grumble, "You have no idea."

"We're almost at our camp for the night. Idris has been riding ahead to set it up for us."

"She was very quiet today," I say as I realize I don't think she spoke once while we were at the camp.

Aneira strokes Barbarian's surprisingly soft fur and says, "She always gets uncomfortable surrounded by the Ice Dominion soldiers. Even though she's been a part of this court for more of her life than she wasn't, many soldiers still hold prejudices against her. Especially now, with tensions increasing."

"That's stupid."

"Yeah, well, most prejudices are. It can be hard to be surrounded by snow when you're made of fire."

"Is that how Sage feels?"

"Sage is both ice and flames. So, no. At least, not to the same extent. But it's obvious to almost everyone that she's more hot than cold."

"No kidding." I knew that from the moment she set my blood on fire.

"You've noticed?" she asks.

"It's kind of hard not to."

Aneira sighs. "I think she feels more at home in the embrace of the flames. Her and Idris definitely connect on that level. But the Ice Dominion is where she grew up. Sure, she visited the Fire Dominion when she was younger, but most of her time was spent on ice. That affinity will always be there."

"Makes sense." Up ahead, Delwyn and Sage have already climbed off their ursas and are illuminated by the glow of a fire.

Before we get close enough for Sage to realize we're talking about her — again — Aneira softly whispers, "None of us know the true extent of her flames. She's always played it off like it's strong, but nothing too insane. But you saw her today, and Del told me that Sage's father secretly trained her at night. So, it's unknown to everyone how strong she really is."

I glance over to her where she's laughing with her cousin and friend. "She hides a lot of who she is."

"It doesn't matter; we all know her heart."

"I hope you're right."

Chapter Twenty-Three

Sage

The intense training session with Aiden followed by hours of riding don't help my joints — they're screaming in pain. I eat my dinner as quickly as possible so I have the tent to myself to apply my salves and massage my joints. I really hope I can sleep with Idris again so I don't have to hide my pain from Aiden.

The sounds of everyone talking make their way into the tent. I'm glad Aiden is finally fitting in, but I hate the way that he saw through me last night. It terrifies me that my mask is invisible when he looks at me. He may not know the true reason for hiding behind my anger, but he's aware there's more to the story.

The flap of the tent moves, and I shove my salves under my pillows until I hear, "Relax, it's me," as Idris walks in. I immediately stop my fussing and take a deep breath.

"He's going to find out eventually," Idris says.

"Why would he?" I ask. I've done everything I could think of to make sure he didn't.

"We're traveling as a small group for several weeks, Sage. Even if none of us slip up by asking you how you feel, I know what that amount of time on the road is going to do to your body. There's no way you're going to be able to completely hide that pain."

"Watch me."

Idris rolls her eyes. "Come here, let me massage your legs." I scoot closer to her and place my legs on her lap.

I'm about to ask if we can create my compression hurricanes when Aiden walks into the tent, stilling when he sees how we're sitting. I imagine that it looks a lot more sexual than it really is.

"Uh, jeez, I'm sorry," Aiden says. "I didn't think I would be interrupting anything. I wanted to- Never mind."

"What is it, Aiden?" I ask.

"I wanted to know if I was sleeping with Aneira tonight, but I guess this answers my question," he says as a blush falls over his face. I study him. Is he jealous?

I can't help but play into it as I rub a hand up and down Idris' arm and answer, "Yeah, that's probably for the best."

He tries to look anywhere but at me as he clears his throat. "Right. Well, goodnight." He leaves the tent, and as soon as he's far enough away, Idris and I burst out laughing.

"You're cruel," Idris says.

"What?" I ask. "I can't help it if he's too polite to ever say what he's really thinking." She gives me a look. "Listen, if he were to ask if we were going to have sex or about the nature of our relationship, I would've told him the truth. Maybe it's an Earth thing or an Aiden thing, but he's constantly worrying about others and being cordial that he doesn't go after what he wants."

"Maybe you could learn a little from him."

I lightly shove her. "I can be cordial. When it suits me."

"Come on, let's do some compression so we can go to bed."

"Thank you, Idris. I can't do this alone."

"Sage, you don't need to thank me for being your friend." But I do.

The next few days follow in the same way. We wake up, travel, stop for lunch where Del or I train Aiden, and travel again until dinner, where Del or Idris hunt some animal for extra meat to go with our pre-packed rations and Aneira forages for edible vegetation.

Unfortunately, our travel route options are slimmer than earlier, so we're forced to pass a number of other travelers along the journey — a group or two every hour or so, some in carriages and sleds, others on horseback.

When we don't cross paths with others, the forest comes alive in ways it never can be when it's surrounded by noise. The light filtering through the trees places a glow on the moss and ferns. Small animals drink out of puddles, staring at us as we pass.

I wake up way too early this morning from a bad dream, so I leave the tent to avoid bothering Idris. I walk around our campsite and hear heavy breathing in the trees surrounding us. I slowly creep towards it, magic at the ready, worried it's either some beast or Fire Dominion spies.

As I approach a clearing, I relax — it's only Aiden training on his own. I can't help but admire his form as he punches the air, throws up ice, and quickly moves positions to defend himself from his own ice attacks. This must be how he's progressing so quickly; he's been doing extra training in the mornings.

I stroll into the clearing. "Looks like you're progressing quickly, Pretty Boy. Want to see how you do against a real warrior?"

He pants as he stares me down. I can't help the rush of heat that floods through my body as his intense gaze slowly roams up and down until it reaches my eyes. "I may be improving, but I'm not stupid enough to believe I have any chance against you."

"Come on, I'll go easy on you."

"Fine," he says as he takes up a defensive position.

I hold two fireballs in my hands as I circle him. "Looks like you've been doing some extra training in secret. Why were you hiding it, *shifrah?*"

His body moves like a mirror image of mine. "I wasn't hiding it. I actually wake up at a reasonable hour, unlike you four." I snort.

Two ice balls form in his hands; I'm impressed with their size. Ice is inherently heavier than fire, so it takes more strength to create weapons of the same size. It all balances out in the end because they can do more damage. I test his reaction time by shooting flames towards him. He shoots his ice balls in the direction of the flames, creating a light mist as he douses the fire.

"Very nice." *But let's see how you do with multiple attacks*, I wind message to him.

Before he can respond, I send two flames towards his head and stomp ice to form under his feet, causing him to lose his stance. Instead of combatting the fire like I thought he would, he allows the ice to drop him to his knees, causing the flames to pass by above his head, leaving him unharmed. He then creates sleet and shoots thousands of tiny ice bullets towards me. I quickly create a wall of fire between us, melting them instantly.

I can't see him through the flames, but I somehow know he's smiling. I won't lie, I'm impressed. I'll never tell him that, though.

How was that? I hear his low, growly voice in my ear.

You're better than I gave you credit for. Guess I'm going to have to up my game.

I tilt my head from side to side, stretching out my neck. I create a circle of flames surrounding him. He shoots ice around him, but as quickly as he douses the fire, it pops right back up. While he's too focused on the flames, I send ice spears straight down towards his body. He yelps as he realizes what I'm doing.

"Do you yield?" I ask.

"Yes, I yield," he says, voice muffled.

I quickly extinguish the flames and startle. About a foot above Aiden's head is a shield of ice he had created to protect him from the spears that stick about four inches past it. His face is strained as he struggles to keep it upright, so I take the ice and throw it away from him.

He takes a large breath. "Holy shit, Sage. I'm still a beginner."

"That's the only way you're going to learn," I say, not bothering to wait for his response as I walk away. I can't control the pit in my stomach that forms at the thought of him getting injured on this mission, so I force myself to dismiss it.

"Isn't the whole point of this mission, so we *don't* have to fight?" he asks as he catches up to me.

I stop walking and turn to face him, staring into his eyes. "Aiden, war is coming. Whether anyone wants to admit it or not. Obtaining this weapon is just delaying the inevitable. If anything, it's probably speeding it up. Not that anyone wants to listen to my opinion."

A low sizzle sounds at our feet and I look down to see a low fire burning into the grass around us. I have to start controlling myself around this man. He's going to cause all my secrets to come out.

Not allowing him to answer, I add, "You're going to have to use this weapon, whether you want to or not. And it's my job to make sure you're ready when it's time. I refuse to allow anyone else to get hurt while I'm around."

Focusing on the ground, I send a wave of water over my fire to douse the flames. I don't allow myself to look back up at Aiden or wait for his response and start walking back to our camp.

He follows me back in silence where everyone is now getting up and ready for the day. I stretch and massage out my joints as I eat my breakfast, stiffer than they've been so far, and we head out for the day.

Chapter Twenty-Four

Aiden

As we continue traveling, we pass several groups of soldiers, but we only stop to inspect them once. They are rigid and stand tall as Sage weaves through their ranks. Aneira, Idris, and Delwyn are close to laughter as she does so, but the soldiers themselves are as stiff as boards and constantly shift their eyes.

Sage's friends are the only ones who understand who she truly is because everyone else here is terrified of her. And I can see that, for sure. But, I've also seen her wit and sarcasm and adoration for her friends-turned-family.

One particularly shaking soldier, who's a solid foot taller than Sage, clenches and unclenches his hands around his shield and sword as she walks in front of him. She notices, of course, and stops directly in front of him.

Looking up into his eyes, she somehow looks down at him. She sneers and says, "Tell me, soldier, why are you so nervous?"

"I'm not, sir. I-I-I mean, ma'am," the soldier says, his voice shaking.

"Sounds to me like you are," Sage says as she circles around his body, only causing him to shake more. "Do I need to test your skills?"

At this, the captain of this squadron clears his throat from the front of their procession and says, "Captain Sage, I assure you, all of my soldiers are trained to the skill required of the Queen's forces."

With one last glare to the terrified soldier, Sage stalks back up through their lines to the captain. "If that's true, why are they so scared to be inspected?"

"Captain Sage, please understand, and I mean no offense, but, well, *you* make them nervous." I'm genuinely impressed with how confidently this captain answered.

She scoffs. "If I make them nervous, then they're in for a rude awakening should we ever have to go to war."

"Yes, ma'am," he says.

Sage walks back towards our group. With one last glance over her shoulder, she simply says, "Pathetic."

"What the fuck was that?" I ask. That was cold, even for her.

"That... was Sage," Idris says.

There's that fire and ice; cold and unfeeling one moment, warm and caring the next.

But then I think back to our conversation in the woods and her fear of the upcoming war. And the weight she's putting on herself to make sure no one else gets hurt. She doesn't allow anyone to know her true reasoning behind her coldness; the truth that she actually cares. Maybe too much.

Chapter Twenty-Five

Sage

Today's journey ruined me. I was even meaner than usual to that passing group of soldiers, which is how I know the pain is getting bad; it's leaking out in ways I can't control.

Between the last several days camping on the ground and our fight this morning, I feel a flare coming.

As we sit down at the fire for dinner, I look at everyone and say, "We're going to stop here for two days." Everyone's brows furrow, but Aiden looks especially confused.

"Sage, what? We're in the middle of nowhere," he exclaims.

I look around us. We're still in the forest, and truth be told, we're only about two days away from the next village. But I can't wait to rest. I won't make it and then I'll be out of commission for even longer.

"It doesn't matter. We'll be stopping for two days," I say

firmly. I look at my friends and they all understand what I'm not saying.

"Okay, Sage," Aneira says.

"Whatever you say, Captain," Del says.

Aiden's hands splay by his sides. "You're all okay with this? This is insane. We can't just stop for no reason for two days." He looks at me, "I know you've had reasons for everything else we've done so far, so what's the reason for this?"

He *has* been so understanding about everything else, I almost want to tell him.

But no. He can't know.

"Aiden, enough." I've never heard Idris speak to him so forcefully. "If Sage says we're stopping, then we're stopping."

I give her a nod. "Good. I'm going to bed early and I'll be taking a tent alone. The rest of you can figure out who sleeps where."

Aiden looks around exasperated. "You've spent this entire time saying that Delwyn needs his own tent because he's a prince. Now because you randomly decide you get one, it's fine. You guys make no sense." I don't bother responding and head into my tent.

I sleep for fourteen hours. When I wake up, I'm in so much pain that I have to bite down on my pillow to keep from screaming. I try to alternate between hot and cold on my joints, but I'm quickly running out of the strength to maintain the control needed over my magic.

By late afternoon, my body feels like it got run over by ten Barbarian's and my joints feel like broken bones. It takes all my years of control to force my tears to come quietly as my sobs try to work their way out of me. Every minuscule movement sends another wave of already excessive pain through my entire body.

Being awake under this much pain is exhausting and I soon need to nap again. My surroundings look as scattered as I feel.

One breath, one step. One breath, one step. One breath, one step.

I repeat my mantra over and over in my head, hoping it will give me the strength to get through this flare.

Chapter Twenty-Six

Aiden

No reason, no explanation, and no complaints from anyone else.

They use today to train, relax, and stretch. I do the same, but every time I try to ask what's really going on, they shake their heads. Even Aneira refuses to speak to me about it. And Sage hasn't left her tent all day. Something weird is going on and I'm determined to figure it out.

All of us, minus Sage, sit around the fire, eating some rabbit that Delwyn caught earlier. No one spoke much all day, just idle chit chat. Idris brought food into Sage's tent, but other than that, she hasn't been seen or spoken to.

Wind flows out of Sage's tent, catching me by surprise. We all look over, but none of them look concerned. A wave of hot air quickly followed by a wave of freezing air hits us. Again, none of them look like they care.

I can't do this anymore. I stand up and look at all of them. "If none of you are going to tell me what's going on,

I'm going to figure it out myself." I march towards Sage's tent.

"Aiden, wait!" Aneira shouts.

I turn back to look at everyone. "I'm done waiting."

Shockingly, none of them use magic or spells to try and stop me. I was expecting more resistance from them, but the only resistance I face is the surprisingly strong wind at the front of Sage's tent. Once I'm inside, the sight alone is enough to keep me glued to the spot.

What I can only describe as mini hurricanes swirl around the tent. Some strain against the top, some are on the sides, but most of them are concentrated around Sage's body. I stare at Sage on the floor. She hasn't realized I'm in the tent, but I'm not surprised once I realize why.

She's clearly in excruciating pain, and the anguish on her face is like nothing I've ever seen before. Her eyes are squeezed shut, her body is contorted in an unnatural form, and she's sweating and shivering simultaneously. Between that and her obvious attempt at controlling these small weather patterns, it's no wonder she doesn't notice me.

I try to use my magic to slow down or stop the hurricanes that float on the sides of the tent. She must sense my magic against hers because her head whips towards where I'm standing. The hurricanes immediately vanish.

"Get out!" She screams, with more emotion in her voice than I've ever heard before.

"What?" I ask.

I can't even comprehend what I'm seeing before she bellows again. "Get the fuck out!"

Someone grabs the back of my arms. I realize it's Aneira as she says, "Come on, Aiden. Let's go back towards the fire."

I glance one last time at Sage then turn away and head back towards the rest of the group. I sit back down on a log, my head in my hands, trying to understand what happened.

I look up at everyone else, who all have varying looks of sympathy, sadness, and guilt.

Taking a deep breath, I ask, "Who's going to tell me what's going on?" They all look at one another. To my surprise, it's Idris who speaks first.

"We don't get sick," she says. "We can get injured in battle, but besides physical wounds and old age, that's the only way we can die. When Sage was around twenty, she started to experience unimaginable pain for no discernible reason. The queen sent for every single healer in the Ice Dominion. Sana was the only one who was able to provide her any form of relief, but even then it was temporary. No one knew what was wrong. She could take a break from fighting for two weeks at a time and still be in intense pain. And if you haven't realized it by now, when Sage says she's in pain, it means the pain has gotten so bad she fears she can no longer hide it. So, we all knew it was bad."

I look at all three of them. I've never seen them look so defeated. Idris can't go on as she sadly shakes her head and looks at the ground.

This may be one of the only times Delwyn's ever looked upset as he says, "We quickly realized whatever was wrong with Sage, it wasn't something Tirlun had ever seen. With no options left, my mother sent Sage to Earth to visit your doctors. That's why we occasionally get sent on missions there — she's the most comfortable in that world because of how many times she needed to travel for medical reasons. Your human doctors told her she has an autoimmune disease, but there's no cure. Their only recommendation was medicine that wouldn't have crossed over the portal. Sage did her own research and found ways of mitigating the symptoms, but nothing ever makes it go away."

Aneira says, "When she finally came back with her diagnosis, I spent a lot of time trying to come up with a spell to help her. Anything I could find was only ever temporary and ended up causing more trouble than it was worth. She learned how to manage what she could — a lot of rest, ice baths, massages, and using what you saw in the tent."

"Yeah, what was that?" I ask. "It looked like tiny storms."

"That's essentially what it is." Aneira nods her head in the direction of Sage's tent. "Using both her fire and ice magic, she can create tiny pressure systems and place them on her joints to relieve pain. But she's not supposed to do it alone. When she's in that much pain, she often can't control her magic precisely enough to use them effectively."

"That's why I've been sleeping with her most nights," Idris says. "I'm the only one with fire magic besides her. When she only uses her ice magic with me using fire, she's able to control them enough to allow it to work."

I'm so fucking stupid. Even though Aneira told me nothing was going on between Idris and Sage, when I saw how close they were in the tent, I assumed she was lying. It was too intimate. I think back to every time one of them was being secretive or suspicious. All the whispering and furtive glances. It was all a cover to hide what was wrong with Sage.

"Why is it treated like some big secret?" I ask.

Delwyn sighs. "There's a lot of reasons, honestly. She's a close relative of the royal family. My mother would never allow a vulnerability like that to be exposed if there was a chance it could be used to weaken her rule. Sage is also the captain of the Queen's Guard. It's a huge title and she would lose it if anyone thought she wasn't fit to have that position."

"I thought she was captain because of her relation to you all and her magic."

Idris snorts. "If you think Queen Neve would ever appoint someone because of nepotism, you didn't learn enough from her speeches she gave while we were in Bruma. No offense Del," she says, looking over at him, "but the queen is ruthless. Everything she does has a strategic purpose."

Delwyn shrugs. "She's right," he says looking at me. "Sage has always trained harder than anyone; even before this illness. She earned that spot. That's why Sage doesn't want anyone to know. She's worried people will look at her differently or doubt her skills."

I shake my head as I process everything they've told me. All this time, I gave her shit for being a princess with her massages and rest. It was all for a medical reason. And she let me believe it — she never once contradicted what I assumed to be the truth. "Wow, I feel like an asshole," I say.

Aneira gives me a sympathetic smile. "She didn't want you to know. We told her you would find out eventually, but she was adamant we didn't tell you. We decided that it was best for you to see it for yourself before we explained."

"Seeing it certainly was something."

Delwyn gets up and claps me on the shoulder. "Come on, Aiden. Let's go do a quick workout before bed. It'll get you out of your head and give you time to process everything."

I stand up. A workout sounds exactly like what I need.

The next morning, I stretch outside my tent before exercises when Sage steps out of her tent. Purple circles sit below her eyes and she's paler than usual — which is hard to believe — and as she looks into my eyes, there's a look on her face I've never seen before. Defeat.

She slowly walks over to me, as if she's scared every step will cause her to break. "Come sit with me?" she asks.

"Of course." We walk over to the logs beside the fire. Aneira brings her a blanket and a pillow without any prompting. Sage gives her a small thank you before turning back to me.

"So, I'm assuming they told you what's wrong."

"Yeah. But why didn't you tell me?"

"I don't know how to tell you what it feels like to have your insides smash together, to have your bones screech into one another. What it feels like is the key — because it's not real, at least not literally. The pain is, but there's no visible effects, so why should anyone believe me?" She sighs as she lightly massages her hands together. "And anyway, I'm supposed to be the strongest, toughest, fiercest warrior. What would people think if they knew I felt imaginary pain? Even my friends and family who care can't ever really know, so it's easier to hide it away than try to explain the unexplainable. You're already looking at me with pity, and there's nothing I hate more than pity."

"Sage." I take her hands in mine. "It's not pity. It's understanding. It explains so much that I wish I knew from the beginning. I feel like such a dick for calling you a princess when everything you were doing was for your health."

A dick is an understatement. I can't believe I ever thought her coldness was just that. The fact that no one else except for her family knows about her disease after five years only attests to her ability to hide her pain.

"Yeah, but I let you believe that. I never told you otherwise." She looks away from me. "The pain is so unbearable at times that it's all I can do to not scream. I've been tempted on more than one occasion to break a bone, if only to have a concentrated center instead of it racing throughout my entire body. The worst part is I can take steps to prevent it from getting worse, but at the end of the day, the only way for me to stop having flares would be to stop living this life that I love — being captain, going on missions with my family, exploring Tirlun. And more than anything, I hate being seen as weak, and this *is* a weakness. We don't get sick. What can this be other than a curse?"

I place my finger under her chin and tilt her head until she has no choice but to make eye contact with me again. "How is it a curse if it's made you stronger than anyone I've ever known?" She tries to turn away, so I grip her chin even more firmly. "You are not cursed, Sage. You may have had to overcome more than you should, but if anything, it's allowed you to be kinder and more empathetic, no matter how hard you try to hide it."

"I am *not* kind."

"If you say so."

She takes a deep breath, and I let her go. "I'm going to go rest again in my tent. I just wanted to talk to you first."

"Thank you. And let me know if I can get you anything." She looks at me with eyes that are more muted today, as if this flare has drained the fire in them too.

I spend the rest of the day training with the rest of the group. Aneira decides it's time I learn some basic spell work. We walk deeper into the woods, away from the clearing we found. The evergreens thicken overhead, turning almost blue with their density, and the snow on the ground sounds stale as it crunches underneath our boots. The further we go, the more quiet envelopes us. When the only sound is the squish of snow beneath our feet, Aneira stops.

She turns to look at me and smiles. "Are you ready?"

"It depends on what we're doing," I say.

"Spell work, of course!"

"I meant what *kind* of spell."

"Ah, see, that is a good question," she begins, "before you can learn, you need to understand a few things. First, spells use your magic. Even though it's not dispelled in its natural form, it will still drain you. Second, the amount of magic you put into the spell determines how long it lasts. On a battlefield, a soldier has to determine where to use their magic. Your power is not endless." I nod. I've definitely been feeling drained after training extra hard these past two days. "Third, which we won't get into today, but it is possible to imbue objects with your spells. For example, if I took the time, I could gradually imbue a carriage to fly. It would probably take months and be very draining, but during a war, it could lead to a huge advantage."

"Like the shower head at the inn."

"Exactly!" She exclaims. "But that was a very simple spell, and it was Open, which is something else I should explain."

"Okay." While I'm once again somewhat frustrated that the group decided to wait until we were this far into the journey to teach me this, I also understand. Mastering my magic and learning how to physically fight has been overwhelming enough. They probably wanted to ease me into this.

"When you imbue an object, you can decide to make the spell Open or Closed. An Open spell means that anyone knowing which spell was cast can use the spelled object as they would like. If it's Closed, only the caster themselves or someone of their blood can use said object."

"That makes sense."

"That's why we needed you for this weapon; the magic used was Closed. Only a descendant can find, unlock, and use the weapon." So that's why I'm only learning about this now. They told me the journey would take around a few weeks and we've been traveling for over two. We must be getting close to where they believe the weapon is located.

Aneira continues. "We assume there will be some cloaking spell that's hidden the weapon. Your power should call to it, but we'll practice that along the way."

"Okay, so where do we start?" I ask.

She claps her hands together. "With one of my favorite spells."

Her excitement is infectious, and I can't help but smile as she explains the first spell. It's a transformation spell, allowing you to turn one object into another. She picks up a pinecone and demonstrates the spell, which has two components — drawing symbols in the air followed by speaking the spell into existence.

She said it can turn into almost anything; the larger the transformation, the more magic that's used. After she says the words, she whispers, "ice cream," and before I can blink, the pinecone turns into a perfect swirl of vanilla ice cream in a cone. She smiles at me, licks the ice cream, and says, "delicious."

"I'm sorry, I'm confused," I say. "If we could've been turning any random object into food this entire time, why have Delwyn and Idris been hunting almost every night? And why are we eating the same meal three times a day?"

"It's not that simple. The flavor is there and it's edible, but it doesn't provide sustenance in the way real food does. It still has the caloric composition of the pinecone within it, it just tastes and looks like ice cream." She picks up another pinecone from the ground. "Okay your turn."

She demonstrates the symbols in the air again and I copy them, then say the spell, ending with "chocolate." A chocolate bar appears in my hand, and I take a bite. She's right; it tastes exactly like chocolate from home.

A pang of sadness comes over me as I think of home. I wonder what my friends are thinking. Do they think I ran away? Was kidnapped? Dead?

Aneira must notice the change on my face. She rests a hand on my arm and asks, "What's wrong?"

"Nothing," I say. "This reminds me of home. I've been so caught up in the craziness of this adventure that I haven't really stopped to think about what it meant for me to leave my friends and my life."

"I know how hard this must be for you, but you've been handling everything so well. And maybe you'll get to go home when this is all over."

I look down at her and see that she's genuine, but I can only give her a sad smile. "I appreciate your optimism, but I think you and I both know I'm never going home."

"Crazier things have happened."

"You mean like getting kidnapped, traveling into another dimension, and realizing I have magical powers?"

"Exactly!" she says as we both laugh.

I sigh. "Truth be told, and I already told Sage this, as much as I do miss Earth, Tirlun is feeling more and more like my home. There's not much left for me there after my parents died."

"I can't imagine what it feels like to not have anyone who cares about you. Ever since I met Del and Sage, all I've known is love," she says.

"I see that," I say, nodding. "And it showed me how much love has been lacking in my life. While there are certain things I'll miss about Earth — chocolate being one of them — I'm becoming more and more okay with the fact that I may be here forever."

Aneira's smile brightens once more. "Aiden, we do have chocolate."

"What?"

"Of course! It's not that processed junk that comes in a bar."

"Well now I'm definitely never leaving."

"Good. Because I like you."

"I like you too."

Chapter Twenty-Seven

Sage

Aiden and Aneira come out of the woods, chatting away. He looks happy, and Aneira, well, always looks happy. It makes me smile that there's at least some joy for him on this journey. Aneira plops down on the log next to me.

"What have you two been up to?" I ask.

"I started teaching him some basic spells," Aneira says.

"Oh, yeah? What did you do?" I look over to Aiden.

"I did some transformation magic, then moved some objects in the air, and ended with a failed attempt to find a hidden object," he says. He still says this more positively than anyone I know who's failed at a task.

"It was a good try!" Aneira exclaims.

"I'm glad spell work is going well," I say.

Aiden settles down next to me and asks, "Why can't you spell the pain away?"

I snort. "If only it were that simple." I don't add that I've tried almost every single spell I could think of to rid myself of the pain and absolutely nothing works.

Idris comes out of the woods from her scouting and sits across from me. "Spells can heal small cuts and bruises. Only a healer can truly fix something major," she says as she looks over at me. "Because Sage's pain doesn't have an actual source, it can't really be healed. Only lessened."

"Good thing food heals everything!" Del shouts as he comes out of the woods dragging a massive deer.

"What is that?" Aiden asks, staring at it.

"A deer," I say, looking at him. They have deer on Earth. I'm almost positive.

"That is not a deer. That looks like a deer bred with a moose and then a horse." I look at the deer again from his perspective; I guess the antlers are rather large and its eyes are closer to the front of his face.

I look back at Aiden and say, "Well these are our deer."

Del expertly skins the deer while Idris blazes the fire. After ten minutes, the deer is tender and ready.

Aiden groans with his first bite. "I stand corrected. This is better than deer."

My friends know better than to ask how I'm feeling, but Aiden can't help himself. "Better," I say. "I'll be ready to travel tomorrow morning."

"Good, because this final leg of the journey will be the toughest," Idris says, saving me from talking about my flare further.

I shoot her a grateful smile as Aiden asks, "Why is that?"

"We have about five days left before we reach the mountains. We'll be out of the Ailec Woods by midday tomorrow, but the closer we get to the border, the more likely we are to cross paths with Fire Dominion soldiers, and we'll no longer have the cover of the forest." Also the more likely we are to face mercenaries, thieves, and our political enemies, but we don't need to scare him any more than necessary.

"Once we hit the mountains, we'll have to leave the ursas and horses and travel the rest of the way on foot." She looks off into the distance like she can see all the way to the Fire Dominion. "The mountains will be the worst part. They're dangerous, not only because of the terrain, but because anyone, from our own Ice Dominion criminals to fire soldiers, could be hiding there. There are massive cave systems and plenty of places to hide."

"What a wonderful end to our adventure," Aiden says.

Del says, "At least for the next three days we won't have to sleep on the ground!" He turns to Aiden and adds, "There's a steady stream of villages and towns once we leave the woods. Actually, the second largest city is right where we'll leave our animals." I smile softly to myself thinking about the amazing food we'll get to eat before we reach the mountains.

"That close to the border? Isn't that dangerous?"

"Slightly," he says. "When our relationship with the Fire Dominion was better, it bustled with trade between the two nations. It's been flourishing for the last three hundred years. They've had to bolster their defenses over the last fifteen years since the attack, but they've still done surprisingly well, all things considered. That's where we'll do our final stock of supplies before the mountains."

Aneira says, "There's still trade; it's much more limited. Cel'a — that's what the city is called — has some of the best food and fashion because of the cultural exchanges that have happened over the centuries. You're going to love it!"

I can't help but shake my head at Aneira. I look over at Idris, expecting her to have the same reaction, but instead she looks like she could soak in Aneira's enthusiasm like a drug.

It's the look of someone hopelessly in love, and while I'm not surprised, I am shocked it's so clearly written on her face. Idris is usually better at hiding her emotions than that. Almost better than me. Maybe she's starting to give into her feelings because she knows what's to come.

She must notice me staring, because she looks at me and quickly returns her face to its normal indifference.

We eat the rest of our meal in comfortable silence, with some small conversations here and there. As I'm about to get up and go to bed, Aiden asks Del, "I'm sorry to keep bringing this up, but, how have you all managed to keep Sage's condition a secret for all this time? Especially if she needs to rest like this on journeys."

I look at my friends, all our grins stretching wide until we break out into laughter. Aiden looks at us all in turn. "What? What did I say?"

I'm still trying to calm myself down from my laughter as I ask, "Who wants to tell him?"

Idris says, "Me, please. This is one of my favorite games." I give her a small nod. "Obviously when it's the four of us on a mission, it doesn't matter. But the first time Sage led a squadron on a mission with her condition, something eerie happened. We were about two weeks into a month-long journey when she had a flare and made the camp stop moving for three days. All the soldiers were confused and started getting stir crazy and complaining by the end."

My family already looks like they're going to break down into hysterics even though they've shared this story a million times.

A rare smile forms on Idris' face. "When we finally started moving, we ran into a ramshackled town. Apparently a three-day massive storm blew through the area, causing a lot of damage and even a few deaths. As we spent the day helping the town clean up, the soldiers started whispering that Sage had prophetic powers and she saved us from getting caught in the storm."

Aneira giggles as she says, "Of course we played into the rumors. What a great cover! Anytime one of the soldiers brought it up to us, we tried to act as coy and suspicious as possible." Aiden starts to smile as he sees where this story is headed.

Del chimes in, "The next time it happened, we had to make sure something similar occurred, so Idris and I snuck out for a few days and created some nature blockades for us to stumble upon once we started moving again."

I shake my head at them all. "They've now turned it into a game. They take turns causing mayhem to give an explanation for my stops. It's made the rumors spread to all corners of our dominion, which is great."

Idris snorts. "Don't lie, you love it."

"Do I love that it makes all the soldiers fear me even more? Absolutely. Do I love that it's caused the three of you to come up with more and more creative ways to cause destruction to our dominion? No."

"Hey, I'm the prince, so it's my right," Del says. "And besides, we always make sure the damage doesn't harm anyone or their livelihood."

I look at Aiden while he takes our story in. His blue eyes are bright with excitement, and his smile widens. "This is fantastic! Sage, you're a *sage*," he says, wiggling his eyebrows at me.

Del laughs. "Oh, trust me, that nickname has certainly made its way around. Anytime Sage hears one of the soldiers say it, she makes them stay an extra two hours after training. Everyone now makes sure to never say it in front of her, but they definitely still call her that behind her back."

What I don't say is that by them taking the wrong meaning of my name, they take away another connection to my parents. And I have so few of those left.

I groan. "While you all have turned this into a fun game, *I'm* the one who has had to deal with the consequences."

"Sage, we gave you more power. You should be *thanking* us."

"Yeah, I'll thank you the day my sage powers let me find a way to punish you three for starting this ridiculous rumor." I stand up to leave because the rest of the night is going to be them telling Aiden more stories of my so-called prophetic powers. "Feel free to chatter into the night about my very humorous illness, but we're heading out bright and early tomorrow." I stretch, give them all a glare, and they smile back. Truth be told, I do think it's funny and they know it too. I just hate all the annoying gossip it started.

Aiden's eyes meet mine and the reflection of the fire in his cerulean eyes feels like home. One side of his mouth lifts as he stares at me, and if I were to stare back long enough, I could almost convince myself he feels the same. But this broken body could never be anyone's home. I clear my throat, nod, and head into my tent.

We're out of the Ailec by midday, like Idris had said. While I love the peace and comfort of the woods, it's nice to be back in the open air again. Everyone else agrees, especially the animals. The woods open to a beautiful meadow filled with wildflowers. The animals run around before continuing our journey, and their eagerness makes for a much faster travel day than expected.

As we get closer to the next town, signs of life start reappearing. First it's the occasional farmer who looks up from their tilling to bow, and next it's children running on the street. Del decides to create an ice slide for them to play on and they shriek with joy. Their emerging ice powers allow them to create sleds to sit on as they slide down.

Aiden watches with unchecked joy and his dimple appears for the second time; his smile for the children's enjoyment is almost as large as their own. He throws some light snowballs for them to dodge as they slide.

We say goodbye to the children and quickly stumble upon a squadron of soldiers going to meet up in the Ailec for war exercises. Now that I'm feeling better, I can't wait to play with them.

Chapter Twenty-Eight

Aiden

Up ahead on the road is a group of twenty soldiers heading towards us. It's been completely arbitrary when we're stopping for the people we pass and when we wave and move on, so I look at the rest of the group for some indication as to what we're going to do.

"Shall we have some fun?" Sage asks.

"Of course, Sage. I'll never miss an opportunity for you to terrify our soldiers," Delwyn says as he grins.

She chuckles as she pulls Blizzard off the road and walks towards the soldiers. "Coming, Pretty Boy?"

I smirk at her as I do the same. "Wouldn't miss it for the world."

"How are they doing?" Sage asks the soldier leading the group, the captain based on the additional decorations on his uniform.

Delwyn whispers in my ear, "Get ready." There's a twinkle in his eye that makes me very nervous.

"Captain Sage," the other captain gives her a respectful nod. "My soldiers are ready for their battle exercises."

"Soldiers," Sage says, turning towards the two lines of soldiers. "This may seem like a game, but that does not mean vacation for you." Before I can blink, she shoots fire down one of the lines. A soldier two rows down flinches and collides with the warrior to her right.

"Why did you flinch, soldier?" Sage asks as she plays with more fire.

"I- I- I'm sorry captain. I just reacted," the soldier says.

"Did you not have faith in your captain?"

"No, no, it's not that-"

"Well, what is it then? You thought I would hurt my own soldier?"

The soldier looks down at her boots and says, "I'm sorry, Captain."

Sage turns back to the group. "Trust. Skill and strength help, but when you're fighting as a unit, trust decides who wins." At that, Sage shoots fire at Delwyn. The heat comes straight towards my face, and while I can't help but flinch, Delwyn stays as still as stone.

Delwyn smiles widely at Sage, and her smug grin in response brings heat to my cheeks. "As you can see, we still need to work on the trust of our new friend," Sage continues. "I hope when we return, you trust one another, as well as your *captain*, the way your prince trusts me with his life."

Sage stalks away as Aneira claps her hands. "You'll all do great!" she says with way too much pep.

Delwyn lightly slaps me on my back. "Come on, the show's over."

Even knowing who Sage truly is, seeing this mask she

wears is still terrifying. Maybe she's both — the woman she portrays and the one she hides. Aren't we all contradictions? Trying our best to hide the parts of ourselves we hate and masking our vulnerabilities with who we wish we were.

Chapter Twenty-Nine

Sage

After about another hour, we approach Rew, a small city of about ten thousand. They're known for their music, and as we walk down the main street, it fills every corner. I can't help but close my eyes as the melodies make their way to my ears. Blizzard and I both sway to the music as we walk through the main street.

We get the stares that our group usually garners, but I can't give my usual glare as the sounds of the city fill my soul. I've always found that music moves me in a way that little else can — it makes me feel hope when I'm defeated and peace when I can't stop fighting.

We reach the inn where we'll be staying, arriving some time after Idris, who had gone ahead to check us in. It's one of my favorite places to stay in all of the Ice Dominion. Even though the inn itself is huge, it's decorated like a whimsical cottage.

The main lobby is filled with dried flowers and herbs that

hang from the exposed wooden rafters. Butterflies flutter around and settle on people's shoulders every now and then. Vines grow from every crevice, with bright red, pink, and orange flowers bursting from every corner.

The temperature here is also tens of degrees warmer than anywhere else in the Ice Dominion, so they have some of my favorite small Fire Dominion animals that wouldn't be able to otherwise live here. It makes me miss Fluffy, who always loved staying here with me. I wish she could've come on this mission.

Calida, the owner, comes out from around the front desk to give us all hugs. She's from the Fire Dominion herself, which is why this inn is able to stay so warm. She married her wife from the Ice Dominion before the conflict fifteen years ago, and even though tensions are high, their inn is doing better than ever. Even ice citizens need to warm up every now and then.

"It's always a pleasure to see my favorite customers," Calida says.

"You only say that because we spend more money here than anyone else," I say as I roll my eyes.

"What can I say, I'm a businesswoman!" She looks at all of us with her warm smile, quirking her head at Aiden.

"Oh, this is Aiden. He's our... companion," Del says.

She chuckles. "No point in lying." She extends her arm fully to pat Delwyn's cheek. "The entire Ice Dominion knows who he is."

I was hoping word wouldn't spread so quickly. The giant parade and festival Queen Neve threw in Bruma did not help things; I told her not to do it, but she can't resist a reason to gloat.

The Columben family line is famous in the Ice Dominion and it's a positive omen from the Mother that he's returned, but the more people that hear about his return, the more speculation will begin as to why he came back now. And the more citizens we'll have watching our every move.

Aneira flits over from where she was playing with the monkeys, pecking Calida on the cheek. "The monkeys are sweeter than ever!"

"Only for you, my girl."

Aneira beams at her. "Where's Idris?"

"Oh, you know Idris," she says. She's one of the few who actually does. There are not many places where Idris feels at home, truly, since pledging herself to the Ice Dominion. This Fire Dominion-esque inn, with its fire owner, is one of them. "She's probably in the hot springs or training at the geysers."

The thought of a soak in the hot springs makes me groan out loud. Aiden gives me a look. "Oh, just you wait, Pretty Boy," I say. "You'll be groaning too once we're in those hot springs."

We head upstairs and I take the room at the end of the hall where Idris has left her stuff. That room is one of the few in this inn that were custom made for people from the Fire Dominion. It's warmer, both in color and temperature, and gives visiting fire citizens a taste of home. Not that there are many of those anymore.

Chapter Thirty

Aiden

The inn is like nothing I've ever seen before. Animals roam around the main floor, there are actual geysers and hot springs inside the building, and it all fits within a too small exterior. There must be a lot of magic at work in this place.

Aneira drags me into a room that I guess we're sharing and shows me several bathing suits to choose from. They're made of a material I can't even begin to guess, but it must be Tirlun's equivalent to Earth's. I select blue and white striped shorts, we grab our towels, and Aneira leads the way to the springs.

Weaving through stairs, we pass a kitchen that smells heavenly as well as several saunas, then go down another floor, where we pass exercise rooms. This building must go several levels into the ground, which would make sense for both its size and temperature. We walk down another set of stairs that's made of raw stone, our gifted sandals slapping against them.

We open a wooden door, and for a moment I can't see anything as we're hit with a wall of steam. After we make our way through the initial wave, I startle and almost run Aneira over.

Sage is lying down on a wooden bench, waiting for us. As she hears our approach, she lifts her upper body to look at us in a move that's so sexual I can't help but blush. Her swimsuit is a one piece, but barely. Her hair is a little unkempt from how she was lying on it, and she might as well be in lingerie.

The few other people in the springs are also looking at her. An involuntary surge of jealousy comes over me, so I walk over to her bench and stand in front of her, blocking their view.

I inadvertently place my shorts directly in front of her face, and she looks up at me and says, "If you want to play Pretty Boy, you just need to ask."

I clear my throat and step back. "Are you ready to go into the hot springs?"

"But of course." Sage stands up from the bench and freezes the tiny pool of water beneath her feet, using it to slide straight to the edge of the closest hot spring before jumping in. Her head emerges from the water, flinging it everywhere. I maintain eye contact and walk over to the stairs, then towards her. She stares back at me with equal intensity, and it's as if there's no one else in the room as we're drawn closer to one another.

By the time we're several inches apart, I'm entranced by the water droplets clinging to her thick lashes. Before I can even say anything, she splashes me and swims away.

"Oh, you little-," she giggles, cutting my sentence off and making my heart skip a beat. That giggle. It reminds me that she's still so young — five years younger than me. And in these moments where she allows herself to just live, it's music to my ears.

I saw her absorbed in the music as we came into the city, and it was mesmerizing. But I would give up every song in both my world and this one if it meant I could hear Sage's giggle every day. I can't help the giant grin that crosses my face as I splash her back. I don't even know where the rest of our group is, and I don't care, as Sage becomes my entire world.

Idris eventually joins us from wherever she ran off to. They said she's in charge of spying and intelligence for their team, but she's gone more than she's present. Idris looks almost as stunning as Sage in her swimsuit. Her golden skin is toned all over and she might as well be wearing nothing, considering how the golden bikini disappears into her skin. I can openly admit she's gorgeous, but compared to Sage and her luscious curves, there's no competition.

She whispers something into Sage's ear who nods and glances over at me. We're now sitting in a different pool than where we started that has a natural seat built into the springs. Sage uses her fire magic to create bubbles, forming a jacuzzi that Delwyn and Aneira quickly come over to take advantage of.

While we certainly are getting stared at, no one dares to join any of the pools we've been in. Whether it's out of respect for their prince or fear of Sage is unclear, but either way, we're able to have plenty of room for ourselves.

Idris sits on the ledge of our pool and dips her feet in. Sage turns to us and says, "Dinner's in an hour. We're getting our regular private dining room. Idris has restocked all our supplies while we were here, so we'll be ready to head out first thing tomorrow."

"Thank you, Idris," I say.

She gives me what I think is a genuine smile. Where Sage is a puzzle, Idris is a locked safe. Both have their secrets and struggle to open up, but once I was able to crack Sage, her true self became clear.

Idris, on the other hand, confounds me. She cares deeply for her friends, but she also hides herself from them. Well, everyone except Sage. They have this connection that I originally mistook for romance. Maybe it's the flames they both have that draw them to one another.

An hour later, we're seated in a cozy private dining room. The table looks like it emerged from the ground beneath us. It's smooth but raw at the same time. The chairs are all ornately carved, portraying flowers and animals on each. Calida comes in with each of the five courses to explain each one and check in on us. It was one of the best meals I've ever had. We're all stuffed and exhausted by the end, but the glint in Sage's eyes tells me our night is not over.

"Are you guys ready?" Sage asks. They all groan.

Great, more secrets. "What? What's going on?" I ask.

"Every time we're in Rew, Sage drags us all to this dance hall. She's obsessed with the musicians that play there," Idris groans.

"They're amazing!" Sage says.

"Okay, Sagey, they are, but we're exhausted," Delwyn says.

"The music will revive you."

"I'll come," I say quietly.

Sage's eyes shoot to my face, and she smiles. "At least Pretty Boy knows how to have fun. Fine, the rest of you go to bed. Aiden, you're with me."

Sage loudly pushes her chair back as she stands up, stares down each of her friends, and heads towards the door. I stand up, wish them all goodnight, and catch up to Sage.

Sage was right; the musicians are amazing. The music flows through my veins and watching Sage dance and sing along is as beautiful as the songs themselves. At some point they sing the tune she was humming that day in the woods and I can't help but reflect on how much has happened in such a short period of time.

My physical connection with Sage has been there from the moment I laid eyes on her at the bar, but the emotional connection has floored me. I know I have a tendency to be too polite and my friends used to tease me for being a people-pleaser; but around Sage, I've never been anything but myself.

That polite mask I wore around others completely disappeared and even though she would sass and taunt me back, there was never any judgement. And Sage — that eye-rolling, bitchy exterior was just that — an exterior. The instant I started spending more time with her, it was obvious that it was a front to hide just how much she actually feels.

The loyalty and devotion she feels towards not only her friends, but her entire realm, is evident through the things she's willing to sacrifice to protect them. Her ruthlessness, her strength, and her callousness were traits forced upon her to care for the ones she loves.

And when those are peeled back, all I see is devotion, hope, and love. I'm confused how nobles who have spent decades around her have never realized who she really is. I've realized in less than a few weeks with her. And I'm captivated.

Towards the end, they sing a love ballad, and to my surprise, Sage grabs my hands and sways with me. I hold her close and breathe in her peony and cinnamon scent. The feeling of peace that comes over me is enchanting and the song is over too soon. She looks up at me, her green eyes shimmering like a forest covered in fresh dew.

I'm dying to kiss her, there's no denying it anymore. But, after seeing her guilt and the emotions she buries, it has to be her decision. Sage needs to make the first move.

And she doesn't.

After the set is done, we head back to the inn. Sage wishes me good night in the hallway before entering our separate rooms. I stare at her until she closes the door. She will be the death of me.

The next few days of traveling are on an actual road through the Ice Dominion. The forest is gone, but it is clear that the people of this society care for nature as deeply as Delwyn had claimed. Every vehicle we pass is powered by magic, and the only exhaust is water or ice. People are kind as they smile and stop to bow to our group. While we can't stop to greet them, Delwyn, and even Sage, to my surprise, bow their heads in return. Delwyn often gives them a smirk and a wink where Sage's face is grim.

As we approach Cel'a, our final stop before we drop off our animals, we veer off the road to make our entrance less of an ordeal than the other stops. I guess Sage is feeling antisocial after all of our public entrances.

When we're close to the city entrance, ten soldiers emerge from the bushes.

"Seriously?" Sage asks, face turned towards the sky.

"Why is she so upset?" I ask Idris. "It's just more soldiers." She's gotten annoyed at all our other interactions, but this is different.

"These aren't our soldiers," Idris says as she grabs her sword out of its scabbard and hops off her horse. I study them again. They're wearing the same clothes as all the other soldiers. But their eyes — all their eyes range from dark brown to yellow. Not a blue eye in sight.

"How did they manage to get this deep into the Ice Dominion without being spotted?"

Aneira sighs. "One of them must have glamour magic and used it to change their eye colors." She studies the soldiers more closely. "They're probably just as shocked as we are to run into other people this far off the road and didn't think they'd need the glamour." Aneira turns back to look at me and gives a soft smile. "Remember your spell lessons? I would imagine only one of them has glamour magic, it's fairly rare, and it must take a lot of energy to maintain it on all of them. Hopefully that will mean at least one of them isn't in fighting shape."

Shit. Are we about to fight them? I've been training, but I don't know if I'm ready for this. It's suddenly all a little too real.

Delwyn hasn't gotten off his ursa. "Don't you know who we are?"

"Of course, Princey," one of the soldiers sneers.

Sage snorts. "Why are you acting like idiots then? You should've stayed hidden." She doesn't grab a weapon or prepare her magic, unfazed by these enemy soldiers. They outnumber us two-to-one, but none of my companions look even remotely nervous.

"The glory we'll get for killing the prince of the Ice Dominion, his bitch of a cousin, and a traitor all while in enemy territory is well worth any fight you can put up," a different soldier boasts, his eyes tracking Delwyn, Sage, and Idris.

I look towards the city that we were about to enter, hoping there's someone there who can go get more help. Sage picked this spot exactly because of its seclusion from the rest of the city — and there's not another soul in sight.

Before Sage can say another sassy taunt, a soldier in the back shoots fire directly into her shoulder. The smell of burning clothes and flesh quickly fills my nostrils.

She hisses. "You're going to regret that."

My mouth opens and closes like a fish. They actually fucking hit her. Any fear I had is replaced with a deep rage — how dare they hurt Sage.

I'm getting ready to dismount and join this fight however I can while Delwyn prepares to attack, but Sage throws her good arm out to stop him. "No. They're all mine," she growls.

I've seen her battle five soldiers with ease, but there's ten *and* she's injured. Now is not the time for her ego.

All ten soldiers have fire in one hand and a sword or similar weapon in the other. Sage bares her teeth. "You're all dust."

The soldier who hit her says, "Why don't you get off your disgusting beast and prove it."

"It's one thing to be rude to me, but Blizzard?" She tsks and leans down to whisper something in Blizzard's ear.

He storms through the soldiers, knocking them over like bowling pins. He picks one to pounce on, his claws ripping the soldier's chest open like tissue paper. At the same time, Sage shoots fire out of her good hand, burning six of the soldiers enough so they can't fight back as Idris and Aneira finish them off with weapons. The three remaining soldiers look like they're ready to run away, but Delwyn has made his way to their backs, so they're closed in.

"Want me to help?" Delwyn asks.

"If you would like, but leave that asshole to me," she says, pointing to the one who hit her.

I look to Aneira and Idris to determine whether or not to get involved. Their hands are placed on their weapons but their eyes are calm. I mimic their stances and wait for someone to tell me what to do. I'm filled with equal parts rage and fear, but as soon as I look at Sage again, the rage takes over and I'm ready to destroy anyone who lays a finger on her perfect head.

While Delwyn takes care of the other two, Blizzard

slowly stalks towards the soldier in a way that's eerily similar to how Sage has stalked others before.

"Wait, wait, wait," the soldier pleads. "Let's talk about this."

Sage tilts her head as she stares down at him. "Which part would you like to talk about? Your ridiculous attempt to hurt me? Or your pathetic bravado? I might be a cocky bitch, but it's a title I've rightfully earned." I can't help the snort that emerges from my mouth. Idris looks at me and smiles before turning back to Sage.

Sage holds ice in one hand and fire in the other. "I'll be generous and let you pick. How would you like to die — fire or ice?"

"Uh- Uh- Uh," the soldier stutters, too terrified to respond.

"Too late," Sage says. "Both it is." With terrifying precision, she burns exactly half of his body while the other turns frozen solid and shatters into pieces. "What a typical weak male." Sage shakes her head as she turns back to us.

One look at her shoulder and my skin turns to ice. "Sage, your wound. It's gushing blood." Her coat has a five-inch tear and blood is oozing, changing the color from navy to a deep purple.

"Annoying," she says as she strips off her layers. That's more than annoying. I can't believe she's so calm. Not a single tear. Just grunts and groans.

When she's down to her bra, the wound is completely visible. It's going to need a dozen stitches, maybe more. We'll have to find a way to stop the bleeding before we get to a healer.

"Anyone have any extra water?" Sage asks. Aneira tosses

her a canteen. Sage dumps the water over the wound, barely wincing.

"Does anyone have a medical kit?" I ask, trying to scan everyone's packs.

"No need," Sage says. Her good hand fills with a flame so hot it's blue. Before I can comprehend what she's doing, she shoots the fire straight into the wound, cauterizing it and stopping the blood flow in seconds. Her face turning red and a clenched jaw is the only indication it causes her any pain at all.

"Holy shit," I say.

"Having my body destroy itself builds up quite a pain tolerance." I look at the rest of the group. Their faces have a mixture of sadness and pride at her strength. The strength it took to willingly cause herself more harm to stop the bleeding, I can't even fathom.

Sage grabs a change of clothes out of her pack and puts them on. "Shall we?"

We've spent the past two nights going over our maps and the history of the final battle, in hopes of an even slightly more precise location to look for this weapon. The magic and spell work surrounding it is strong; none of them were alive at the time of the battle, but stories have been passed down orally and in writing, and every time the location of the final battle gets discussed, the words get vague and abstract.

Aneira has also been working with me on locator magic. I would spell an item, and she would hide it, forcing me to use my magic to find it. They're all counting on me to locate this weapon, and the closer we get, the more nervous I become. It doesn't help that they don't know the exact location. Or even what it is.

We're supposed to head in the general direction and hope for the best. Well, they're hoping I'll feel some sort of tug and be able to guide us the rest of the way. Based on the knowledge they do have, they believe the weapon is hidden underneath the final battle site from the war three hundred years ago. Unfortunately, battles occurred in many places in the mountains, so it doesn't help us all that much.

And they're assuming I'm the only one who can find and use this weapon because of the lore that only the Columben line can wield it.

But what if it's not even me? What if there's another descendant and they're the one who's meant to be on this mission?

They're all so confident I don't want to question them, but I can't help worrying that this entire journey will have been for nothing when it turns out I'm not the one meant to find this weapon.

As we walk into Cel'a, it's clear why they're all so excited to come here. It reminds me of a cleaner combination of New York and Paris. The architecture is intricate, and individuals fill the streets in a range of fashions. Everywhere I look, there's something different.

While the tallest buildings are only about five stories tall, each one is crafted from only the finest materials. And the food. Each step brings about a new smell, every one as complex and delicious as the last. I'm giving myself whiplash as I look from side to side, trying to glimpse where each of these smells are coming from.

The city's slightly smaller than their capital, so it takes about an hour until we reach a smaller version of the palace in Bruma. Ice Dominion soldiers open the gate into the palace and close it behind us.

Delwyn takes a deep breath and sighs. "Feels good to be back."

"Where are we?" I ask.

Delwyn looks over at me and smiles. "The seasonal palace." I look up at the light snowfall all around us. "The closest thing to seasons we get, I suppose. It's where the royal family, A.K.A. me," he says puffing out his chest, "stays whenever we need to have dealings with the Fire Dominion. Of course, we come here much less often than we used to, but we also use it as a vacation home when we want to get out of the capital. Or during our short summers; the closer we are to the Fire Dominion, the warmer it gets."

"Right, because the two other vacation homes aren't enough," Idris snorts.

"You're welcome to go sleep somewhere else," Delwyn shouts as he walks into the palace.

"Come on, let's go," Sage says.

Inside is as beautiful as the other palace. The walls are gilded in silver and there's art depicting everything from war to gardens covering the walls. Beautifully carved molding lines the tops and bottoms of the walls and ornate blue rugs cover the ground.

Five servants wait in the foyer, curtseying to us as we walk in. "Prince Delwyn, Captain Sage," they say in unison.

The one in the middle says, "All of the rooms are ready to your specifications. Dinner will be ready at seven."

"Thank you," Delwyn says as he puts a hand on his heart. Delwyn turns back to look at us, "Who wants to play?"

Aneira jumps up and down. "Me! Me! Me!"

"Play what?" I ask. Here I am, confused again.

"Come on, we'll show you." Sage grabs my hand and pulls me along. I think I would follow her anywhere as long as my hand is in hers.

We reach a massive court, still inside the palace, where they explain the game. It sounds like a combination of baseball and soccer and uses a ball about the size of a melon. The game is called "Fireball" and starts with one person hitting the ball (thankfully not on fire) with a wide paddle onto the other team's side. From there, we use our feet to pass the ball back and forth. Instead of a net, there's a square of stones that a player needs to pass over while in possession of the ball to score.

Delwyn decides it's women versus men. I appreciate his confidence in me, but I've never played anything like this. I tell him so and he replies, "Don't worry, I'm good enough for the both of us." I see Sage's arrogance runs in the family.

"Are you sure you can play with your wound?" I ask Sage.

Sage scoffs "Don't worry, Pretty Boy. I can still beat you with only one good arm." The arrogance.

They're all crazy competitive. I appreciate it, coming from a sports background myself, but when I'm learning the game, it's very frustrating. After half an hour, the score is two to one, with the women in the lead. Sage is wicked fast for someone with such short legs. Idris, unsurprisingly, is graceful and swift.

Even Aneira surprises me with her intensity and

strength. It's clear why she's their war strategist; she gets the other women to run weaving, complex plays that we're unable to defend, despite Delwyn knowing them.

Watching them play as a team, it makes sense how they're able to defeat a group of soldiers eight times their size. They play off each other's strengths, can predict where the other will go, and can communicate next steps without words.

We take a break to drink water, panting from the exertion. Delwyn looks over at me and says, "I think we can add magic now."

Sage gives what I can only describe as an evil grin. "Finally."

I put my head in my hands and ask, "Alright, what are the rules for magic?" Of course there has to be a fucking twist.

Aneira says, "Only defensive spells, nothing offensive. And powers can be used in any way except when it comes to moving the actual ball. For example, I can use ice to slide across the field quicker, but I still need to be physically dribbling the ball myself the entire time."

If there was even a chance at me and Delwyn beating them, adding magic will completely take it away. I'm so far behind them in that respect, it's no competition.

I take another sip of water. "Can someone at least teach me how to glide on ice before we start?"

"Did you see the villagers entering the castle gates and how it looked like they were moving on ice?" Aneira asks.

I nod.

"When we need to get somewhere in the city, we put ice under our feet and can move quicker than we would by walking."

"That's cool," I admit.

"Okay, so that's what we're going to do. Have you ever slid on a hardwood floor while wearing socks?" she asks.

"Yeah, of course."

"That's basically what this is, except it's ice and you need to imagine the floor moving with your feet." Right. So simple. The floor is moving. Got it.

Aneira envelopes her feet in a thin layer of ice and steps. She slowly moves in circles around us, allowing me to study her movements and the ice that moves with her.

After a few laps, she stops. "Now you try."

I create giant blocks of ice under my feet which promptly slip out from underneath me, causing my arms to windmill as I fall.

Sage and Delwyn start laughing and I can't control the blush of embarrassment that reddens my face.

"Think thin," Del comments, still chuckling.

"Cut him some slack, Del. It can be hard to think thin when your head is so thick," Sage teases.

I give her a mocking glare and she winks at me, quickly dissolving any ire I had.

Shaking out my arms, I try again. A slow circle of ice spreads out from underneath my feet.

"Perfect!" Aneira exclaims. She slowly moves next to me, allowing me to mimic her movements.

I'm a quick learner and rapidly get comfortable moving around on the ice. I jump and spin; it's like ice skating, but freer. Sage joins in next to me, a soft, genuine smile on her face.

She grabs my hands and begins spinning us in a circle. I

laugh with unfettered joy. Her low chuckle follows her scent as we spin all over the court.

"Lovebirds," Idris shouts from where she stayed by our waters. "Can we get back to the game please?"

Sage and I stop spinning, but my smile doesn't budge. "What are we waiting for?"

It's my team's first hit. Delwyn lets me take it, opting to head onto the court to receive it. Sage stands at the ready to pitch. "Ready, Pretty Boy?"

No. "Yes," I say. She lights the ball on fire. Ah — hence the name, *Fireball*. "I thought you said no powers to move the ball!"

"I'm still going to physically throw it. It's just going to be on fire," she says like it's the most normal thing in the world.

Wonderful. I will my ice magic to coat the paddle. Hopefully it'll be enough to douse the flames before they come in contact with the wood so I can still actually hit the ball. Sage throws the ball, and I take a deep breath, trying to block out the heat that's gradually increasing and get ready to hit the ball. The sound is deafening as it echoes through the court.

It worked! The ball goes sailing towards their side of the court.

"Well done, Pretty Boy," Sage says before entering the playing field again.

"Why thank you, Princess," I say.

The next half hour is harder than any of the training they've put me through. I try to use my ice to reach the women faster, but often end up shooting too much power and flying past them, having to double back. Idris blocks almost every defensive power I send her way, using a massive fire wall to stop anything from getting through. This is the first time I'm really seeing her powers in action and they're strong. Delwyn's ice is really the only thing that can beat her flames down.

Sage is unbelievable with her magic; using ice and fire in equal measure, constantly switching so we're unprepared for how to defend when she approaches. Her defensive spells also build bubbles of protection around her that don't last long, but certainly allow her to dribble further than without it.

Aneira primarily uses defensive spells, only using her ice magic when necessary, but her spells are more than enough. They're complicated and strong — she's able to lock us in an air box for a solid thirty seconds before Delwyn can break us out.

And Delwyn. Well, he's a beast, there's no way around it. He's surprisingly agile for someone who's even broader than me. He would've dominated the lacrosse field if he lived on Earth. He complements his strong ice power with his physical prowess, causing the girls to frequently have to go two on one to defend when he's in possession of the ball.

By the end of the second half, the women win the game four to three. We're all sweaty and smiling, covered in a few scrapes and bruises from being unable to block each other's magic completely. We grab towels and head out of the court, then walk to our rooms to wash up before dinner. Once again, Sage's room is right next to mine and Delwyn's is further down in a separate wing.

After I shower and change, I knock on Sage's door to ask if she wants to head down to dinner together.

"Come in." I open the door, and Sage is massaging her legs with some sort of salve. "Oh, it's you," she says.

"Were you expecting someone else?" I ask.

"Idris said she would stop by before dinner to do compression, but I guess she's running late."

"Ah. Did you see a healer for your arm?" I still can't believe she played an entire sports game with her arm barely healed, cauterized herself.

"Yes, Pretty Boy, don't worry. I'll be in tip-top shape for tomorrow."

I give her a tight smile as I look down at her spot on the carpet to see a massage roller and some other tools I can't identify.

Sage notices me staring and says, "I always leave these in the palace here so I don't have to transport them back and forth. These are compression clothes I wear under my normal ones," gesturing to clothes on the floor. Next, she points to armor. "These are braces should the pain get so bad I need extra support. We designed them like this to look like armor so no one questions it." She puts the braces on her joints. "This is what was in the room I hid from you back in the palace," she admits with a shrug. "My massage table, creams, braces, and other tools."

I sit down in a chair next to her. "Do you ever get tired of hiding it all?"

She sighs. "Sometimes. But, I can't imagine the gossip that would rise from the truth and the questions that would be asked. If the people don't have trust in me, then my credibility plummets. I need the citizens I protect to know that I'm strong enough to fight for them."

"If anything, I would think they would believe you to be even stronger, since you're doing all of this while fighting through this disease."

"Aiden," my name on her lips making me want to beg her for a taste, "while I appreciate your positivity, you've only just arrived in our world. You don't know these people like I do."

"Maybe not, but I know strength. And there's no denying that you're one of the strongest people I've ever met." She surprises me by breaking eye contact. Her eyes glaze over, and I can only imagine what she's remembering.

I try to bring her back to the present by saying, "Besides, I'm super strong too, so you must be powerful to constantly beat me."

She gives me the smirk that I love so much. "Don't be getting a big head on me now, Pretty Boy." I chuckle and offer her a hand to help her up. She takes it, shocking me again. "Let's go eat, I'm starving."

Dinner was delicious, as it has been for every single meal here. It's clear that this world has zero processed foods and it makes everything taste that much richer. Even the simplest ingredients taste fresh, juicy, and flavorful. We walk back to our rooms until it's just Sage and I left at our doors.

I want her. There's no denying that anymore. She's the most incredible woman I've ever met. Her ferocity is balanced with equal parts kindness, as much as she tries to hide it. Her beauty only parallels her strength. And while I can tell she feels the attraction between us the same as me, she's hesitant to cross that final boundary, whatever the reason may be. As I look at her, I see her trying to read my face, as she does with everyone around her.

"What are you looking at, Princess?"

"Oh, nothing. Just your hair sticking up." I blush and pat down the back of my hair with my hands. I realize she's pulling my leg, and I look over at her laughing. I blush even harder as I awkwardly put my hands back to my sides. Not the best start to a romantic move.

I can't help but stare at her as she stops laughing. She still wears a soft smile on her face and seems almost content.

As she looks back at me, a question forms on her face. "What?" I ask.

She shakes off the emotion. "Nothing, Pretty Boy. Good night."

Before I can think of a response, she walks into her room and shuts the door.

That went well.

Chapter Thirty-One

Sage

I want him.

I want him so badly it hurts. But I'm terrified to give in; this attraction is like nothing I've ever felt. He's kind and caring and so positive for a man whose life has been turned upside down. And he sees me. Every single scar, flaw, and wound I've tried my whole life to hide. He sees it all and he's never once looked away.

We spend one more day in the palace, resting and restoring our magic for the most intense part of the journey. The game yesterday shouldn't have drained any of our magic too much, except maybe Aiden's. Shit. I should've thought of that.

I was so excited to share something fun with him, I didn't even think of the consequences. Not smart. If this ends in him getting injured, I'll never forgive myself.

The table is filled with all of our favorite foods; the chef here isn't as amazing as Genie, but she's still pretty close.

For most people, knowing we're about to head into the most dangerous part of our journey would make them not want to eat. But if anything, we're all stuffing our faces even more.

Everyone except Aiden.

He clears his throat. "Can you guys tell me a little bit more about the previous war?"

"Why?" Del asks.

"Well, it's the whole reason we're on this mission, right?" He looks at each of us before continuing. "I mean, clearly things never resolved completely. And besides, it's why the weapon is hidden in these mountains. I feel like any information will be useful."

He's right. And while I appreciate his desire for knowledge, Mother knows I'm the same way, I really don't want to spend my last good meal talking about the darkest period in Tirlun's history.

Thankfully, Del decides to take his question. "It was carnage. Long story short, the Fire Dominion decided they wanted to rule over both dominions and tried to invade the Ice Dominion to do it."

A snort escapes me before I can stop it. Del whips his head to me. "What?"

I really did not want to get into this right now. But maybe, if Del hears the truth, he'll be more inclined to believe me later on.

"It wasn't the Fire Dominion," I say. "It was Ice."

Del shakes his head. "That would mean my mother."

"Correct."

"Don't you think I would know if my own *mother* had plans to take over half of our world?"

Del looks at Aneira and Idris for support. They both smartly keep their mouths shut and avert their eyes.

I sigh. "You weren't born. You weren't there. Of course, now, she would never admit it." I glance at Idris; she subtly shakes her head no. I can't get into this right now. Not when we're so close to the weapon. "Both dominions obviously claimed it was the other's fault. Truthfully, they're probably both somewhat to blame."

Del begins to settle at that.

I look back at Aiden who's been shocked into silence. "The war started the way they all do; power hungry elites hungry for more power. Seizing an opportunity to incite conflicts and escalate prejudices as an excuse to intervene and grab more power in the process. And, elites never change. So, here we are, three centuries later, trying to prevent the same thing."

My food has gotten cold over the course of this conversation. With my heart racing from our discussion it takes barely a thought to send a wave of warmth over my plate to reheat it.

"Right," Aiden says, at a loss for words.

Del takes a few more bites of his food, also trying to calm down, before adding, "If we can get the weapon that's infamous for ending the last war, hopefully it will discourage both sides from intensifying to physical altercations and we can find a diplomatic path to peace."

"And finally restart cultural exchange so we can get some new fashions!" Aneira butts in.

Low chuckles spread around the table, all of us grateful for the break in tension.

We head out early the next morning. While we've not been as incognito as I would've liked on this journey so far, the closer we get to the weapon, the more stealth matters.

Saying goodbye to our animals, we leave the city on foot. According to the map we found in the Ice Dominion's archives, the weapon should be about a two days walk south from the city. We'll have to walk through the mountains in case it's wrong and Aiden senses something earlier. I've continually been impressed by his dedication to his magic and spell work through the already arduous journey.

It has to be enough.

Everyone is transfixed when we reach the mountain range. "I always forget how big these mountains are," Del says quietly next to me, our tense conversation from last night forgotten.

As I stand at the base of the first mountain, I have to crane my neck almost straight up to see the top. Not to mention the fact that there are hundreds of these mountains practically stacked on top of one another; rows and rows of sharp black rock dusted in white snow like the mountains bit the sky.

Very few paths snake through the shale and boulders scattered across each towering range, which is going to make the hike slow and treacherous.

"Okay everyone, let's huddle up," I say. "This is going to be the hardest part of the journey. We need to use magic as a last resort, only if we really need it to climb over an obstacle. These mountains are dangerous, and we have no idea what to expect. Aiden," I turn to him, "You've been working with

Aneira to sense your magic. If at any point you feel a tug towards something, let us know, and we'll stop to investigate. Is that clear?" Everyone nods their heads. "Alright. Let's go."

We stop for lunch after four hours of intense climbing. Luckily, we only had to use our magic twice to push ourselves over two impossible hurdles.

I'm already exhausted. These mountains are impassable for a reason. My mind wanders, thinking about how the old dominions fought in these mountains during the war and how I can barely climb them.

Aiden hasn't sensed anything so far, but I'm not surprised. We look over the map and read the notes we took again, hoping that some revelation will magically come to us.

I stretch and layer ice over all my joints before we get moving again. We're all too focused for conversation; between having to walk single file through impossibly thin passageways to needing both our hands and feet to climb portions of the mountains, there's little time for talking. Aneira starts to sing at one point and we yell at her to stop.

As the sun starts to set, we come upon a small stream with several caves: a perfect place to stop for the night. Idris builds a fire as the rest of us set up our sleeping packs. No tents for these two nights — it wasn't worth the extra weight. We all sit around the fire, chatting and eating our dried meat and cheese, when I hear a loud crack in the distance.

"Everyone shut up." They all look at me. "Id, put out the fire." She quickly douses it, not asking any questions.

We sit in silence for a minute. The sound cracks again,

closer this time. It could be a mountain lion looking for a meal, but my gut doesn't think so.

Aiden whispers to me, "What's that noise?"

"I'm not sure," I say. "But you better get ready to fight, Pretty Boy."

As I finish speaking, a shout comes from in front of me. A body moves towards our group, illuminated in the dim light. Without thinking, I shoot flames in their direction that are quickly redirected. That means fire soldiers.

"Everyone up and at 'em," I say. "Time to get dirty."

We grab our weapons and form battle-ready positions. Even Aiden shows no hesitation as he gets ready to fight.

A small flame ignites in someone's hand, showing a smiling fire soldier. He slowly walks towards us. "Well, what do we have here?"

"Your worst nightmare," I say, giving him my best feral grin.

"Oh, Captain Sage. I've heard so much about you, but I must say, your ferocity is a little disappointing." He looks around the group, landing on Idris' face and sneers. "Traitor," he spits at her.

"Better traitor than asshole," she cooly says.

I'm familiar with the more important fire captains and generals from political meetings over the years but I don't recognize this one, although he clearly recognizes me. Not that I'm surprised.

"What do you want?" I sneer.

"A little birdie told us you were on a mission for something invaluable. I want it," he says simply, like he's asking for a cup of tea.

I scoff. "Why on Tirlun would we ever give you anything?"

"Because if you don't, we'll kill you."

Now it's Del's turn to laugh. "While I'm sure there are several friends of yours hiding in the shadows, you must've heard enough about us to know it won't end well for you."

"Well, Princey," the male sneers, repeating that condescending title all the Fire Dominion citizens use for him. "The thing is, there are only five of you. And no matter how good you are, there's no way you can beat forty of us," he says as more faces emerge from the shadows.

My eyes flit from face to face as I try to recognize anyone. It's hard to tell in the dark, but they all look like strangers. We've beaten forty soldiers before, but that was without Aiden and not without injury. As long as he doesn't hinder us during this fight, we should be okay.

But, forty, it's still a lot, even for us. And we've been traveling hard for the last several weeks. I'm getting a little nervous, but I'll never show it.

I casually lean against my sword. "Forty against five? I think we've beaten worse odds than that."

"I'd like to see you try."

"Then what are we waiting for?"

Before he can respond, I build a fifteen-foot-tall ice wall, shielding us in. While I'm sure they'll have it down in a matter of seconds, it gives us time to collect ourselves and prepare to fight. We form our usual fighting formation, Del on my right, Aneira on my left, Idris at my back. Only this time, Aiden squeezes in between Del and me.

I nod at Aiden. "Are you ready?"

"As ready as I'll ever be," he says.

I take a second to study his face. His jaw is clenched, but he doesn't seem scared. If anything, he's steady as his eyes fill with determination and his grip tightens on his sword. I nod at him and turn back towards the rapidly melting ice wall.

The ice wall drops and we pounce. I take on the leader as he throws fireballs to get closer to me. I coat everything but my head in a thin layer of ice so I don't even need to worry about the fire hitting my body, ensuring that I reinforce the ice every time it melts. It's draining magic, but better than risking an injury and weakening that way.

I shoot ice under his feet, causing him to stumble before he can melt it. I hurtle a spear of ice towards him, but he spins out of the way, causing it to only graze his arm. He yells out in pain but quickly recovers.

Three of his soldiers come towards me while he wraps his arm. They all smile like they want to eat me alive. I give them an even worse smile back, taunting them. They take the bait, merging towards one another and me.

When they get close enough, I circle them in a ring of fire. They look at each other and then at the fire, smiling, because they can easily remove the flames, but by the time they separate them, I'm ready with my reinforced ice spears. I shoot one into each of their chests and they drop like flies. The leader watches all of this, biting his lip as worry crosses his face and he runs away from me. Coward.

I take a moment to catch my breath as I quickly glance to my right as Aiden and Del fight in tandem. Del uses his massive weight to simultaneously slice down soldiers and stop any fire from hitting him or Aiden. I'm not worried about Del in the slightest, but I'm glad Aiden has someone watching his back. I was so focused on the leader that I forgot to worry about him, but as I look over, it appears I've had no reason to. He has a few scrapes and his tunic is torn, but I already see three fallen soldiers in his path. Del already has five.

"Del, does the leader count as three?" I shout over the sounds of ice, flames, and swords.

He glances over at me. "No way! One soldier is one soldier. Looks like I'm winning by two. Wait." He pushes five ice spikes through a fire soldier's chest. "Sorry, three!"

I growl, "Fine." Jerk.

This leader is going to mess up my win. Aneira runs up next to me and I quickly scan her body for any injuries. Somehow, she still looks perfect. Not even a scuff of dirt.

She smiles. "Hi, Sagey, how's it going?" We both take our swords out and fight with two soldiers as we talk.

I quickly dispatch mine and turn to her. "Del is winning. But it's not fair; the leader picked me."

She slices off her soldier's head in one, swift movement. "Sorry, Sagey, you know the rules. And besides, I think Idris might have him beat."

Aneira guards my front as the sounds of the battle fill my ears while I slowly turn towards Idris glowing. Literally glowing. She's coated herself in an armor of flames, burning hotter than anything the soldiers can send her way. What looks to be about ten bodies are littered around her — and she's currently fighting three more.

While she appears unscathed, a quick glance in her eyes shows her exhaustion. She's hiding it well, but it's there. There's still so many soldiers to kill before we can rest. I settle my nerves — panicking will get me nowhere. If I portray confidence, maybe I'll eventually feel it.

"Ugh, I need to step up my game," I say as I turn back to Aneira acrobatically jumping up and over our enemies, dangling two fire soldiers in the air by their arms. She drops them as she smoothly lands next to me. Her strength never ceases to amaze me; both soldiers had to be easily double her size and she held them like they were birds she hunted.

"Where's that asshole?" I scan the rocks and small bushes, looking for the coward who fled to nurse his wounds.

I have a small break from attacks as my family works through their opponents, so I use the opportunity to study Aiden and his fighting tactics more closely. Those early morning training sessions have been working; while his ice weapons aren't super clean and his sword swipes a little sloppy, they're still extremely effective. I wince as a fire soldier's dagger slices his upper thigh.

Alright, it's time to end this.

Their leader still hasn't reappeared; I guess he's still too scared to face me again. That won't do. This next move will cause the pace of the battle to increase, but hopefully will end it faster too. I can handle one more push. Probably.

I take a deep breath, stomp my feet twice, and quickly whisper a spell. Slowly, an ice dome is built, closing both us and the fire soldiers in. My friends, minus Aiden, are prepared for this move, as we've done this before. I slowly bring the ice closer, pushing us all in a tighter and tighter circle. Any fire soldiers still alive try to directly melt the dome through my magic and I grunt as the strain to keep the ice intact takes hold.

Any spots that weaken are reinforced by Delwyn, with the addition of ice spears that pierce through the Fire

Dominion soldiers as the dome shrinks. They're certainly not expecting the dome itself to attack them and quickly fall.

As the dome brings us all into tighter quarters, the fire soldiers get desperate. They shoot their flames at random, hoping to make a mark. We're all out of breath, but with the adrenaline running through my veins, I'm unstoppable.

When the dome has a radius of about thirty feet, there are five soldiers left, including their idiot leader. He finally looks scared. I give him a smirk as I strut towards him. Two of his soldiers try to defend him by sealing me in a bubble of flames, trying to burn me alive.

I take a deep breath and let the flames lick my body. I break out in sweat as I copy Idris' fire armor, and the flames become harmless as they meet the even hotter fire that coats my body. The fire soldiers' flames get completely absorbed into mine and I'm left standing in front of them like a phoenix reborn.

A phoenix who's fucking exhausted and just about out of magic, but a phoenix nonetheless.

Almost done. A few more soldiers and then we can rest. Assuming we're not attacked again.

The fire soldiers' put their hands out, trying to placate me. I quickly strike the first one down with my sword and stab the second in the jugular with my favorite dagger. I've found that the stronger soldiers tend to forget about physical fighting, to their detriment. They believe that their magic is stronger and can protect them no matter what, always forgetting that metal can pierce them just as easily.

"The little leader's mine!" I shout at my group. "Someone else can take the other two."

"I got it," Aiden growls to my right. He's bloody, but he snarls with anger. So fucking hot.

I turn back to their leader whose arms are out as if he's ready to fight, but they're shaking. "What was that about us being unable to beat forty of you?" I ask as I twirl small flames through my fingers on my left hand and water through my right. I chuckle. "You see, while we may all be cocky assholes, there's a reason. We're just that good."

He sends fire up his sword, ready to make his final stand. I smile, doing the same, hiding the shaking in my arms. "In fact, to prove to you how good we are, I'll only fight you with this sword. No other magic." This is really probably very stupid of me considering how exhausted I am, but I can't let him know and this is a great way to not show how drained I am.

He scoffs. "Fine. Let hubris be your death."

"No. Let it be yours." I attack, moving like the flame itself. I weave around his sword, ducking and jumping as he tries to find some part of me to hit. He manages a slice on my upper right arm, and I hiss through the pain. He smiles to himself.

I narrow my eyes, take a deep breath, and attack him with full force. Our swords collide, the flames mixing then separating like they want nothing to do with one another. I scream with rage and manage to cut straight through his left shoulder and his severed arm drops to the ground. He collapses, shrieking in pain.

I slowly circle his body as he scrambles to grab his sword with his right hand. I kick it out of his grasp, stepping on his hand in the process. His shrieks get even louder. I look up to see how the rest of my friends are doing, and they're all huddled around Aiden resting on the floor. Del catches my eye, looking way too worried for my liking. Shit. I turn back to the fire soldier.

"While I would love to have the time to play with you a little more, one of your soldiers hurt one of my friends. And nothing makes me more furious than my friends getting hurt." Before he can respond, I shove my sword through his heart, sending ice through the sword and into his body. His body quickly freezes from the inside out, his face now frozen in an endless scream. I give him one last look and jog over to my friends.

They all have a few scrapes and slashes, nothing too bad. But, they're staring at Aiden, who I finally look at as he's lying on the dirt against a rock. His hand covers the left side of his stomach, which is covered in blood. My heart lurches in my chest. There's way too much blood and with the minimal healing we're capable of, never mind the fact that we're all exhausted, it doesn't look good.

I crouch down next to him, and seeing me, he tries to smile.

"Hey, Princess," he chokes out. "Looks like I could've used a little more training before my first battle." Blood dribbles out of his mouth and he chokes on it as he speaks.

No, no, no, not now. He's not allowed to die. Not when I've finally started giving my heart to someone else. Not when it's my fault that he's here.

I curse quietly. "Shut up and let me think." I look at each of my friends. He's losing blood too quickly and they know it. We should've brought a healer.

Fuck. I'm not losing him. Not now. Not when we need him. Not when *I* need him.

"Okay, we can do a joint spell," I say. "The four of us. Aneira, you're the most talented. Pick your strongest healing spell and we will lend our magic to it."

Aneira looks at me with way too much love. "We'll try, Sage, but I'm not a healer. It may not be enough."

"I don't care! It'll be enough. It has to be enough." I nod like I'm encouraging her to begin, when really, I'm trying to convince myself. If he dies, it'll be my fault. Both his death and the repercussions to my realm.

"Okay," she nods. She takes a moment and draws two symbols in the air — I would think a more complex spell would need more than that. She takes our hands in hers and teaches us the spell. We repeat the words over and over with her, her other hand resting over Aiden's wound.

Slowly, too slowly, the flow of blood is decreasing. It's not going to be enough, he's already lost too much blood.

I dig deeper into my magic source, finding my dragon and begging her to push harder. I can almost feel her looking at me, nodding, and roaring through her flames. I jolt as my magic comes out of me stronger than ever before. I didn't think I had that much power left after our battle.

Aneira whips her head to look at me, sapphire eyes bewildered. We turn back to Aiden, whose breathing begins to level out. The blood flow is finally slowing to a stop. I let out a huge sigh of relief as we all slowly remove our hands.

Aneira mutters under her breath, "We shouldn't have been able to heal him that completely." She looks at me. I shake my head. I can't have this conversation right now. Not with Aiden still so injured.

Everyone else gradually gets up and leaves Aiden and I alone, knowing I'm not going to be leaving his side anytime soon. I stare at him, my heart in my throat, unable to speak. He's still focusing on calming his breathing. I can't believe I almost lost him. I've known him for less than a month and I already don't know what I would do without him.

Pathetic, but true.

Somehow along this journey I've found myself opening up to him in ways I've never done before, and I didn't hate the way it felt. He took everything I threw at him and accepted it like it was nothing. No one's ever done that before. He made me feel like my mess wasn't so messy; made me feel like it was okay to share my pain.

"Thank you," Aiden says. Is he joking?

I scoff. "For what?"

"Saving my life."

"I'm the one who put it in jeopardy." I look away, trying to blink away the tears that begin to form.

He grabs my hand and makes me look at him before responding, "No, Sage, you didn't. I chose this." I shake my head, but before I can respond, he continues. "I see the weight you place on yourself; constantly shouldering the burden of everyone's life around you. But we all chose to be here. Maybe not initially, for me," he says, trying to get me to smile. "But I already told you, I've forgiven you several times over for what you did. In fact, I should thank you. You've allowed me to become part of something bigger than myself. Even though I didn't grow up in this world, the connection I have through my magic is unmistakable. It's an honor to be able to help save it."

My heart's in my throat and I don't want him to see me cry. "Come on, let's go into one of those caves so you can rest properly," I say, gesturing to the largest cave in front of us. "I'll apply some salve to your wounds."

I carry my pack in one arm and support him as much as I can with the other, and he must be in excruciating pain based on how heavily he's leaning on me. I don't even look to see where the rest of my friends are. If they need me, they'll call.

I start a fire and lay out the minimal healing supplies I have next to our bedrolls. Aiden takes off his shirt and I freeze. Even with the gash slicing through his stomach, he's still beautiful. He leans against the wall of the cave and slowly slides down to the ground. I lightly apply the salve onto his wound, pushing some heat through my fingers as I do so. He sighs in relief, and I can't help the small smile that crosses my face.

"What?" he asks.

"I'm glad you're feeling better," I say.

"I don't think I've ever seen you smile because someone else is feeling *better*."

"Hey! I'm not that cruel." I lightly slap his arm, and he grabs my hand before I can remove it.

"I know. You're one of the kindest people I've ever met." I look away from him before he can realize how much those words impacted me.

"Now *that* is cruel."

He shakes his head. "Sage, it's true. You-"

"You don't need to lie to me just because I'm feeling sorry for myself."

"It's not a lie."

"I know I'm not as mean as I like to portray, but I'm certainly not one of the kindest individuals you've ever met."

"It's not in what you say, it's what you do. And that

matters more than anything else." I stare into his eyes as he speaks straight into my heart, watching his blue eyes sparkle in the light of the fire and the warmth of his soul. I'm breathing heavier than I did during our battle.

Our breath starts to mingle as I lightly trace his lips with my finger. His mouth opens and I'm entranced. Am I really about to kiss him? Why would he want to kiss me after all I've put him through?

But I'm done fighting as my gaze moves up his face and our eyes meet; the tension in his jaw and the strain in his eyes indicate he's holding himself back and is waiting for me to make the decision.

And that, that choice he's leaving entirely up to me, undos me.

I bring my lips to his and melt into the kiss, tilting my head and grabbing his hair with my hands. He lifts his hand off the ground, grabbing my waist and moving my body on top of his. As I straddle his waist, he winces.

I look down at his wound. "Maybe we shouldn't." I don't want to hurt him anymore than I already have.

"Yes, we should," he growls, pulling my head back down to his.

He nips my lip with his teeth, and I can't help the soft moan that escapes my lips as I lean back into the kiss with even more fervor than before. My hands rove around his chest, moving up and down every plane and dip of his chiseled body. He grabs my hair and pulls my head to the side, giving himself access to my neck. He kisses, nips, and licks, moving from one side to the other. My eyes flutter shut in ecstasy. He moves his mouth lower as he lifts my shirt away from my chest, pulls down my bra, and closes his mouth over one of my nipples.

I moan again, arching my back to push my nipple further into his mouth. He groans and I look down, the hunger in his eyes blazing as he looks up at me, his mouth firmly sucking on my tit.

Heat pulses through me, starting in my core and working its way outward. He takes his mouth off me, only to immediately begin kissing me again. I pull away for a moment, breathing heavily and looking into his eyes. His breath is as heavy as mine as he stares straight into my soul.

"Sage," he whispers, his fingers tracing my lips down to my neck.

"Aiden." I move down his lap.

"Sage," he growls as he realizes what I'm doing.

I inch my body back slowly, until my head is parallel with his belly button. I need to find some way to show him what this means to me — it's not a decision I'm making lightly to give into this attraction. Because the truth, as much as I'm loath to admit it — even to myself — is that this is so much more than lust.

I undo the buttons on his pants and huskily reply, "Aiden."

His cock releases from his pants, hard and gorgeous. I lick my lips in anticipation, giving him one more look before I lick him from his base to tip. I take my time, slowly working up and down. He moans as he puts one hand in my hair and softly grabs my head. Once I've licked every inch of him, I take him in my mouth, once, twice, working my way down his entire length.

I speed up, slowing when I reach his head, twirling my

tongue before moving back down. Aiden's chest rises and falls rapidly as I continue, which only turns me on even more. He lightly pushes my head, and I moan in pleasure at his need to take control. He pulls me off him, grabbing the back of my neck and staring into my eyes.

"I need to be inside you. Now."

I can't even speak; I want him so badly. I quickly nod my head in response. He picks me up like I weigh nothing and like he has no injuries. He stops, staring at my exposed breasts and licking his lips. He gently pushes me onto my back, kissing his way down my body until he reaches my pants, unbuttoning them and practically ripping them off me with impatience.

"I wish those bastards were still alive so I could kill them all over again for hurting you," he says as he looks at my various cuts and burns.

"I think they got the worst of it. And right now, I don't want you to be thinking about anyone else but me." I've never cared if someone I'm with only wanted me, but with Aiden, the thought of anyone else on his mind — sexually or not — makes the fire next to us blaze higher in response to my anger.

He smirks over at the now roaring fire as he moves back up my body and kisses me as he enters me. We moan into each other's mouths. The kissing gets wild and feral as he pumps himself into me at a relentless pace. I nip at Aiden's neck as he buries his face into mine and hooks my legs around his torso, trying to bring him impossibly closer.

He moves one hand down to my clit, moving two fingers in time with his cock. Our breath begins to sync, panting into one another as he moves faster and faster.

We stare into each other's eyes, and a spark moves

through my body. He must feel it too as his eyes widen slightly at the heat. That gives me the idea to send a wave of heat through the air where we're joined together. Once he feels what I'm doing, he falls into my neck, murmuring, "Fuck, Sage."

He lightly circles my neck with one hand covered in a thin layer of ice while the other still plays with me. The contrast of temperatures, plus his relentless pace, pushes us over the edge and we climax together. I see stars as waves of pleasure flood my body. Aiden grunts several times before coming to a stop, his now softening cock still inside of me. We both pant, staring at each other. He gives me a soft kiss before slowly pulling out of me and laying on his back.

"That was something," I say, still catching my breath.

He chuckles. "Yeah, something."

He looks down at me, pulling my body into his and kissing the top of my head. We lie together in comfortable silence as our breath evens back out. I'm content and at peace; this sensation is something I've never experienced around a man before.

Once our heart rates are back to normal, he asks, "What does *shifrah* mean?"

"What?" My eyes blink rapidly as I process what he's asking.

"Shifrah. I hear that and 'Pretty Boy' come out of your mouth more than my name." I tilt my head up from where it rests on his chest to him smirking down at me.

A smile grows across my face. "Are you sure you want to know?"

He leans up on his elbows as a flash of concern flits across his face. ".... I think so?"

I lightly chuckle. "It's a compliment... mostly. It's from an ancient language that my parents taught me growing up. It can mean many things: beauty, cleverness, fairness, peace, and calm. Even before I knew you, I somehow knew it would suit you. And every day, it fits better and better." His eyes shine with joy and something else as he listens.

"Okay, but what else?" The shine of joy turns more mischievous.

"Whatever do you mean?"

"You wouldn't be that hesitant to tell me if it was only those good things."

I drag my fingers up and down the tattoos on his upper body to avoid his face. "Well, it also happens to be a name only given to females." My fingers stop their tracing as all of his muscles tense.

"You gave me a woman's nickname. Who else knows how to speak this ancient language?"

"Um, I mean who can really say? My parents taught it to me and Del, and I taught it to Aneira —"

Aiden grabs my chin. I'm terrified to see the anger on his face. When I'm met with only amusement, I let go of the breath I didn't realize I was holding in. "Who else knows?"

"Mostly everyone," I say as I cringe. "But it's really a compliment more than anything else, so you should really feel honored."

He laughs and pulls me back down to his chest before responding. "Relax, Princess. I think it's endearing. And I don't mind that it's only used on women. You chose it for me and that means more to me than any silly little gender definition."

Mother, this man. Taking everything in stride with a grin.

I stare at the top of the cave and realize there are intertwining ice and burn marks.

"Look," I say, pointing at the pattern. "I guess my magic was a little out of control."

"You mean *both* of our magic." The ice was definitely him. When I'm around him, it's like my fire wants to see what boundaries it can push on my normally tight leash.

"True. I struggle to control myself around you," I admit. I hate feeling out of control.

"I do too," he whispers. "But it's a lack of control I can get used to."

"It scares me. How fast I felt connected to you."

"I'm not scared." He gently brushes my hair with his fingers. "I'm home."

I am too. But I'm not ready to admit that to him. I can't until he knows all of my secrets. If he still wants me then, maybe I'll let myself fall.

I'll never be called gentle or sweet, but I'd tear into the flesh of anyone who threatens Aiden and claw through the depths of my tortured mind if it means carving a safe space for him. Maybe someone else's horror can be his home.

Chapter Thirty-Two

Aiden

The sound of birds chirping wakes me up as small rays of soft sunlight trickle into the entrance of the cave. The smell of cinnamon and peonies floods my nose. Last night started like a nightmare but ended like a dream. I would gladly go through that hell if it meant it would lead to Sage and I finally getting together. Her steady, warm breath tickles my chest and I'm more content than I've been in a while.

My stomach's still in pain, but it's nothing compared to the joy I feel. I slowly pick Sage off me, who moans slightly in protest.

She covers her eyes with her arms. "What time is it?" she mumbles.

I chuckle into her shoulder, kissing it as I respond, "It's still early."

"So why are we awake?"

"Because I need to repay you."

"For what?" She rubs her eyes, slowly waking up. I look down at her stunning naked body. Her porcelain skin is smooth and soft except where she has scrapes and one bad gash from our fight last night. Anger rushes through me at the thought of those assholes that hurt her.

"For this." I smile as I go down on her.

As soon as my mouth closes over her, she whimpers and twists her body in pleasure. I suck and pull, lightly biting and then licking away any pain. She writhes as I continue, pulling my hair in satisfaction. I continue to suck and swirl my tongue as I place a finger inside of her. Her breathing picks up and her moans get louder. The sounds that come out of this woman's mouth are enough to undo me without her ever laying a finger on me.

"Fuck," she whispers, and I smile into her.

I add another finger, pumping in and out in time with my mouth. She pants harder and I suck as I hook my fingers inside of her. I hear her breath hitch, and I know she's close, so I moan into her, causing her to push over the edge as she comes.

She catches her breath as I pull my fingers out of her. As I look up into her bright eyes, I slowly put my fingers in my mouth, licking her cum as I close my eyes. She tastes like heaven, and I'm addicted. I give her a light peck and get up to collect my clothes.

Sage stares, looking satiated, and I'm more than tempted to lie back down when Delwyn shouts, "Are you lovebirds done in there?" I blush.

"Yes, Del!" Sage shouts in response.

"Good, because we need to get moving."

I look over at Sage rolling her eyes. I smile at her as she stands up, so comfortable in her nudity. I can understand why — her curves and soft belly are enchanting, and as she stretches with her back to me, her perfectly round ass is on full display. My mouth literally waters and I force myself to turn away before I make us stay in this cave all day.

Sage and I leave the cave to find the rest of the group gathered around a fire, cooking meat one of them must have hunted this morning.

"Finally," Idris groans. Sage sneers at her as she grabs the piece of meat out of her hand and plops on the log next to her. "Glad you two finally got one out of your system." I cringe; that can't be all it was, right?

Aneira blows on her meat. "Now is not the time to be messing with Aiden's head, Id."

I look back at Idris as a smirk sweeps across her face. "I'm kidding, Pretty Boy. We're all just glad we no longer have to deal with sexual tension that we can cut with a knife."

"What she means to say," Aneira adds, "is that we're so happy. For both of you."

Delwyn's grinning in agreement as he looks at me surveying the surprisingly empty ground. "We buried the bodies last night. The two of you must have been a little too busy to realize."

Aneira giggles as she glances between Sage and I. Sage, queen of the eye roll, gives Aneira a look, and I can't help but chuckle.

"How's everyone doing?" Sage asks.

"None of us were as badly injured as Aiden," Aneira says, looking over at me. "Just a few cuts, so we're ready to continue as long as he is." I feel shockingly okay, considering how hours ago I was genuinely scared last night would be my last. And based on how it ended, I'll do anything to make sure I stay okay, if only so I can spend more time with Sage.

I nod. "I feel up to it."

Sage looks over at me. "Are you sure?"

"Yes. Definitely. Are you?" Her injuries weren't nearly as bad as mine, but she's too good at hiding her pain and I want to make sure she isn't just for my sake. She continues to look wary but nods in agreement.

"Good," Delwyn says. "Because our fight last night will definitely attract unwanted attention to this area. Whether it's more soldiers or animals, I don't want to wait and see what will come sniffing."

"Do you think we'll get to the weapon today?" I ask.

Idris says, "Hopefully by the end of the day. If not, tomorrow. But that all depends on you."

Delwyn puts an arm around me. "Don't worry, Aiden. I'm sure we'll find it."

Sage scoffs and we all turn to look at her. "What? Listen, I'm sure we'll find it too, but I don't think it's going to be easy." She looks at each of us in turn. "We need to be prepared for anything."

After we finish eating, Aneira reapplies salve to my wound, wraps it, and we get on our way. More trekking through the mountains, more climbing over massive rocks, and many more hours later, my stomach is killing me. I don't want to tell them to stop but I'm not sure how much longer I can go.

There's an uncomfortable tug along with small sears of pain. Sage keeps looking back at me to make sure I'm okay and I smile to reassure her, but I think she's starting to not believe me.

Her voice sounds in my ear. *Are you alright?*

I close my eyes, take a deep breath, and wind message back. *Yes, just a little tired.*

She looks back at me and must send a wind message up to Delwyn because eventually I hear him in my ear say, *I see a good resting spot over this ridge. We'll stop for lunch there.*

I dump all my stuff on the ground and gulp down the water in my canteen. Sage comes over and sits next to me.

"Take off your shirt," she commands.

I choke on my water. "Excuse me?"

"You heard me, take off your shirt." I mean, I'm down if she is, but we're surrounded by her family and it's the middle of the day.

"Sage, I hardly think now is the time-"

"I want to see your wound." That makes more sense.

I slowly take off my shirt and hear her take a sharp breath in. My wound has opened back up, the blood mixing with sweat as it drips down my stomach. Sage curses in shockingly imaginative ways and pulls out her first aid kit. She dabs my wound and now it's my turn to wince.

"Hold still," Sage says. "If you had told us it was bothering you earlier, it might not have gotten this bad."

"I didn't want to slow us down," I say.

She looks up from the wound to pierce me with her gaze. "Your health is more important than any mission."

"Do you take your own advice?" I'm as shocked as she is at my response; the pain must be making me mean.

Before I can apologize, she shakes her head and gets back to cleaning out my wound. She summons a stream of water, places it directly over my gash, then freezes it on top. "This should stop the blood flow without the pain of me cauterizing it. I hope."

"Thank you," I say, grabbing her hand before she can get up. I snapped at her and she was trying to help. Before I can apologize, she gives me a small smile and walks over to Idris.

I drink more water and sit in silence, breathing through the slowly decreasing pain and listening to the rest of the group chat. Eventually, Delwyn comes over and hands me a tonic. "This should help with any lingering pain."

"Thank you," I say. I take a big swig of the mysterious liquid and gag, forcing myself to swallow it. Delwyn chuckles as he sits down next to me. We both stare at Sage with her head down, eyes staring intently as she talks to Idris. "I can't get a read on her," I say. "Every time I think she's finally opening up to me, I say something stupid, and she shuts down again."

Delwyn looks at me. "Listen, Aiden. I've known Sage my entire life. She doesn't share things until she's ready to share them. She's very slow to open up to others, but once she does, she'll be the fiercest and most loyal person in your life. Besides, if it's any consolation, she's sharing things with you that took her years to share with the rest of us."

I shake my head. "I wish there was a way for me to show her that I understand. We've only known each other for a few weeks, but without sounding like some cheesy guy from a rom com, it's like I've known her my entire life."

"Well, I don't know what a rom com is, but you don't sound cheesy. Here, we believe in soulmates. It's a choice to devote yourself to another person for your entire long life, but we believe there's one individual that's meant to be your other half. Some people will go so far as to fall in love with one another without feeling that soulmate connection. They might refuse to do the binding ritual for fear that one day they'll meet their soulmate."

The thought of having a relationship that deep is something I've wanted my whole life. Without getting ahead of myself, I've felt such a strong connection to Sage since the moment I laid eyes on her. A soulmate like Sage would certainly keep me on my toes.

"What's a binding ritual?"

"It's like your weddings, I suppose, only it uses magic to bind your entire beings together. It means if one of you dies, you both die. You can share each other's power, and with practice, you're able to communicate directly into one another's heads no matter where you are in Tirlun."

"Isn't that the same as wind messages?"

Delwyn shakes his head. "Wind messages can only be sent over smaller distances. And, you can choose to ignore a wind message. That's what happened the night you tried to escape and why it took so long for us to find you; we all ignored Sage's message to keep track of you."

I cringe; he laughs. "It's alright, it all worked out. But, speaking into each other's heads. That, you can't ignore even if you want to."

"That's intense." But beautiful.

"That's why it's a choice. It can't be forced upon either party; that kind of trust needs to be given willingly. My parents weren't soulmates; at least, they didn't think so. But Sage's..." Delwyn takes a deep breath. "I don't know how they got so lucky with it being a politically arranged marriage, but they were the truest soulmates I've ever seen. Sage saw it too. I think that's another reason she can be so closed off — she's scared she'll one day give herself up to that kind of love."

"It doesn't sound scary, it sounds lovely."

"Truth be told, I think she's more scared that she'll never find it." I look over at her sitting next to Idris and have a bone-deep sense that maybe she already did.

We trek through the mountains for about an hour until I feel another tug in my gut. This time, my limbs refuse to move forward, and Idris practically bumps into me.

"What is it?" she asks.

"I felt something," I say. It felt like the tug from earlier, but with no pain, I can't imagine it's from my wound. They did tell me I would feel something when we neared the weapon and I don't want to risk missing any signs.

Sage turns around from her spot up the path. "What did you feel?"

"A tug, deep in my gut." I'm not sure what it was, but it definitely wasn't natural.

"Are you sure it's not your wound reopening?" I don't think so, but I lift my shirt to double check. The wound is unopened, so I look up at Sage, waiting for our next move.

"What are we waiting for? Lead the way, Aiden," Delwyn says.

I move to the front of the line until Sage is in front of me. She stares at me like she's trying to see through my body to the tug that I felt. I approach her and feel the heat off her body. She's entirely focused on me and my movements, so she doesn't realize there are flames in her hands. I take her hands in mine and freeze them until her palms are back to a normal temperature. She jumps at the shock, surprised as she looks down at our hands clasped together.

I give her a sheepish smile. "Felt like you needed me."

She rolls her eyes. "Come on, Pretty Boy. Let's see where your gut takes us."

Every time I think I've gotten used to the magic of this world, something new pops up and surprises me. We reach a fork in the path and my body is pushed towards the left. Whatever magic is tied to this weapon wants me to find it. I can practically feel it hurrying me along.

We spend the next three hours following this thread until we're so deep within the mountain range that I have no idea how we'll find our way out. We pass a few little creatures, who scurry away when they hear us. But even the predators of these mountains must be scared of this weapon, because the closer we get, the less signs of life there are.

Where there was very little vegetation to begin with, there's now none. Where the temperature was tepid, it's now frigid. Where there were traces of individuals traveling before us, it's now empty.

The sun begins to set, casting long shadows on our bodies from the rocks overhead. The magic drags me to the entrance of a cave that's unremarkable in every way, one in a network of thousands.

I'm held captive by whatever magic connects me to this weapon. "It's in here," I say.

"This is sort of anticlimactic," Sage retorts.

"Let's not jinx anything," Idris says.

Sage dramatically looks at Idris before creating a fireball in her hand and dramatically bowing. "Shall we?" Idris creates a fireball as well, and Aneira and Delwyn both quickly cast a spell, creating balls of light in their hands.

"Uh," I say and look at all of them, unsure of what to do.

"Focus on guiding us towards the weapon. We'll handle the light," Aneira says, giving me a reassuring smile.

I nod before leading the way into the cave with Sage at my side. She gives me an arrogant smile. "Time to play, Pretty Boy."

My nerves almost got the better of me, but Sage's sass has a funny way of calming me down.

I snort. "I think your definition of playing is far different from most. So, let's hope there's very minimal *playing* involved."

Sage twirls the flame around her fingers. "I don't know, I'm feeling a little stabby this evening." A chuckle escapes my lips despite our literal life-or-death situation.

"Why's that?"

"You see, this man I've been hanging out with gave me a little taste of what our time together is like. And instead of being able to spend my time slowly exploring that, I'm forced to be in a disgusting, dirty, dark cave system surrounded by my family."

Delwyn pipes up from behind us. "This cave really reverberates sound, so your *family* can hear every word you're saying!"

My shoulders rise to my ears as I cringe in embarrassment. I'm still not used to Sage being so nonchalant about sex.

"Don't forget the smell," Idris says.

"What smell?" I ask Sage.

"Oh, Pretty Boy," she says. "Your senses haven't fully acclimated yet, I suppose. When a person is... enamored... their scent tends to shift." Does she mean the scent she's been exuding since I met her?

"Like your cinnamon-peony scent?"

"Sorry?"

I blush, grateful for the dark for hiding the color blooming on my cheeks. I clear my throat and say, "Your scent, it definitely gets stronger when you're... enamored." It's also constantly there, but now might not be the time to bring that up.

Sage shrugs with indifference. "I suppose it could be worse."

"Not for your cousin!" Delwyn shouts. Sage and I look at one another before laughing together.

Hey lovebirds, Idris wind messages into both of our ears. *Every sound in this bug-infested cave echoes, and I'd rather avoid meeting any creatures that are most definitely guarding this centuries-old weapon. So how about we stop with the flirting and focus on the mission.*

Sorry, we both send back.

We walk in near silence, interrupted only by the occasional drip of water or scurry of feet of some creature that I'm grateful we're unable to see. The magic in my blood guides me to the weapon, and the vibration of its power moves through my veins. I turn a corner only to hit Sage's arm. I look at her and she places one finger to her lips. I look behind us to the rest of the group slowly approaching as quietly as possible.

Sage picks up a rock the size of her hand and throws it

around the corner. It clicks against the rough stone floor, but the sound is quickly drowned out by ripping and shrieking as something attacks it. It must be huge, because it causes some stones to scrape off the ceiling from the reverberation of the movement and noise. After it settles down again, we're all left breathing heavily.

I look at everyone else, and it's clear that not only have they never faced this beast, but they have no clue what it is. Sage creates a second fireball and stares at all of us. She smirks, and, before any of us realize what she's doing, she tosses the fireball into the hallway. None of us can even stop her from doing what is sure to get us all killed.

But there's nothing — no movement from whatever creature is around the corner. It must be blind, and Sage must've guessed that. She looks back at us with a smug look on her face.

"Way to go Sagey!" Aneira exclaims as quietly as possible, oblivious to the potential danger Sage put us in.

Delwyn leans in and whispers, "Okay. Thanks to Sage's reckless plan, we know this creature can't see. We'll use the light to our advantage to avoid it. But that also means its other senses are heightened. We must be as quiet as possible and try to not be scared."

I give him a look. "How the fuck are we not supposed to be scared?"

Sage grins, her canines looking sharper in the firelight. "If we make it through this alive, I'll let you fuck me against the cave wall." I can't help the wave of arousal that floods through my entire body.

Aneira says, "That worked."

Idris mumbles, "There's no way this monster can't smell that either."

Sage smiles. "I'm sure it's not used to *that* scent, so maybe it'll be confused?"

"Let's fight this thing and get it done with," Idris says. She adds another fireball to increase the light in the natural hallway and we all turn the corner.

Chapter Thirty-Three

Sage

We step into a massive cavern. It has to be made of magic because there's no way it could otherwise fit under the mountains. It's probably even bigger than the throne room in the palace — between three and four hundred feet in length and at least triple Aiden's height.

As I look up, stalactites of different shapes and sizes point down from the ceiling like death waiting to devour us. An altar rests in the back of the space, illuminated in artificial blue light. Blocking my entire view from the altar itself is one of the most disgusting creatures I've ever seen.

It has four legs and is at least the length of my body. It's furry and scaly at the same time, like whatever hell this beast came out of couldn't decide which would look worse and chose both. It has the body of a spider — an ovular shape, covered in scars. And its head. Where eyes should be are three sets of massive fangs, each the size of my forearm and covered in what I hope is non-poisonous black saliva. It can definitely smell our arrival, but without eyes, we all quickly spread out along the wall as it scurries to the entrance of the cavern, tracking the scent to where it's strongest.

We use this opportunity to circle around the abomination that doesn't deserve to be called a spider. I test its strength by shooting a fireball at the leg closest to me. It shrieks and whips around to face me. I quickly roll underneath its body as its fangs snap the air where I had just been.

I take my sword out of its scabbard and shove it into its underbelly. I try to drag it through, but its insides are too thick, so I quickly pull it out and run to the other side of the beast.

Idris whips fireballs at it on one side while Delwyn does the same with ice on the other side. Aneira quickly moves her hands, most likely creating some crazy spell that will give us a much-needed advantage, as fire and ice aren't doing anything except annoy it.

I peek around the beast's body as Aiden shoots ice directly at its face. Stupid. But brave. Its fangs get closer to Aiden with each spray. Shit. I try to find a way to get to him without being crushed by its legs or getting hit by one of my friends' magic.

I'm about to risk it when the beast freezes midair. Aneira shouts, "This won't hold very long!"

I look at Delwyn on my right and say, "Del, give me stairs." Del nods and I back up as far as I can from the spider, my back hitting the wall behind me. When I can't move any further, I sprint. As I do, steps of ice appear in front of me, gradually getting higher and higher the closer I get to the monster. When I'm about two steps from its body, it begins to shift. I'm running out of time. With one last burst, I jump onto the spider's back as it begins moving towards Aiden.

I slam my sword into its back, and it roars, rearing its head and threatening to throw me right off its body. I hold on tight to my sword as I dangle off its back. "Now would be a really great time for someone to kill it," I say through gritted teeth.

Aiden, who's still the closest to the beast, moves forward with ice in his hands. The creature still struggles to buck me off it, causing the sword to slowly carve its way down. I can no longer see Aiden from my position, but I slowly hear the crackling of ice. Del runs to where Aiden is, and I hope that it's not because he's injured.

Idris is staring at him with wide eyes. I don't think I've ever seen her so surprised. After about thirty seconds, a cool breeze emerges from underneath me. I look down as ice slowly crawls up its legs and underbelly. The ice creeps up and up until the cold seeps through my clothes as I hang on its body.

I push my legs against the creature's body like I'm rock climbing so I can gain leverage to pull out my sword. My sword loosens and I create an ice slide off the beast's body and onto the floor, gliding down. As I touch the ground, the entire body collapses onto the floor as the ice cracks and the beast's body crumbles into a thousand frozen pieces.

"What happened?" Aneira asks.

"I slayed it," I say.

"Oh, no, no, no, Sagey, I don't think so," Del says.

"Um, I'm sorry. A sword into the underbelly as well as on the top doesn't count as slaying?" Why aren't they giving me credit for this kill? I earned it.

"Not when it's not what killed it."

"And what killed it?"

Aiden quietly says, "I did." He doesn't even have a scratch on him; how did he kill it?

I raise my eyebrows as I look at him. "You? How?"

"Well, as it was trying to get you off its back, I noticed the open wound you made, so I started throwing ice into its body. I thought I could freeze it from the inside out." I wish I thought of that.

"And when I saw what he was doing, I ran over to help. Hence, the crumbled ice on the floor where this thing used to be," Del gestures toward the ice on the floor.

I roll my eyes. "Whatever. We'll never know what actually killed it." I can't accept my complete loss, I deserve at least partial credit.

Idris comes over from where she was playing with the ice shards on the floor. "Actually, Sage, I hate to admit it, but they're right. It's definitely what killed it."

I look at Del and Aiden and see two very smug assholes. "Ugh, fine. Congratulations."

Del comes to me and swings his arm over my shoulders. "Don't worry Sagey, you'll get the next one." He tries to ruffle my hair, so I shove him away before he gets the chance.

"Should we continue on the mission then?"

Aiden looks at me. "Since when are you the one who's keeping us on track?" Since I didn't get credit for a kill.

"Since there was a magical glowing pedestal in a magical cavern." We look past the broken body to stare at what's undoubtedly the location of the weapon. But there's nothing on top of the pedestal; only several raised steps, each glowing blue and leading up to a podium with nothing on top.

"So is the weapon this stone?" Idris asks.

"Definitely not," Aiden says. "I would've felt that. It's on or in the pedestal — the magic is pulling me there."

We walk towards the podium in the center of the room, Aiden leading the charge. He stops short and we all skid to a stop to avoid hitting him.

There's a ring of water, inches away from lapping at our shoes, twenty-feet wide and who knows how deep, circling the entire podium. I'd rather not have to swim across — I don't even want to guess what's lurking in the water that's guarding the weapon.

I try to throw my ice on top to create a bridge, but nothing happens. Del tries as well, and we're faced with the same thing. Aneira attempts to cast a spell and build a bridge with the stones, and once again, no luck.

"Looks like we'll have to wait here for you, Pretty Boy," I say.

Aiden looks at me with flared nostrils and shallow breaths. His eyes glow in the blue light. An uncomfortable lurching fills my gut; I'm scared. Not for what's going to happen now, but what will happen after. The chance that I'm going to lose him. Before I can think twice, I stand on my toes, grab his face with both hands, and kiss him.

He grabs my body, lifting me up close to him and sears his lips to mine. I angle my head better as he deepens the kiss and the world around us disappears. There's nothing but him and me, this kiss, this moment. Whatever happens next, at least I'll have this. Too soon, he pulls away, still holding me close to his chest.

He stares into my eyes, his own glistening. "Sage, I-"

I hush him and put a finger to his lips before he can finish his sentence. "You're just going to have to tell me after." He nods and softly kisses my finger. As he sets me down, he looks at the rest of my family and gives them all firm nods. When he looks at Aneira last, she runs up to him and gives him a hug.

"You're going to be fine," I hear her whisper to him. He nods and kisses the top of her head. He gives me one last look, longing in his eyes, turns back to the pedestal, and prepares to make a bridge.

Chapter Thirty-Four

Aiden

It's probably twenty feet to the other side of the water, which makes it impossible to make it across without building a bridge. As I stare into the abyss, something long and scaly swims towards the surface of the water. I can't help the chill that runs through my body. I hope whatever it is doesn't mind a little ice over its head.

I take a deep breath and hold my hands, slowly building a bridge from my side of the ring to the other. I make sure it's at least six inches thick so it won't break under my feet, as well as twice my width.

As I get the bridge about halfway across, the creature under the water begins to increase in speed as it approaches my spot on the ring. Before I can contemplate how to keep it from breaking the bridge, it leaps out of the water. It looks like a massive eel with the scales of a snake and the mouth of an alligator. It lands directly on my bridge and breaks it into pieces.

It continues to swim around as if it didn't destroy my only hope of reaching the pedestal. I look behind me where the rest of the group stares with mouths slightly agape.

"Any ideas?" I ask.

"You're going to have to kill it," Sage says.

"How?"

"Well, considering that none of our magic works past this point, that's on you. I would suggest some ice spears. Or, you know, you could always freeze it from the inside out." She puts one hand on her hip and a finger to her lip and adds, "Oh, wait. You can't. Because without *my* slaying, that wouldn't have been possible."

Delwyn's eyes go wide. "Seriously Sage? Now is *not* the time."

She shrugs. "I'm just saying."

"Okay," I say, getting back to the task at hand. "Ice spears. I can do that." The creature makes slow circles around the ring. I don't see any other animals in the water, so what it eats is beyond me. Granted, if it's been here since this cave was made, maybe it doesn't need to eat.

It takes around two minutes for it to make a full loop. That gives me two minutes to prepare an attack. Plenty of time. It passes me, and even though its eyes face forward, I can feel it looking at me through the water. In case that's somehow possible, I wait until it passes before I begin to build ice spears, daggers, and spikes as fast as I can. I place the extras next to me so they're ready when I need more.

After I count to a minute in my head, I have as much as I anticipate I'll need. I turn to look back at Sage for what I hope is not the last time. She grins at me and gives me two thumbs up. I can't help the soft chuckle that escapes my mouth. *Oh, you'll definitely be rewarded for this when we're out of this Mother-forsaken cave, Pretty Boy,* she sends to me.

Looking forward to it, I wind message back.

"Whatever nasty things you guys are saying to each other can wait until we're done here!" Idris shouts, drawing my attention away from Sage. I turn back to the ring and the creature's approaching. Fuck. Okay. I got this.

I create a three-foot spear in my hand and make it as sharp as possible. I grip the top, aim, and shoot the spear out of my hand using more ice. It hits its upper back, and I'm soaked in water as the creature screeches, contorting itself half out of the water as it tries to get the spear out of its back. It swings its head back and forth but can't dislodge the spear. Unfortunately, it doesn't seem like it caused all that much damage. I pick up several of my daggers and rapidly throw them along its body. A few miss because of its constant movement, but three strike home on its back.

Its back is made of thick scales and the ice won't be able to kill it. I need to somehow get it to turn over or hit its head.

I look back at the group to see what they think. "You need to get it to flip," Delwyn says.

"How?" I ask.

"I hate to be the one to say this, but I think you need to get in the water," Idris says. Shit, she may be right. I look at the rest of them and take their lack of protests as agreement.

"Sage," I plead. "Please tell me you have another idea that doesn't involve me getting into the water with a twelve-foot eel monster?"

She looks at me and slowly shakes her head. "Idris is right. It's never going to voluntarily flip onto its back. You either need to force it or attack from underneath. Cast a spell to throw some lights in the water first so you have more visibility." This is not going to be easy, but I need to stay positive.

Things will always work out if I'm positive.

"Okay, I can do that." I look at Aneira and she quickly demonstrates how to cast the spell. I repeat her movements and words, and soon enough I have five balls of light that I toss into the water. Now that I can truly see what I'm fighting, I want to get into the water even less.

Its scales are black and mucus green, and its body is as wide as mine. It continues to thrash, showing three rows of razor-sharp teeth. Great. I give Sage another glance, unable to stop myself.

Somehow, covered in beast guts, dirt, and blood, she still looks like an oasis in the desert. Her auburn hair is strewn about, but her eyes are as bright as ever. They peek through her loose strands like the last green leaves in the fall. She leans against her sword in one hand and holds a small dagger in the other.

She must notice me looking because she whistles. "Hey, Pretty Boy," she says and tosses me the dagger. I catch it and take it out of its sheath. It's beautiful. The hilt is made of interwoven brass and gold, forming what looks like vines around the handle. A massive emerald sits in the center. And the blade, well, looks like it could cut through bone in one swipe.

Thank you, I send.

One breath, one step, she wind messages me.

What does that mean?

She gives me a sad smile. *It's something my parents used to say. You can do anything, as long as you start with one breath and one step.*

I like that. One breath, one step. I smile down at the dagger she gave me.

Just make sure you're alive to bring it back to me.

I give her what I hope is a confident smile and turn back to the creature. It dislodged at least two of my ice daggers and is working hard on the spear. Before I can think better of it, I jump into the water, aiming for its back. I land with a loud smack and try to push my dagger through its scales. I manage to get it underneath one, causing it to shriek, piercing my ears and throwing me off its back.

I splash into the water and realize that Sage's dagger is still lodged in its back. I swim back up to the surface and look for the eel, getting ready for its next attack.

And it's not there. There's no eel.

I look up at Sage. She shouts something but I can't hear her. I turn in a circle until I see the crocodile head with a wide-open mouth coming at me from the other direction. I shoot ice directly into its open mouth and it veers around me, inches away from my face, with its jaw now stuck open.

A smug grin involuntarily crosses my face as I approach it from behind to grab Sage's dagger and finish this once and for all. I'm about a foot away when I hear a large crunch, and I crane my neck over its body — it's snapped the ice out of its mouth. Swimming as fast as I can to the dagger before it turns around, I grab it and hold on for dear life as the creature tries to turn its head to bite me.

Between the splashing, snapping, and my attempts to hold on, I barely hear anything else that may be going on. The sound is broken when someone sends a wind message to me. *Make an ice dagger and shove it underneath.* I can't pinpoint who said it — it doesn't sound male or female — but

I'll have time to think on that later. I create an ice dagger in my right hand, still using the left to hold onto the dagger embedded in its back.

With as much strength as I can muster, I take a deep breath then duck under the water. Extending both arms as far as they can go so I can get the ice into the softest part of its belly, I drive the dagger into it, and finally there's actual blood. The thrashing gets even more intense, but I hold on for dear life and drag the dagger back and forth as far as my arm can reach.

The eel is weakening, but I don't want to leave anything to chance. Swimming up to the surface, I use the dagger in its back to swing onto the beast. Then, I yank the dagger out of its scales and look inside myself to the magic that shows itself as hands. Taking those hands, I shove all the magic I can muster into the tiny hole Sage's dagger made.

Once again, the monster slowly freezes from the inside out. Between that and the large open wound on its stomach, it's only a matter of moments before the thrashing stops and the beast goes limp underneath me. I let go of my magic and tread water as it slowly sinks to the bottom of the water. As I catch my breath, I look up at my companions. All of them look slightly shocked, except for Sage, who just looks proud.

I shout to her, "See! It *was* the ice that killed the other creature!" I can't help the large smile that crosses my face. Before I can find out if there's anything else lurking in this moat, I swim to the other side of the ring and pull myself up to the bottom stair of the pedestal. I lie on my back and take a few moments to catch my breath. I'm soaking wet and exhausted, but there's a buzzing energy running through me.

The energy's not coming from me, but the ground itself. I

sit up and place my hands on the surprisingly warm stone. Yup, that buzzing is coming from the ground beneath me.

I stand up and look at the plinth at the top of the stairs. I slowly make my way up, wary of any other surprises that could emerge. Five concentric rings of stairs encircle the podium, each getting progressively warmer as I reach the top. On the surface of the plinth are symbols that are far beyond my understanding.

I send a wind message to my group. *Does anyone know how to unlock this?* But there's no response. I guess not even their wind messages work here.

Okay, think.

Sage did say only someone only of my *bloodline* can access this weapon.

I use Sage's dagger to slice my palm, letting the blood drip into the symbol on the podium. I watch as the blood slowly fills the divots in the stone and realize it's a hand. It can't be a coincidence that I view my magic as a hand — maybe this really is going to work. I didn't let myself think about the possibility of this mission ending in a failure, but the fear was always there.

But now I'm afraid of what's going to happen if it succeeds. What will this weapon be? Will I have to use it? Will it change me?

The blue light that lined each stair disappears and a large column of light shines around the podium. Slowly, something rises out of the plinth. In a glass display case emerges... a pair of gloves. I look over at my companions on the other side of the water, who're all as confused and wary as I am. They look like any regular pair of gloves: black leather, plain, with no designs or embellishments.

I slowly lift the glass in case it triggers something. When nothing happens, I place it on the stair below me and look back at the gloves. Yup, plain black gloves. No floating or glowing or anything magical happens. I pick them up and put them on.

Well, they do fit like a glove if I say so myself. I chuckle at my own joke and hold the gloves up to the light to see if anything has changed. Slowly, right in front of my eyes, the gloves disappear into my skin.

I can still feel them, but there's no discernible way to tell. I look over at Sage and she looks as bewildered as I feel. I test them out, flexing and wiggling my fingers. They're definitely still there, but invisible to the naked eye. I take a deep breath and attempt to draw on my magic.

In the blink of an eye, the largest spear I've ever made appears in my hand. It took barely a thought. I try to think of something more complex — thinking back to when I first saw Sage's true magical strength, I attempt to build a snowstorm vortex around myself. And just like that, it's there. Massive clumps of snow, whipping winds, in a perfect circle around the pedestal. Once again, a fraction of my magic.

With one thought, the storm disappears. In its wake, my friends cheer and shout, but looking over at them, there's wariness too. Even though I can't hear what they're saying, I feel equal parts excitement and fear.

These gloves obviously enhance my magic. Since I don't want to bring this entire cave system down on us, I decide to wait until we leave to test them further. With a flick of my wrist, an ice staircase is built from the top of the pedestal to the other side of the moat. I run down the stairs and swing Sage into my arms.

Breathless, I kiss her with all the joy I have in my heart. I put her back on the ground, only to have her beaming up at me. "You did it!" she exclaims.

"Amazing job," Delwyn says. Aneira and Idris both share their congratulations as well, although their gazes are still nervous.

Sage holds my hands in hers. "Where did they go? I can't even feel them."

"I think they sort of became a part of me?" I say, and her eyes widen. "I could take them off if I wanted to, but when they're on, they sort of melt into my body." And it strangely feels like they've always been a part of me.

At that comment, Idris gives a much more enthusiastic, "Sick."

I look at my hands dwarfing Sage's and create a massive, intricate snowflake in our joined palms. On the other one, she creates an equally large flame.

"I've barely tested these gloves out, but I can already tell the magic in them exceeds anything I've seen so far," I say. "I'm a little scared." This kind of power; I mean, I've barely gotten used to having any magic, let alone massive amounts.

"I'm not," Sage says as she gives me a soft smile. She *is* the only one who has not looked worried or nervous at the power I've shown.

"You're not?"

"Nope. I've had to come to terms with how much magic I have, and it used to scare me. To be completely honest with you, I'm still not sure I know its full extent. But it never scared *you*. And if there's one thing I know, it's that you're the best kind of person to handle this kind of power. We'll figure it out. Together."

My heart warms at her faith in me. I know how hard it is for her to put her trust in someone else and I'll do whatever it takes to be worthy of it.

"Together," I agree, squeezing her hands.

"Now let's get the fuck out of here."

"Please," Idris says.

I take Sage's hand, which she surprisingly doesn't pull away from, and we head out of the cave.

Chapter Thirty-Five

Sage

As we leave the cave, we shield our eyes from the brightness of the dawn after so long in the dim light. Once our eyes fully adjust, everyone gets into fighting positions — we're surrounded by fire soldiers. I can practically feel their bodies tensing. Standing directly in front of us is one of the highest-ranking officers in the Fire Dominion's military.

"Captain Sage," she says. "Was your mission a success?" The leather on my family's weapons make a stretching sound as they're clenched tighter, but I stay relaxed and composed.

"Indeed, General. Apologies, but we did have to kill some of your soldiers we ran into. They didn't get the memo to leave us alone." Thank the Mother most of my wounds are hidden under my clothes; it would not be good for my reputation if they knew how close our battle was last night.

"That's alright, Captain. The cost of war." I did always love her pragmatism.

I let go of Aiden as we meet in the middle and shake hands.

One breath, one step.

All I can do is hope my family will give me time to explain. Finally, no more secrets. I turn back to them — everyone but Idris looks confused.

"Surprise!"

Chapter Thirty-Six

Delwyn

My mouth hangs open like a broken door after a storm as I watch Sage casually stroll towards our immortal enemy and shake her hand.

What the fuck is going on?

Standing next to General Elata, one of the highest-ranking generals in the Fire Dominion army, Sage turns back to us. "Surprise!"

I look down the line at Aneira, Aiden, and Idris; Aneira and Aiden share looks that rival mine in confusion, but Idris seems perfectly at ease, leaning against her sword like a cane.

My cousin may look self-assured to everyone else, but I know her well enough to tell she's nervous. She massages her wrist joints — stress makes her pain worse. It appears as if she's stretching and loosening up, but I know better.

"Sage, you better have a good ass explanation why you're now all chummy with this scum," I say, jutting my chin in General Elata's direction.

Since the attack fifteen years ago, too many Ice Dominion soldiers have died at the hand of the Fire Dominion. Sage wouldn't befriend them without reason. Mother, her own parents were killed by them. My father was killed by them.

She looks at Aiden — her first glance at him since leaving the cave. They gave into their undeniable connection, but with this revelation, even I don't know how Aiden will take it.

I look at him as well; his eyes are wide and his fists are clenched, but more than anything, he doesn't look betrayed. On the other hand, Aneira's eyes glisten with unshed tears and my heart hurts all over again for what Sage is doing to our family.

"Just come with me back to the Fire Dominion and I'll explain everything," Sage pleads. "We don't have much time."

The pounding that I thought was my blood racing through my body is actually the sound of soldiers making their way to our location. Ice Dominion soldiers, I'd guess by the looks of fear beginning to spread on the Fire warrior's faces.

I shake my head again. "I'm sorry Sage. I'm not going to abandon my home for reasons you won't even explain."

Her shoulders slump with a look of defeat that she usually reserves for when her body betrays her. It's never been directed at me and I hate the way it makes my heart ache. She looks at Aneira next. "Aneira?"

A few silent tears glide down Aneira's obsidian cheeks. "I'm sorry, Sagey."

Idris has been her usual silent self throughout this entire conversation and remains that way as she walks over to Sage's side of the clearing; creating a divide that feels much larger than the ten feet it really is.

Based on her lack of shock, she must've been in on Sage's plan from the beginning. And left me and Aneira in the dark.

I can tell Sage is dreading the last decision to be made in our group. I also know that if Aiden refuses to come with her, she will take him by force. She's come too far to give in now.

With one more look at his hands in gloves only he can see, he makes eye contact with Sage and I practically feel the surge of energy created as their gazes meet. "I gave you my trust. And you gave me yours. I'm not breaking that now over some conflict I can't possibly understand."

Sage's face breaks out in a soft but genuine smile as he reaches her and places a gentle kiss on her lips.

"I'm so sorry Del," Sage says. "I wish it didn't have to end this way. All I ask is when you return home to think about why I would do this. You too, Aneira. You are my family and I hope you know at the end of the day, everything I do is to protect you. Should you change your mind, the Fire Dominion guards know to let you both through. You'll always be safe with me."

Without waiting for me to respond, Sage turns around and follows the Fire Dominion soldiers in the direction that will ultimately lead them through the mountains dividing our two lands.

I could try to stop her. But, there's no way Aneira and I can defeat an entire squadron of enemy soldiers, especially with Idris and Sage on their side. Not that I'm sure I'd even be capable of hurting my cousin. And by the still faint sound of my soldiers' boots, they're too far away to aid in a fight.

And Sage knows it.

So I'm left to watch, helplessly, as my family and the most powerful weapon in all of Tirlun head directly into my enemy's territory.

What's Next?

If you enjoyed *The Lost Weapon*, I would love if you would consider leaving a review on Goodreads, Amazon, or wherever you purchased your copy!

Want to stay up to date with book two and other updates? Subscribe to Sophie's newsletter now!

Thank you so much for sharing in Sage and Aiden's adventure with me — but it's not over yet.

Book two is coming; Sage, Aiden, and Idris bring the weapon back to the Fire Dominion and Aneira and Delwyn head back to the Ice Dominion defeated and confused.

Acknowledgments

This story was simultaneously one of the easiest and most difficult things I've ever done. Easy because this story poured out of me; once I had the initial idea, the entire plot came to me like it was just waiting for me to tell it. Difficult because the decision to self-publish and take on all that entailed was complicated; there were so many factors that played a role in my ultimate choice to move forward with this story. But at the end of the day, I was so proud of what I had done and wanted to share it with the world.

Sage was a woman after my own heart and if even one part of her and her family's story resonated with you, that's all I could ask for.

That being said, this book would not have been possible without my amazing support system.

First and foremost, thank you to my parents for being shockingly onboard with my choice to pursue self-publishing. Your encouragement means the world to me.

Thank you to Hannah for listening to ten-minute long voice notes of me rambling about my plot ideas as well as explaining the scientific process of hurricanes (if my compression hurricanes didn't make sense, blame her).

Thank you to Morgan for explaining how hallucinogenic drugs work.

Thank you to Nora for being a mentor as well as an amazing developmental editor.

Thank you to Hanni for begrudgingly reading the book, especially the sex scenes.

A huge thank you to my beta readers for their invaluable feedback.

And finally you, dear reader. Thank you for giving my debut story a chance. I hope you enjoyed reading it as much as I did writing it; and if you didn't, please don't tell anyone.

About the Author

Sophie Jay was born in NYC (a fact she is very proud of) and raised in the suburbs. She currently lives on the Upper West Side with her golden doodle Maple.

Sophie graduated with her BA in Political Science and French from the University of Pennsylvania and received her Master of Arts in International Affairs in May of 2023 from Columbia University. While writing a novel is not where she foresaw the implementation of this degree, but she's finding that her knowledge in international politics, warfare, and persuasive writing has translated into an exciting new career field.

When she's not writing, Sophie is playing with her dog, drinking too much coffee, and reading.

This is Sophie's first book.